# As Those Above Fall

# AS THOSE ABOVE FALL

CATLYN LADD

NEW YORK | LOS ANGELES

Jacket design by Rejenne Pavon

Jacket Copyright 2024 by Winding Road Stories

Interior book design by Winding Road Stories

ISBN#:  978-1-960724-26-7 (pbk)
ISBN#: 978-1-960724-27-4 (ebook)

Published by Winding Road Stories

www.windingroadstories.com

*Courtney, Dena, and Robyn,
who love vampires as much as
I do, this book is for you.*

# CHAPTER 1

# RECOGNITION

I T FELT LIKE RECOGNITION. I did not know him but everything about him haunted my memory, the planes of his face, his scent, the taste of his skin. The buttons of his shirt melted under my fingers and I ran my hands down his stomach, nails teasing through the golden hair below his navel, a trail disappearing, tantalizing, into the waistband of his jeans.

The bourbon roared in my veins, pulsing heat between my ears. For this moment everything outside blissfully faded, and there was only space for me and this man. This beautiful man who tasted of light and warmth and everything I craved.

It felt like recognition. I pushed into him, inhaling his breath. He seemed so hard, more than solid, a statue of marble and silk. His hands caressed the length of my body and lifted me by the hips, pushing me into the wall at my back as his body returned home, holding me suspended between him and the plaster behind me.

"Who are you?" I spoke in breath, a whispered question into his mouth. I felt his teeth bite into my lower lip, consuming, almost painful. "Who are you?"

His only response came in the form of fingers slipping like thieves under the hem of my skirt. It felt so familiar. I pushed him back, bringing that face into focus. His hands grazed upward, adulterous lovers drawing my skirt tight over my hips. He smiled slowly.

"I don't know you?" It came as a question and I searched his eyes, probing.

An hour earlier I'd been by myself in the living room, the party surging around, playing with candle flame. I could make the candle go out and relight with a thought. No one noticed, too preoccupied with the music pulse, the company, the flowing alcohol.

I saw him across the room. He brought the glass to his mouth, tilting his head back to draw the liquor, the line of his jaw and throat exquisite in the shifting shadow. The act of drinking transformed his mouth from something sculpted and hard into another thing, soft, seductive. When my eyes met his I knew I did not know him. Yet the recognition would not allow me to look away. He'd been talking to a woman, but he'd walked away from her, leaving her in the middle of a sentence, her eyes following him to me. The look on her face. She knew I'd called him.

I watched him walk toward me, feeling my mouth curl up. He had a player's swagger, looking good, knowing it, aware of the eyes drawn to follow him. I would never know a man like that, but I knew him.

I stood to meet him, startled by his height. I had to tilt my head back, something I rarely found necessary. He came into my personal space, invasive, and my nerves responded with shock waves. I felt my pupils dilate.

"I know you," he said.

His voice held some slight trace of an accent, but I could not place it.

"No, you don't," I responded, my lips curving up.

"You know I do."

The accent sounded clipped, exotic but faint, barely there. I reached for the glass he held to buy myself time. The bourbon burned a hot trail in my throat, and I took a cooling breath.

He took the glass back, his mouth going soft again as he swallowed. Finished, he dropped it to the floor and it rolled away into the shadows. He ran one finger up the bare flesh of my arm. "I've always known you."

"Your pickup line work on all the girls?" I asked.

His eyes traveled slowly up my body to meet mine. "It's not a line."

I stared back into his gaze, captivated. His eyes shifted from gray to silver in the amorphous light. His mouth thinned, lush but hard, his narrow chin tilting down, creating caverns in the concave wells of his cheeks. His eyes softened, boring into me, invasive and intimate.

I knew this man. Had known him in another life. Every cell cried with recognition, but I recoiled from the feeling, afraid of drowning. He called to the darkness in me, and I felt my tenuous hold on sanity slip another notch. I held onto reality with my fingernails, aided by bourbon and wine. I had been living as a shadow for months and I felt myself slip into his void.

Now this, his mouth on mine, the tingles of heat from his lips flashing in my skin. The room faded away, all the people gone. His tongue twisted in my mouth, brutal and delicious. The fabric of his jeans rubbed raw against my thighs, his fingers music on my bones.

As I pushed him back, into focus, my mouth opened to say his name, but I called forth silence as I realized I did not know it. I reformed to ask but found myself dumb in the face of his face, framed by a halo of light hair, glowing against the candle flames.

He glowed, every part of him, the white skin, the silver eyes, the red hair dyed bright blonde, almost white, but grown out so it wreathed his head in fire.

"What's your name?" I asked.

He dropped his chin again and the shadows swam across his features. "You don't know?"

I laughed. "I have no idea."

"Let's get out of here."

His words brought the party crashing back. People laughed, ice tinkled against glass, music pounded. "Okay."

The night air enveloped me and I felt my entire body dilate. His hand holding mine sent quivers of warmth up my arm. I laughed again when I saw the motorcycle, black and chrome and lurking at the curb.

"Are you for real?"

"No." His smile curved upward, vulpine and tricksterish over perfect, sharp teeth. "You conjured me." He reached playfully for the silver pentagram glinting at my throat, but pulled back before touching it. "Witch."

I laughed up at the sky and the waxing moon laughed back. For the first time in months, I felt happy. I wanted to howl with the relief of it. I knew it wouldn't last. Right now, I didn't care.

The motorcycle roared and I placed my hands on his hips, slipping my legs around him, skirt riding up, curling my fingers around the spiked belt he wore. The machine throbbed, powerful beneath me.

"Where are we going?" he asked over his shoulder.

I pointed and we leaped forward as he gunned the engine, testing me. I let my body find the balance easily and I heard him laugh, the sound snatched by the wind.

It seemed the trees danced in the silver light. The whole night world shimmered with energy only witches like me could see. Each tree sparkled with a distinct aura, its life told in shifting colors. The magic roared in my veins. I rested my head against a leather clad shoulder, inhaling the musky perfume. This magic provided me with a reason to keep living, the only reason in a world gone dark. It sustained me when no other force on earth could have kept me above the yawning grief.

Magic had been with me my entire life, before I even knew what to call it, manipulating reality with forces I took for granted. But my will could not bring Alex back. I entered a dream world constructed through my desperate grief only to have it crash down. Magic is the most powerful natural force in the universe, but it cannot turn back time. It cannot make the dead live. I'd begun to think seriously of joining Alex.

But this man had come to me. He seemed nothing like Alex and yet my body burned with the same desire.

I pointed the way home and reveled in the wind in my face, watering my eyes, numbing my cheeks. My home, the small house I had shared with my lost one, my Alex, set back from the street, wreathed in shadow. The light burning over the mailbox in the stone wall surrounding the property did not sustain past the gate, and the walk danced with ivy fronds weaving spells in the breeze. I swiveled myself off the motorcycle and waited for him to park at the curb. The silence of the stilled motor crashed in and I spun in a circle, the magic of the night too much to contain.

He laughed at me and drew me in, his hands reaching around my waist. His mouth tasted sweet and metallic. The recognition struck me in shatters.

"I must know your name," I said, pulling back, knees weak with alcohol and desire.

His mouth grazed across my lips, sending shivers down my spine. "Zeke. My name is Zeke."

I opened the gate behind me without looking and pulled him forward by the hand. He carefully avoided the glass evil eye, blue in the concrete, and came with me into the gloom.

I heard his breath quicken as we came out from under the arbor shading the walk. My little cottage shone in the bright moon, a crystal glimmering in the front window. Vines crawled up the wall beside the door and the side porch lurked, dark and inviting. I reached for my keys, but his hands stopped me, pulling me into him. His mouth sucked in my breath and I melted to him, the soft material of his shirt indistinguishable from his flesh.

Finally pulling back he contemplated my door, his eyes wandering over the dragon snarling from the wall. "A protection spell," he said, his fingers reaching but not touching the plaster statue.

"It's under the mat, actually," I said. "How do you know that?"

"I can feel it." He turned back, his eyes oddly lit in the bright light.

"You can't cross it." His hand still enclosed mine warmly, but I pulled away, my consciousness sparking with awareness. I was starting to sober up. "Who are you?"

"I told you. You conjured me." His lips curved up.

I backed up until my back rested against the wood of the door. My head spun from the night, from the alcohol, from the scent of him, like desert after the rain. "Don't lie to me."

He tilted his head back toward the sky, his profile sharp and exquisite against the stars. "I could never lie to you." He shifted, his boots grazing the mat but not crossing it. "I will not hurt you." He cocked his head back down, chin dropping, so beautiful I felt like screaming. "And that has nothing to do with your protection spells." He reached and twisted a strand of my hair between his fingers. "And everything to do with you."

It felt like recognition. Everything about him, the strength in his body, the sharpness of his features, the power radiating from him, seemed dangerous, and yet I did not fear him. The worst he could do was kill me and I longed for that.

"I need more to drink," I whispered.

"Do you want me to go?"

"No." Never that. "Meet me on the deck." I found the lock with my key and let myself inside. I watched from behind the window as he walked across the grass. Stopping in the center of the lawn he stretched his arms wide to drink in the night. I felt the dark power swirling around him in a vortex of negative space. I craved that power.

I grabbed a bottle of wine from the case in the kitchen and let myself out onto the side porch. Zeke sat on the bench built down one side, his face hidden in the darkness. I stood just out of reach, tipping the wine bottle back, the sweet, musty taste wonderful on my tongue. Fortified, I asked the question I desperately needed to know. "What are you?"

He held a hand out for the bottle, silver rings glinting on his white fingers. "You tell me."

"Why did you avoid the evil eye? How did you know about the spell at the front door? Why did you call me a witch?" I paced left, seeking to penetrate the shadow in which he sat. "I mean, everyone knows I am a witch. The pentagrams are kind of a giveaway. But lots of people play at witchcraft. Everyone just thinks I'm playing pagan. They don't know it's real. But you do."

His legs shifted and he stood, stepping toward me. I still could not see his face. "Of course I feel it. The power pours off you like..." He paused and took another sip of wine. "Well, it pours off of you like wine. I can taste it." He set the bottle down and moved closer, his features becoming visible, mouth soft, chin lowered toward me. I stood frozen as he slid his arms around me, his hands up under my shirt, fingers dancing across my spine. "I can taste your grief."

I felt the tears on my cheeks but did not weep, mesmerized. He lowered his head toward me and his breath moved across my face. "Your grief is like wormwood. Rank and poisonous and delicious."

His tongue flicked the salt on my cheek and I could not contain the sigh. "I thought only crosses repelled vampires."

Surprisingly, he laughed, waving a flippant hand. "*Power* repels vampires. Faith repels vampires. The symbol doesn't matter. If enough people believe, or if one person believes hard enough, I can't touch them."

"But you're not running."

His teeth glinted in his grin. "You're not trying."

I laughed. I could not help it. "Maybe I've lost my faith."

His mouth descended to mine. "You could repel me if you wanted."

I pulled back, looking up into his eyes. "And you can't come in unless I invite you."

His fingers dipped down, tracing fire over my hip bones and under the elastic of my skirt. I moaned into his mouth before I could stop myself. "That's true for things besides your house."

The sunlight woke me and I sat up, groggy and light dazzled. My skirt lay across my lap like a blanket. I drew it over my shoulders against the cool morning air.

Zeke sat in a pool of deep shadow in the corner of the deck watching me, dregs of wine stirring in the bottom of the bottle in his hand. He looked just as pale and flawless as in dark light, a statue wreathed in flames against the dark siding of the house.

"I thought vampires didn't come out in the sunlight."

He shot that cocky grin at me. "I'm not in the sunlight, am I?"

I stood up, letting the fabric fall, and stretched in the warmth of the sun.

His chin dropped. "You're a flirt."

I gathered remnants of clothing, watching him watch me. I skirted the shade, staying in the light, staring him down.

"Tell me you want me."

His nostrils flared and his eyes went from silver to gray. "I've always wanted you."

"Then come inside."

# CHAPTER 2

# SUICIDE IN FLESH

A VAMPIRE SLEPT IN my bed. He'd said his name the night before: Zeke. In the blue holiday lights wrapped around my bed frame his white skin glimmered and his hair appeared purple.

I did not believe in vampires even though I knew the magic in the world. But there he lay, in the flesh.

Outside, darkness approached on teasing feet, shadowing the trees in skeletal fingers against the dark curtains. I'd shuttered the windows against the sun's light; it would burn my lover to bones.

I had been sitting in the same position against the wall beside the fireplace for almost an hour watching him. He had not moved, though his brow furrowed with dreaming. My eyes wandered over his slim hips, muscular stomach. I could almost feel the heat from his skin from where I sat. I'd assumed vampires cold, but he burned.

When I'd awoken an hour earlier, I had traced my bite marks on his pale shoulders with my tongue, tasting the broken flesh as he slumbered. Now, the last of the bruising faded before my eyes. His skin appeared flawless, as perfect as the night before.

I'd been surprised to find him still here but then it occurred to me that he couldn't leave into the sun. Not if he was what he said.

A vampire. Or something not human. Magic come to life.

I twisted my fingers together and rose for another bottle of wine. I could only think when the alcohol roared through me, deadening reality to a manageable hum.

A bottle, half gone, rested on the mantle and I upended it into my mouth. My pentagram, sparkling silver in the dancing flame light, twisted a serpentine shape on the dark wood of the mantle and I picked it up, letting it run through my fingers.

Alex stood next to the fireplace wearing those white jeans I loved. His hazel eyes glinted gold in the shifting light from the dying fire. He held out a hand and the silver chain dropped from his fingers, the small star twirling to catch the light. He'd stood right there, in that exact spot, when he'd given it to me.

I closed my eyes, blotting him out. He wasn't really there. Seeing him like this reopened the wound his death made inside me. But he was everywhere I looked, like he'd been burned on my retinas.

I fastened the chain around my throat, keeping my eyes closed. Zeke had not been able to touch the pentagram. He had claimed that faith, that power such as mine, and not the symbol, repelled vampires. I opened my eyes. Alex had gone.

But Zeke stood fewer than two feet away, his red and blonde hair bounding up in wild spikes. I had not heard him rise and I jumped.

He reached for the star glittering at my throat, his fingers grazing the skin over my collar bones.

"Don't be frightened of me, love."

"I'm not scared. Because you're not real." I grinned at him over the bottle as I fortified myself some more. "You're a hallucination. I've finally gone mad."

He took my hand, turning it palm up, and placed his lips against the vulnerable skin of my wrist, his breath against my flesh. The hair on my arm stood up. "I'm real enough to make you tremble." His lips drew back over carnivoristic teeth, glinting and sharp in the blue light. The candle lit on the mantle glowed golden, turning him into a fantasy of fire and ice. He was Alexander the Great, Jim Morrison, and Johnny Depp. He looked like God should look.

With his silver eyes on me, I began to believe again, just a little. I reached out and pulled my nails down his chest, leaving faint white lines that blushed red a moment later.

"I don't believe in vampires," I told him and he laughed.

"Neither does anyone else. Trust me, that's what ensures our survival."

I paused over the plural. "How many of you are there?"

He shrugged. "A few thousand, maybe. We are very solitary creatures."

"And you feed off blood?"

He nibbled on my finger, dropping his jaw so that blue shadows swarmed into the caverns of his cheeks. He looked dangerous and my stomach flipped over. He had told me that he could not hurt me, that the power embedded in my cells protected me, but there is more than one way to lose a soul. I reached out with all my considerable psychic power, searching for his vibe.

He bit down on my finger and I gasped. "I know what you're doing," he whispered. "You can't read my thoughts."

"I'm not reading your thoughts," I told him.

He released my finger and I examined the puncture wounds, filling with dark blood trapped in deep wells of flesh.

"So what are you doing?" he asked. "Because you are doing something."

I turned away from him and moved to the bed. I sat on the edge and gazed at him. He turned, backlit by the candle and all I could see of his features was a strong jaw haloed with glowing hair.

"You don't feel human," I admitted. In fact, he felt psychically cold, like swirling arctic air. I breathed out and let the auras creep in. I kept them damped most of the time and alcohol dimmed my abilities further. But now I invited that sight and the world bloomed with color. He cocked his head, watching me with his silver eyes.

I looked at him again. His aura radiated out a good five feet, much bigger than most humans and deep red except for a silver streak rising straight up from the top of his head. There were glimpses of emotion, a hot streak of desire, a cool hunger that twisted out from his chest, darker red than the rest. Most humans teemed with emotions like oil slicks but here only the red, darker in places, with that shock of silver. Many creatures had a white glow or line rising from their crowns, but I had never seen one so bright.

He called to my self-destructive nature with such seductive sweetness that I closed my eyes to shut him out. I wanted to jump into him, I wanted to be enveloped, I wanted to drown.

I wanted to die. Alex had loved my courage, and so I'd been dragging myself along, but I was so tired. Now Zeke appeared like a magic trick: a solution. How fitting for a witch to end in the bite of a vampire.

I opened my eyes when he touched me, gently moving my legs apart to crawl into the space between my thighs, his exquisite face tilted up toward mine. "You conjured me," he whispered the words he spoke last night. "You called me like a scream in my head. I am powerless to resist." That lush mouth curved up.

"The only thing that I have been calling is death," I whispered back.

"What do you think I am?"

I gazed sightlessly up at the ceiling, gleaming with glow-in-the-dark stars. I dreamed of crawling into the grave beside Alex, letting my decaying juices mingle with his. The grief of losing him ate into me, creeping along my nerves like acid. But I had been powerless to act. All I could do was wait, my psyche screaming, deafening all of reality, drinking to die. I had always been able to get whatever I wanted by focusing my desire, charming everyone I met, using glamour to transform myself into whoever I needed to be. But I could not charm death.

Instead, I had summoned a vampire, a creature that should not exist. I laughed with the absurdity of it, and Zeke's red eyebrows rose inquisitively.

"What is a vampire, exactly?" I inquired. I could not resist touching him, running my fingers along his cheekbones and up into his hair.

"I don't know. I only know what I am."

"What are you?"

He gently disentangled my fingers from his hair, kissing my knuckles and making me shiver. "Well, I know I need blood to survive."

"How much?"

"About the same as the amount of food humans need, as far as I can figure." His accent, faint but distinctive shifted for a moment, confusing my ear. "I need three or four pints a day."

"Does it have to be human?"

He laughed softly, his breath warm on my wrist. "No." The silver of his eyes glimmered up at me, and I felt a recoil in my viscera. The danger lurked in his eyes, the deadly speed of his body, camouflaged by his beauty, hiding beneath the surface. "But humans taste best."

I shivered, and he smiled. "Do you have an aversion to killing humans?" he asked.

I hesitated. It was a difficult question. I had never considered the actuality of it, the literal taking of a life. "I don't know," I said finally.

"I don't have to kill," he said, sitting back. "I can take a sip from several victims and be perfectly satisfied."

"So how often do you kill?"

He shrugged, a lovely motion of rippling muscle across bare shoulders. "I don't keep track."

"Who was the last person you killed?" I pressed.

His eyes turned silver in the shifting shadow light. "I killed a hooker two nights ago."

I gasped. He said it so flatly. "Why did you kill her?"

He hunched his shoulders, looking in that moment so playful that I almost laughed. Mischief danced in the curl of his lips. "He," he glanced up and now there was no question of the laughter in his eyes. "He was high on heroin and I wanted to be, too."

I laughed, appalled. It was the last answer I expected. "You can't get addicted?"

"Oh, no." His eyes darkened. "Us vampires are way too sophisticated for anything so banal as addiction." He chuckled. "Except for that whole blood thing, of course."

"Of course." I stood, forcing him back onto his heels. My new posture brought my thighs level with his face and his eyes traced upward. He pushed his face into my crotch.

My skin responded to his touch with a heat I could not control, sending fire into my groin and down to my toes. But I pushed past him. I needed to know if he really was a vampire. If so, there was more power in the world than I knew. I wanted it. He could be my suicide in flesh, an answer to my dark dreams.

"Are you hungry?" I asked. He'd been with me for almost 24 hours and all he'd had was the alcohol.

He knelt on the floor where I'd left him, turning to watch as I pulled jeans out of a dresser drawer and stepped into them. The shirt from the night before lay in a tangle and I began to turn it right side out.

He stood up and I couldn't help but admire the long length of him, thin and strong. "Yes. I am hungry."

"Unfortunately, I don't have any blood for you."

"You mean you weren't planning to have a vampire over for dinner?" He grinned at me and picked up his clothes, putting them on the bed and beginning to sort them out.

"Only for dessert."

That made him laugh. "Dessert accomplished. Several times."

A sliver of feeling, something I refused to recognize as guilt, wormed through me. Zeke was the first since Alex. I had been avoiding firsts. I didn't want to have any new experiences. But Zeke was beyond my control, something entirely novel.

"What happens if you sip from someone? Do they remember? Call the cops? Hemorrhage?"

"They don't remember if I don't let them." He pulled on his jeans, buckling the spiked belt with quick movements. "Vampires are just as magical as you are, love. It's a form of glamour, I guess. We construct ourselves, encounters with us, however we see fit."

"So what would it feel like if you drank from me?"

His eyes flashed dark and then back to silver in an instant. His chin dropped, his countenance shifted with dizzying speed. He changed from vulnerable to menacing, two different beings with the same lovely face. In a shift of light, a tilt of his head, he transformed from a Botticelli angel to a predator.

Daring, I approached him and he rocked backward on his heels, drawing imperceptibly away from me. I became the stalker.

"Zorah..." he whispered my name, as a plea or in longing I could not tell.

"What would it feel like?" I tilted my head to look up at him, close enough now to feel the heat from his skin.

"It's like..." his voice cracked and he cleared his throat before beginning again. "It's like sex. I can make it like sex, orgasmic."

"Don't people offer you their blood?" I asked. "You're acting like it's never happened before."

"Of course. People offer all the time. But you know exactly what I am and you're offering anyway."

I paused over his words, considering. It occurred to me that he must get offers from people playing at danger, not taking him seriously, or coveting his power. The little goth girls and boys would love him, naturally. But he's right, I knew exactly what he was, I felt him, read him, knew him in a way others could not. It was all right there in that red aura, rapacious and rabid.

"Would it make me a vampire? The legends disagree on that point."

He smiled slightly. "No. It's almost impossible to make a vampire. The process kills most people. It might make you lightheaded, though. Depending on how much I take."

"Fine. You can make me dinner after. Or order out if you don't know how to cook."

"You are too much." He stepped away, pulling his shirt on with quick, forceful movements.

"Don't you want to?" I felt brazen, pursuing him like this. I had conjured him, my suicide. He was mine. "Have you ever tasted a witch's blood?"

The silver chain of my pentagram burned as he tore it away, moving with speed I never imagined, on me before I knew it, an attack from nowhere. I saw a flash of his face as he buried it in my neck, his lips drawn back, the shine of his white teeth, his eyes closed. His hands pulled me into him with a strength beyond comprehension, bending me to his will.

My instincts flashed, repelling him, and he froze, his mouth on my throat. I felt his hot breath on my skin. And I relaxed, sighing into him, withdrawing my defenses, lowering my psychic guard, letting him in.

The penetration felt like sex, just like he said. I felt the pain but remotely, part of the pleasure. I sensed the control he wielded over my mind and I did not struggle, allowing him to sweep me up in his glamour, making my body flush, the tingle curling my toes. The sensation of being consumed overwhelmed me and I felt my heartbeat align with his. It felt oddly more intimate than anything we'd done before. I glimpsed fragments of images, too fast to see. Then the beat was all I heard, primordial rhythm of hearts beating as one. Like romance and dying. I made an inarticulate sound of longing.

He dropped me, withdrawing to the other side of the room at a speed I could not see or understand. I simply found myself on the floor, cold. "What?" I said, not sure what I was asking.

He stood on the other side of the room, a hot flush rising over his collarbones into his pale cheeks. The sharp tip of his tongue found a seep of blood and licked it away. "I'm not your death, Zorah," he said.

I sat up, drawing my arms around me. "Isn't that my decision?"

His brows drew down. "No. I am not your suicide. Not unless I choose to be."

I felt like I had been spinning on a swing and I laughed, tucking a long strand of hair behind my ear. My throat burned and I traced fingertips across the puncture wounds, seeping blood. I tried to stand but almost fell from the light headiness. So instead, I crawled to him across the plush blue carpet.

He shrank when I touched him but finally looked at me, the expression in his eyes some combination of fear and awe.

"I can see auras," he whispered.

I smiled. "Distracting, aren't they?"

His pupils dilated. "Yours is blue," he said.

"How does my blood taste?"

He laughed with a tinge of hysteria. "Dear god, Zorah."

"What was it like?"

"The closest I will ever come to heaven."

# CHAPTER 3

# DEATH INCARNATE

M Y FINGERS FOUND THE wound in my throat and wandered around the edges of the puncture. The seep of blood had stopped and I traced the drying stream over my collar bone, sending flakes, black in the dim light, scattering over my knees. I felt no pain and I did not feel any effect other than a passing dizziness, but my emotions roared, clouding my thoughts.

I'd expected pain from the bite, the pleasure he assured me he could cause, blood, a pounding heart, but it had been like trying to imagine death: impossible until the experience unfolds. I had not been prepared for the pleasure, acute and intoxicating, or the feeling of loss and coldness when he withdrew.

"Why doesn't it hurt more?" I asked.

"My saliva is healing you." He stepped away from me to the bed, buttoning his shirt quickly.

I laughed, disturbed by the tinge of hysteria in the sound. "Well, aren't you just the fountain of youth."

I asked for this, but I had not understood my request and now I reeled from it, off balance. Still on all fours, my hand found my necklace, torn from my throat when he bit, buried in the plush pile of the carpet. I held it before my eyes, letting the star-shaped pendant swing. His silver eyes in the gloom followed the movement, hypnotized.

I stood, facing him. I felt all too sober, not ready for a reality that included vampires. My life had spun off without me, out of control.

Alex stood in the doorway behind Zeke, his dark curls tousled as though from sleep. I looked into his eyes and his generous mouth curved up in that special smile he had for me. I took a deep breath, knowing that he would be gone in a minute. Every time I saw him it reminded me that he wasn't really there. It reminded me of what I'd lost.

I had loved life. I loved the magic that poured out of me. Alex had loved it too. Together, we created the perfect world of just the two of us. Then he had died while I lay sleeping. The injustice of it burned through me.

Alex's eyes left mine and went to Zeke, narrowing slightly. He wondered at this creature, too.

I had resolved to die but now this: Zeke. A mystery I had not known existed, a glimpse of power beyond my imagination. Now I had to live, just a little longer. I had to see what it meant that there were vampires in the world. What else existed? What other powers?

Zeke looked up, meeting my eyes and behind him, Alex flickered out. Gone. Again.

I could not take those silver eyes on me, and I flung the pendant at him as hard as I could.

It glimmered in the ghost light, and his eyes widened in surprise. Reflexively, he caught it and then yelped in pain, dropping it. Intrigued, I walked across the carpet toward him. He allowed me to take his hand, curling his fingers away from his palm, to reveal the star, burned into his flesh. As I watched it healed, the skin drawing smoothly together.

"Why?" I asked. "It's just a piece of metal."

He pulled his hand away. "It shares your essence, your power."

"For how long?"

He shrugged. "Until you forget about it, I guess." He ran his hand, fingers sheathed in silver rings, through his bleached hair, making it stand up. I wondered about the whim or vanity that made him bleach it and I glimpsed him in a small room, head bent over a sink, dye kit in hand. It was such a human image that my assumptions about him shook and I remembered that, despite the vampire in his veins, he had started out human. Or so I assumed.

He turned away, sitting on the end of the bed with his back to me, pulling on his boots, trying them with quick gestures. "I think you might be the first human I've ever feared."

I walked around so I could see his face, but he kept it lowered, focused on wrapping the long laces around the tops of his boots. Bypassing the wine on the mantle, I opened the bourbon instead. I needed to get rid of the sick pulse of sobriety.

"You fear me because you can't kill me?" The liquor burned and I welcomed the heat, taking another swig.

He laughed but without humor. "I guess you could put it that way." He stood up, boots tied, clothed and back to punk rock glory. "I fear you because I never dreamed that anyone like you existed. I have been all over this planet, met thousands of humans, but no one like you." The predator had left his features and it was only him in all his human beauty, the shadows swarming in the caverns of his cheeks, lips curling upward at the corners, full and lushly inviting. Him as I first saw him, an evening ago now, watching me from across the room at a party I had attended out of boredom. I went for the free booze. And to stave off suicide one more night.

I looked into his silver eyes and felt the same thing I had felt the night before: recognition so strong it left me dizzy. "I know you," I whispered.

"And I know you." He said it right back. "I knew it from the second I saw you: you are a new thing, something I was looking for without knowing it. Zorah, this power is incredible." He shook his head in wonderment. "Where did it come from? How can it be?"

I realized that he felt the same way about me. We were impossible to one another.

"When I was three years old it was raining outside and I wanted to go out into my playhouse. So I made the sun shine," I told him.

His lips parted in wonderment.

"Five miles away it rained so hard that a mudslide swept down the mountain and killed four people."

His eyes widened. "Did your parents know?"

"No. They just thought the sun came out. But weird shit happened around me all the time. By the time I turned seven I'd figured out how to focus the reaction, make it part of the plan."

"Did they ever figure it out?"

"They suspected. They feared it. So I got really good at using glamour to change people's perceptions. And then I just..." I closed my eyes. My world had been so perfect. I ached at the loss.

"Just what?"

"I just made the world whatever I wanted it to be. The right grades. The right friends. The right college. I just made it all happen."

"And then you lost the one you love."

That brought my eyes open quick, like a slap. "How do you know that?"

"The only thing not covered in dust in this room is that photo." He pointed.

I didn't have to look. "You're perceptive."

His lips curled up. "I've had some practice."

"I can't think with you here," I told him, taking another swallow.

"Do you want me to leave?"

"No, " I decided. "I want to leave."

His red brows rose. "Can I come?"

I considered him in all of his impossibility. "Yes. You can come.

I stood looking out across the bay. The Golden Gate Bridge glowed over the water, orange and alien. I had come here with Alex, long ago. He appeared, conjured by my thought of him, stepping up beside me, the soft light glowing on his swarthy skin.

"What have you done?" he asked, his tone amused.

Sometimes he spoke to me. I answered him in my mind. Long ago I'd figured out how to speak to him telepathically. It was a hard habit to break.

*I'm summoning a way to get to you.*

"This is not what I had in mind when we worked together to make your powers stronger," he replied, amusement in his voice. "Did you know vampires exist?"

*Of course not. But I want to die. Zeke can make me die.*

He looked at me, serious. "Slitting your wrists or swallowing a bunch of pills too easy for you? You have to call a vampire to do it?"

*I don't think I called him. I think he just found me.*

"If anyone could call a vampire, you could." He laughed and my heart hurt. I loved his laugh.

"Remember when you glamoured the bank into giving you the money for our house?"

*You told me to magic us up some furniture, too.*

"So the next day you did."

I laughed. *That sales boy didn't know what hit him.* I turned to look at him. He didn't look like a ghost. I couldn't see through him, he didn't glow. He just stood there with his hands in the pockets of the leather jacket he liked best. He'd died in it; it had shredded on the pavement. So had his skin.

*You convinced me that I could do anything and then demonstrated to me that I can't.*

"What can you not do, pretty Zorah?"

That pet name for me. It brought tears to my eyes. *I can't bring you back. I can't make you live.*

This time I saw his lips move. "You haven't tried everything yet."

Zeke stepped into his space and Alex blew away on the breeze. Apparently, I'd conjured a man who could not die, my fantasy made flesh. He tilted his head back, sharp profile tilted up toward the sky. He took my hand and his rings made a soft clink against the wedding band I still wore.

"I'm hungry," he whispered.

I took his hand in mine and pulled him toward the light of El Embarcadero where tourists strolled in the cool evening air. I felt the human regard as we passed through the crowds, hearing whispers of thought. They stared at us in wonder.

Zeke topped six feet, his head crowned by the flaming hair, his skin pale and flawless under the sodium lights. I saw us as they saw us: I as pale as him, platinum hair curling to my waist. I hadn't brushed it in awhile and it tangled down my back. They thought us beautiful, famous.

He basked in the attention, glowing and gluttonous. He seemed used to being watched.

"Her," I whispered and directed his gaze.

She sat against a light post, meager belongings in a pack beside her, a cardboard sign propped against her knees, *Hungry, please help* printed in careful blue letters. She wore a white lace camisole over ripped jeans and feathers had been tied into her black dreadlocks with beads and bells that whispered to themselves in the breeze. I saw the track marks on her arms and between her fingers.

I could barely see her aura, sickly green and dying. A pulse of scarlet surrounded her head and I imagined how beautiful she must have been before.

I reached into her mind. She thought herself on a grand quest, an adventure, a cog in the status quo, but I saw no new ideas, no grand schemes. Fated to die in the gutter, the disease in her blood spreading in a viral wave to infect anyone she encountered. I watched her aura in fascination, violent scarlet and a dull greenish gray twisting together in an endless search for sustenance. She was like a vampire herself, a weak, addicted creature.

She saw us watching her and smiled wanly, her face lighting with hope. She had beauty, like nightshade, destruction encoded in the essence of her being.

I reached into my bag for money, but Zeke dropped my hand and moved ahead of me, kneeling before the girl. I watched her pupils dilate and felt her psychic response to him as his face came level with hers.

"What's your name?" He took her hand and she didn't even realize it, mesmerized by his silver eyes.

"Star."

"That's beautiful," he said, bringing her hand to his lips, raising goose bumps along her wrist as he exhaled. "Why don't you come with me, Star?"

She rose, not even remembering to take her bag, the lettered sign falling forgotten into the street. He had her, utterly.

He slipped his arm around her waist, guiding her, and glanced back over his shoulder at me. His chin dropped, eyes shifting molten in an instant. He was all predator, changing from seductive to feral in a heartbeat. His lips curled up over sharp teeth and I realized that this was the reason he existed, I was foolish to think that I ever could have conjured this being. He had been created to hunt, to prey, to feed.

I stooped to grab the girl's bag, a battered and scuffed leather backpack. Then I followed my vampire lover and his kill into the dark.

He took her down the boardwalk and into the shadows of the docks, whispering in the delicate shell of her ear the entire time, his fingers weaving though her wild hair.

The wood of the docks had silvered with time and glowed in the senseless light reflected off the clouds. Someone laughed far off, the sound eerie over the water. Zeke stopped in the recessed gateway of a pier, turning Star toward him, his hands cupping her shoulders. She looked up, childlike in her waif's clothes.

"You are so beautiful," she whispered.

His hand wrapped around her neck, pulling her to him, glancing at me over the top of her head, eyes flashing. His aura consumed the girl in his arms, so deep red it was almost black. The rings on his fingers glinted as he wrapped his hand into her snakelike hair. She seemed to sense his intent at last but it was too late; he pulled her head back and sank into her throat before she could call out. A whisper escaped her lips and her world spun away.

I couldn't believe how quickly it happened, how rapidly it was over. When he drank from me it had seemed leisurely, but this was violent and sudden. Her hands clutched his arms then fell as she went limp. Her aura flashed once, bright, almost blinding and then went out like a light. The greenish color of her lost vitality seemed to melt into Zeke, absorbed into his hunger. Her skin paled and then cracked. At first, I credited what I saw to the amorphous light, but then I could not deny it.

She fell to dust before my eyes; her hair came out in his fist and he dropped it as her entire body turned to sand. Her form held together for an instant and then her clothing fell to the ground, empty. I heard a faint patter and realized that it was her jewelry falling to earth. And her teeth. The breeze picked up a whirl of grit I felt blow against my skin and then she was entirely gone.

Zeke looked up at me, his aura brightening, the predator glow. He was insanity, my death trip, pilot error, fetal distress, the cancer in the system.

I should have felt horror at this annihilation, but I did not. I felt only awe. He was death incarnate. And he came to me.

# Chapter 4

# HUNGER

I picked the girl's teeth out of the cracks in the wooden planking, struggling to remember how many the average person has. I couldn't believe how long they were, double pronged where they had been buried in her jaw. I'd read somewhere that teeth were not exposed skeleton but instead dead bone. Inside, our bones lived.

When her hair brushed against my ankle, I almost screamed.

I flashed to a memory of Alex, his face lit with sunlight and laughter. He had blown away as well when I scattered his ashes over the ocean. I wondered if this girl had someone to miss her, someone to mourn.

I looked up at Zeke, this impossible creature I had called into my life. He stood watching me, his predator features lit by the moon, shadows swarming in the hollows of his cheeks and in his eye sockets. A gleam of moisture shined on his curving lower lip and I watched him lick it away with the tip of his pointed tongue.

"Ecstasy," he said, laughter in his voice.

I stood, picking up one of the serpentine dreadlocks, wrapping it through my fingers. "I guess this explains why vampires don't leave bodies lying about all over the world." I recognized shock in the chill on my skin and the way everything seemed sluggish, how it became difficult to think. My tongue felt thick. I was too sober for this.

He laughed, stretching his arms out as though to catch the wind. The breeze opened his shirt across the white velvet of his skin and I reached for him.

He caught my fingers and brought them to his lips. I felt the points of his teeth against my fingertip, but he did not bite, only ran my flesh against the cruel tips, sending shivers up my skin. Finding the girl's teeth in my palm he smiled.

"I'll make you a necklace."

"Is that what the vampires are giving their lovers this year?" I asked.

"It's all the rage." Zeke spun in a circle, his head back, eyes closed. "There is ecstasy in her veins."

"The drug?"

He ran his hands down his chest, feeling the texture of his own skin. "Yes."

"Great." I knelt down and pulled the girl's bag into my lap. "A tripping vampire."

He sank down beside me, laying back against the boards. "It won't last long," he said. "My body metabolizes drugs very quickly. But it's fun while it's happening." His face did that shift, from violent to innocent and I watched the play of the moonlight over his cheekbones for a moment before I opened the bag.

Magic spells fell into my lap. I sifted through crystals and incense and baby witch charms. A tab of ecstasy fell into my palm. I brushed lint away and placed it under my tongue.

Alex appeared again, sitting next to me. "Why do you think magic spells and charms repel him? Do you think crosses do the same thing?"

Let's *find out*. A cross lay tangled with other necklaces at the bottom of the bag and I pulled it out.

"Zeke?"

He rolled over to look at me, his pupils dilated and strange from the drug.

"Have a look at this." I dropped it into his outstretched palm.

He looked at it without flinching, red brows lifting. "Bloody hell, love. What are you trying to do to me?"

I laughed at the outrage in his voice. "Just testing a theory. It doesn't burn you?"

"No. It has no power over me."

"Crosses have no power over me either. I got over that a long time ago."

He lifted his eyebrows at me.

I waved away his question. "Super religious upbringing. Childhood indoctrination. Blah, blah."

He nodded, his lips quirking up. "Is that why you turned to witchcraft? Been suckered in by the devil?"

I grinned. "That's certainly what my family thinks!" Sobering, I asked, "So the cross didn't burn you because no one believes in it? But people do believe in it."

He let it dangle from his fingers. "No one believes in this one. Not right now. I told you: faith is what repels vampires. And the symbols of faith when wielded by someone who believes in them. But most people don't." He grinned. "Have faith, I mean." His fingers caressed the metal, seeming to enjoy the texture.

"So...priests?"

He stretched out and inhaled deeply, as though drinking in the night. "A callow lot mostly." He flung the cross into the dark.

I pulled an envelope from the bag and opened it absently. Alex leaned over my shoulder and we read "Congratulations on your acceptance to Claremont."

My vision dimmed. The waif had a college acceptance to a very good school. I had condemned her at a whim. I put the letter back in the bag and dumped the junk in my lap in on top.

"You said you've never met anyone like me."

He glanced at me. "Absolutely not. There is magic in this world, sure. People wield it, though as far as I can tell, it's mostly unconscious. They have faith in people, symbols, buildings like temples and churches, sometimes their homes. It's like a reflex. They don't employ it intentionally."

"So you've never met someone like me?"

"I've met people with some latent psychic ability, a little more power than others. I've met lots of people with profoundly deep faith. It all feels the same." He stretched out on the old wood, his fingers picking at rough patches. His voice had gone dreamy. "But no. I have never met anyone like you."

"How does faith feel?"

"Like a tingle or a burn if I push it. Like a barrier preventing me from entering certain places or touching certain things."

"Like my house." Beside me, Alex nodded as though confirming my words.

"Have *you* ever met anyone like you?" Zeke asked, rolling over onto his stomach. Sand clung to his shirt and I realized that he lay in Star's dust.

"No. I mean, same as you. A few people with some mild psychic ability but I could never figure out if it was real magic or just intuitive observation skills. And priests have never struck me as magical."

"Like I said, most of them aren't."

"I even tried to find people like me. Alex and I opened an apothecary after college and specialized in craft supplies: potions and charms and such. All I ever met were wanna be witches. Playing at paganism." Alex smiled, laying his hand over mine where it rested on my thigh. I could not feel his touch.

"I call myself a witch because I don't know what else to call myself," I said.

"Wizard? Warlock? Charmed?" Zeke pushed himself up onto his knees and laughed up at the stars.

"You watched *Charmed*?" I did not hide the disbelief in my voice.

He shrugged and pushed himself to his feet. "I prefer *Buffy*."

Alex shook his head, bemused. "Of course you did," I said.

Zeke threw back his head and howled, laughter lurking beneath the madness. Down in the dark someone howled back, and a shiver worked down my spine.

"Zeke?" I inquired. "Was that girl a witch?" He claimed that my blood, witch's blood, tasted different.

"No. She was nothing like you." He lifted his hands to the moon, captivated by the light against his skin.

"This is a dream," I said, turning a piece of painted bone in my fingers. Of all the things in the bag, this one held some small bit of ancient power, the power of life. It hummed, emitting a soft glow.

Zeke looked down at me. "I am not a dream." His eyes burned molten in the silver light, and his chin dropped. I saw his teeth, sharp in the soft corners of his mouth. "I'm hungry."

"You just ate. Didn't you say that you only need a few pints a day?"

"More." His lips drew up in a snarl, sending shadows across the surface of his aura, and a chill ran down my spine. I needed to remember that this creature was not a game, not some beautifully tormented soul from the pages of an Anne Rice novel. He's impossible, madness. He had stepped from my unconscious, the epiphany of my insanity. I wanted to drown in him, I wanted to die in him. The drug lit my veins with fire.

As my guard dropped, the lines of color flooded back; turning to Zeke, I saw him in all his dark splendor. His aura overpowered me, black and silver and red. His features shifted, the innocence he put on like a mask fading in an instant as the predator surfaced. His delicate chin dropped, cheekbones like razors as the night flooded his features. "I am hungry!" He screamed it at the sky, bestial and mad. His fists clenched and the muscles leapt across his shoulders.

"Hunt," I told him. "I want to watch you feed."

"Why aren't you afraid of me?"

"I want the whole world to die," I said.

He looked at me, eyes narrowed. His pupils had returned to normal size. "Then who would I eat?"

"Come on." I took his hand. "I know just the place." I heaved the bag over the railing and heard it splash in the water below.

"Him." I pointed to a suit sitting at the bar, nursing a martini. I saw the intoxication rise into his lurid aura as an olive green darkness in the glow of his vitality.

I have been able to see auras my entire life. As a child I had thought everyone could, perplexed when others did not understand references to the colors I saw, oil-slick swirls around all things, vivid lines of connection between objects.

The olive did not obscure the cruel maroon of the man's vibe, it enhanced it. I saw the sadism on him like tar across his expensive exterior. Reaching into his mind I saw the faces of those he hurt, how he fed on fear.

"Why him?" Zeke lowered his chin to my shoulder, bringing his eyes even with mine as though he looked through my optics to see what I saw.

"What does cruelty taste like?" I asked him, lifting my hand to his cheek as smooth as mine.

"Whiskey."

"Do you like whiskey?"

He laughed, his breath caressing my ear. "You know I do. But who are you to judge?"

I looked at him, surprised. "Who are *you* to judge?" I countered.

"I am a predator. They are prey. But you are one of them."

"I am not prey," I hissed. "I have never been one of them."

"Because you have power?"

"Exactly."

His eyes narrowed at me again. I could feel him thinking but I could not see his thoughts, only the turmoil in the overlapping reds of his aura.

His lips curved up. "Then carry on." He gestured toward the dark interior of the bar.

"Watch this." I pulled away and left him standing in the shadows as I walked toward the bar, sending out my psychic signal. Everyone in the room turned to look at me, their heads swiveling as one in choreographed time. Their lips parted, their eyes shone, swept up by my glamour.

Behind me, Zeke laughed. "Holy shit," I heard him say.

I found hypnotizing people easy, a simple matter of showing them what they wanted to see, as easy as plucking an apple from a tree. I transformed into Helen of Troy, Liz Taylor, Princess Diana. A collective sigh pulsed down the bar and I focused on the man with the olive green aura.

He started as my eyes met his, pupils dilating as my lips curved up. He was not bad looking, probably about thirty-five, silver along his temples, complementing his healthy, tan skin. The expensive suit fit him well and he knew it.

I slipped in next to him, my body close to his, inhaling his musky aftershave. "Buy me a drink."

"What would you like?"

"I'll have a martini," I told the hovering bartender. "With vodka. Extra dirty, lots of olives."

"What's your name?" he asked, running his fingertip over the back of the hand I rested on the arm of his chair.

"Sophia," I said.

"The goddess of wisdom," he replied and a smug stain of color worked its way through his aura.

I leaned into him. "Did you learn that in the Humanities class you had to take in college?"

His grin slipped but he caught it. As he pulled his wallet out to pay for my drink I glimpsed bills, dozens of them. I lifted an olive into my mouth and sucked the vodka from it to hide my prying gaze. I watched him watch my lips on the fruit. "My name is John," he said.

"I don't care." I took a swallow of the drink and sighed as it worked a warm path down my throat. The X in my veins made me hyper aware of every sensation, internal and external.

He chuckled. "I know about women like you," he said, taking a sip of his own drink.

"Yeah?" I arched a brow at him.

"You're just mooching drinks," he said and ran his fingertip across the back of my hand again.

"You think so?" I leaned into him, bringing my mouth close enough to inhale the cigarette he had smoked an hour earlier. Behind me, I felt Zeke tense and my smile was not for John. "You have what I need." I took another swallow of my drink, a big one, and risked a glance over my shoulder, leaning into John, letting him look into my cleavage as distraction.

Zeke leaned against the wall in the corner, his head tilted, his lips drawn up in that sardonic smirk. So punk rock in this light, with his bleached crown of red and white hair.

I finished the rest of my drink and set the glass carefully on the bar, the alcohol roaring in my veins. "Why don't you come with me." I took John's glass from his fingers and swallowed the rest of it, grimacing as the gin hit my vodka flavored taste buds.

He followed me willingly, laughing under his breath, making assumptions about what I wanted. He was so wrong and I laughed back, hating him and glorifying in my ability to finish him. Alex had died on the highway while men like this lived.

Zeke stepped away from his place against the wall and led the way into the street, John so focused on my ass that he didn't notice.

I followed Zeke down the sidewalk, loving the way he moved, a dancer's swagger in the sultry night air. The moon shimmered on the white tips of Zeke's hair as I guided John into the darkened mouth of an alley, turning him so that he stepped into the dark backward. I pushed him into Zeke's arms.

Though I watched closely, the vampire still surfaced in Zeke too quickly to see, his features feral in a heartbeat as he pulled John into his embrace, biting down, drawing in.

John fell to dust in his arms in less than a minute, his aura absorbed into Zeke's pores, his moisture feeding the monster. I saw his green suffuse the red of Zeke for an instant and then he was all gone.

Zeke caught his wallet as it fell with the expensive suit and tossed it to me. His white features flushed for a moment with the new influx of blood and his fangs gleamed red before he licked the drops away.

"You're wonderful bait," he said, making me laugh.

He caught me, pulling me in, his mouth coming down on mine. I tasted copper for a second but drew his tongue deeper, and then his flavor flooded everything away. He tasted of sunshine, warmth, and wine. He could be my vengeance, an illusion of life. I had died and he had revitalized me. He lived, and I became the vampire.

# CHAPTER 5

# LOST

Z ORAH PLACES THE PHONE down, her expression annoyed. "What's up?" I ask her.

"My friend Nicholas is about to call the cops if I don't get in touch with him," she says. "They're worried about me."

"Who's Nicholas?"

She twists a strand of light hair around her finger. "One of Alex's colleagues. He and his wife are...we were all close."

"Call him back. Cops are annoying."

"They're having a get together this evening." She glances at her phone. "In a couple hours, I guess."

I sit up. "Want to go? Be seen?"

She looks at me gravely with an expression I can't quite read. "Will you go with me?"

I grin at her, showing a bit of fang. "You sure it's a good idea to show up with the new boy toy?"

Her lips curve up. "Is that what you are? My 'boy toy'?"

I run my tongue over the tips of my sharp teeth and give her my best eyebrow waggle. "I'm whatever you want, baby." I'm gratified by her laugh.

"Thank you for offering to go."

"I love get togethers. Mingling with civilians."

She shoots me a stern look. "No eating anyone."

I cross my heart with my finger, making her laugh again. "Get dressed. I'll pick you up in an hour. Gotta run home and get cleaned up." I'd been in her house for a week and, though vampires don't sweat, our clothing does accumulate grime. I want new jeans.

Zorah had piled her long hair on top of her head and soft tendrils brush my fingers as I place my palm between her shoulder blades, escorting her up the walk of an opulent townhome in the university neighborhood of San Francisco.

"Who's hosting again?" I ask.

"Dr. Nicholas Weal. The chair of the Arts and Humanities Department. He and Alex worked together."

"I thought Alex ran the shop with you."

"He did. But not full time. He was finishing a doctorate."

She glances at me over her shoulder. "Nicholas became a friend. He invested a bit in the shop."

The inside door is open and a woman appears, backlit against the bright. But I see perfectly in the shadows. I get to watch her when she thinks herself unseen. Her gaze narrows when she spots me.

Zorah strides up the steps to the entry and the woman opens the glass door and sweeps Zorah into her arms. Cool hazel eyes regard me over Zorah's shoulder. I keep my expression blank, meeting her gaze.

Zorah pulls away, close enough for me to feel the heat from her. "This is Zeke," she says. "Zeke, Annette Weal."

Red nails pinch into my palm as I take the woman's hand, bringing the back close enough to my mouth for her to feel my breath against her flesh, bowing straight from the waist at a perfect angle. I had been trained in etiquette in the Spanish court of Queen Isabella; I always make a good impression.

Annette swallows hard. "It's a pleasure, I'm sure," she says, her tone cool. "Please come in."

I appreciate the invitation. Homes can be difficult for me to enter unless explicitly welcomed. There is all sorts of magic in this world, but it exists beyond human consciousness or understanding. It doesn't work the way people of faith believe it does. Homes are protected places because the humans who live in them believe in the inviolability of the spaces they craft to hold their identities. That power works to keep creatures like me out. Though not one another, ironically.

I follow Zorah into a white tiled hall with a formal staircase climbing to a second floor. Framed photos cover one wall and curve up with the stairs, and I realize that Nicholas is a lot closer of a friend than I'd thought. Zorah's face looks at me from many of the photos and she's with a man who can only be Alex.

She has a photo of him on her bedside table, but it had been taken in profile, only giving me an impression of a Roman nose and dark, curling hair. Here I can see his full face and form.

I drop back and walk to the nearest photo. I recognize the room as the one just to the left of the entry; same overstuffed furniture, fireplace, and mantle, though hung with stockings in the photo, the furniture shoved aside to accommodate a large tree draped with sparkling ornaments and white lights.

Annette stands next to a thin man with a goatee, both of them smiling broadly. Zorah and Alex stand between them. Alex is a couple inches shorter than Zorah and he's been caught in a laugh, generous mouth and perfect teeth, strong jaw, dark hair framing his face. Zorah's eyes are on him, her mouth curved up in a smile. She looks healthy, radiant. I hadn't known how tan and glowing she could be.

Annette materializes beside me and I tilt my head toward the photo. "I see you know them well."

She nods, her eyes misting. "Such a tragedy, what happened. They're like family."

"How did you meet?"

"Alex was in one of Nicholas's classes as an undergrad. Then they became friends as Alex worked through grad school. Finally, colleagues."

"And Zorah?"

A tiny frown appears between Annette's brows and then fades. There's some worry there. "Alex and Zorah met his junior year. Inseparable. But she didn't have family who came to the wedding. Just his family and their friends."

"Zeke!"

I turn to see Zorah standing in a doorway toward the back of the house. She glances at the photo, a line appearing between her brows. She gestures me to follow her into a spacious kitchen opening through two sets of French doors onto a stone terrace. Annette hurries in behind us.

People stand about in small groups near citronella torches, laughing and drinking from crystal glasses. The conversation falters as we enter, and I feel Zorah pause. I place my hand on the small of her back, running the tip of my finger in a small circle over the tight muscles there.

A man with silvering hair detaches himself from a group and comes toward us, reaching toward Zorah without glancing at me. He's the man from the photo. She steps into his arms without a hint of hesitation.

They hug a long time, not speaking. I examine the other man curiously, free to do so since his eyes close over her shoulder. Unlike Annette he is completely focused on Zorah. He is trim, dressed in linen slacks and a cream-colored shirt open at the neck. A perfectly groomed goatee, silvering like his hair, gives him a certain flair.

When they part, I observe a slight sheen of tears in Zorah's eyes, but she appears otherwise composed. The man turns and offers me his hand. "I'm Nicholas."

I shake, my grip perfectly firm without squeezing. "Zeke."

"Welcome to my home, Zeke," he says. "What do you drink?"

"Scotch."

He laughs, releasing my hand. "Good man. Let me escort you to the bar."

I glance at Zorah and she nods imperceptibly, so I follow Nicholas onto the patio to an elegant bamboo serving cart. He sets three bottles, each more expensive than the last, next to the ice for my inspection. I select an aged single malt, the most expensive of the three.

"Ice?"

"Not today." Too much water gives me indigestion.

He pours three fingers worth into a cut crystal glass and I take a sip, smiling as the liquor burns down my throat. I could drink the whole bottle and only get a rush from the sugar. My body burns through calories, proteins, and amino acids at an incredibly fast rate. But in exchange, I'm virtually invincible. It's a fair trade.

"Zeke." Nicholas says my name in a speculative voice. "How did you meet Zorah?"

"I saw her at a party last weekend."

"The English Department party? I've heard they can get kind of wild." He laughs, his eyes twinkling.

"Been to a few yourself, Doctor?" I laugh back.

"Well, not since the new wife but I have tied on a few in my time." His mirth subsides. "Zorah is a very special person to all of us here. I would hate to see her come to any harm."

Ah, the warning. I meet his eyes. "I would say that she's already come to a great deal of harm. Life has inflicted it upon her."

Nicholas nods and places his hand on my shoulder. "I see you know about Alex."

I try to decide if the hand is condescending. I leave it for the time being and reply, "It's impossible not to know. The grief pours off her like..." I begin to say, 'like wine,' the line I had spoken to

Zorah herself, but I hesitate. "Well, it's obvious to anyone who knows how to look."

"It's good you got her here tonight. She needs to start coming out again."

I wonder how much Zorah has glamoured this man. It seems like an unconscious reflex, subtly altering how people see her. I feel her try to do it with me. But I don't need her enchantments. I have become Zorah obsessed. She is a new and fascinating thing.

"You recognize that she's vulnerable," he says, squeezing my shoulder. "Are you taking care of her?"

I step back and he releases me. "As much as she'll let me," I parrot what a good human would say. "She's working through some stuff but she's healing." Actually, she might be getting worse. I am curious as to what she'll do next.

Nicholas looks over at her fondly. The object of our discussion is deep in conversation with a tall, gawky woman in ill fitted tweed slacks and a musty cardigan too heavy for the balmy evening. Zorah twines a tendril of light hair around one finger as she speaks, and I admire the way the light plays on her silvery skin.

"She's strong but I'm glad she's found someone. I hope your intentions toward her are pure," he says.

I meditate on the irony of a vampire with pure intentions but that is superseded by the connection of Zorah with vulnerability. Insane with anguish and flirting with alcoholism, yes but vulnerable? Never.

"Losing Alex was a blow and Zorah has led a charmed life," Nicholas shakes his head. "And she's young. The young always think they're indestructible."

"You knew them well?"

"I'm sure that Zorah mentioned that she was a student. Alex was as well. Brilliant, both of them. They collaborated on honors theses under my mentorship. Some of the best work I've ever seen. Alex continued his education. He had the makings of an inspired professor."

"You miss him."

Nicholas did not hide the tears in his eyes. "Initially I thought of them like the children I never had but then they grew up and became friends." He gestured toward the house. "This place was like a second home. I'd hoped they would fill it with children."

I'm watching Zorah. I can't imagine her as a mother. Would she use that glamour on her own children? Could she let them be their own people?

"What was the topic of Zorah's thesis?"

Nicholas smiles, delighted by my question. "An analysis of the similarities and differences between the Aztec goddess of death, Mictlancihuatl, and the Hindu goddess Kali."

"And Alex's?"

"Witchcraft across cultures."

I laugh before I can help myself. Of course. Alex had been trying to figure out Zorah just like I am.

Nicolas looks at me inquisitively. "What's funny?"

"So Alex researched witchcraft," I manage. "Is that what caused them to open the shop? Are they interested in witchcraft?"

He looks at me, puzzled. "I mean, they own the shop. I know their clientele are involved in Wicca and paganism. But Alex and Zorah don't believe in that." He blinks at me. "They're atheists." His tone conveys that all sensible people are.

"Annette mentioned that Zorah didn't have family come to the wedding."

He shrugs. "You'll need to ask Zorah about the details. Her family is..." he hesitates. "Religious."

"Christian, you mean."

He nods. "In the worst way."

I sense that he's not willing to say more and switch topics. "I think a person can be an atheist and still be a witch. Those are not mutually exclusive."

Nicholas grins. "Sounds like a great thesis topic."

I smile back, automatically keeping the points of my teeth covered with my lip. "My thesis topic was an application of Stoic philosophy to the ethical question of murder."

"Fascinating! Where did you study?"

"Humboldt."

"I love Berlin! Who did you study under?"

Tricky question; I'd been there right before the university closed due to World War Two. I should know better than to share such details about my life.

"I argued that Stoicism and existentialism have the same attitudes toward death."

"What a fascinating comparison!"

I love academics. They're so easy to distract.

My eyes have never left Zorah. She's taken a new glass of wine every time the waiter in her white jacket passes but she never wobbles on her tall heels. The woman's tolerance is impressive.

She turns and meets my eyes, and then walks away from the awkward woman without another word. The other woman trails off, apparently in mid sentence.

"Excuse me," I say, pulling away from Nicholas and meeting her in the center of the patio. Her dark eyes turn up to mine as her lips curve up.

"Are you hungry?" she asks.

"For you." She laughs, the light sound at odds with the turbulent energy pouring from her. "But we've been here for twenty minutes and I thought the whole point of this was to let everyone see that you're okay."

"I haven't been seen enough, is that what you're saying?" she smiles and takes a sip of wine. I smell the sweetness of the liquor on her skin, flowing from her pores. I've never actually seen her eat anything, and I cannot gauge how drunk she is.

"Well, you're certainly being watched now."

Her dark blue eyes glance over my shoulder and she laughs again. "I think they're all looking at you, actually."

The buzz of conversation has muted and I am aware of sly glances thrown in our direction. "Only because they're worried about you."

She wrinkles her nose in irritation. "I'm fine." She turns sharply and moves toward the bar, leaving me alone in the middle of the floor, smelling the sweet, herbal scent of her, my skin burning from her presence.

I follow her and accept three more fingers of scotch.

"I hate this house," Zorah says.

That explains the turmoil. "Nicholas said that you and Alex came here a lot."

She glances quickly at me and I see her eyes are red. "We did," she confirms. Her gaze darts away from me and fixes on something over my shoulder. I glance back but there's nothing there, only an empty chair. But she watches it like it's alive. I wonder what she can see that I cannot. Since I've been a vampire, I've always been the one with enhanced sight. But I can't imagine how she sees the world. Or what she sees in it.

"Have you ever been married?' she asks. "Or partnered? In love?"

I see Yrsa's face, the fleck of gold in her left eye, the cleft in her chin. "Of course. You think you're the only one of us who has lost someone?"

Her lips part and I realize that she hasn't considered this. No one exists in Zorah's world except Zorah.

"Who was she?"

I'm angry suddenly, angry at her narcissism, angry at how swiftly she's ensnared me. "I don't remember her name. It's been centuries."

"You don't remember the name of someone you loved and lost?"

"I've had plenty of time to get over it." I swallow the rest of the scotch in a gulp.

"Get over it," she repeats.

"That's one thing love and grief have in common."

"What's that?"

I set my glass carefully on the bar to avoid slamming it down and shattering it. "They fade."

Her expression — lips parted, groove between her brows — makes me angrier but I don't know if it's me or her I'm really mad at. I'm lying to her about Yrsa because I don't trust her with that knowledge. Her knowing that I still thought of a wife with longing would increase her conviction that we are alike, that she'd somehow conjured me as a way of working her will. I am my own vampire. I will not be sucked into her void. If I step into her, it will be my choice.

"They fade," she repeats.

"I know it's hard to imagine. But grief ends. Life goes on."

"Maybe for you." She turns her back and walks away, leaving me on the lawn amidst strangers.

# CHAPTER 6

# WHEN THE DEAD SPEAK

**"I** 'M GOING TO RAISE your wife from the dead."

I carefully set the bottle of wine I'm holding on the counter. "What did you say?" I'd heard her but I need a minute.

She takes a sip from the glass in her hand, her blue eyes widening at me over the crystal rim. "Would you like to speak with her again?"

I consider Zorah in her astounding improbability. She'd left me at the party the other night, and I'd considered being done with her. But then she called and I came running. In all my years I have never dreamed someone like her possible. The magic glimmers on her pale skin, sparking my nerve endings, sending tingles of heat into my flesh.

I had lied to Zorah; I remember my wife with perfect clarity, from the freckles on her nose to her small toes callused on the tops from her sandals. She had smelled of elder flowers in the spring and had been named for her grandmother.

I had lied to Zorah, telling her that my wife's name had faded into the immense span of my life. I hadn't been willing to share Yrsa with anyone, least of all a woman convinced that her grief is more powerful than any grief experienced by anyone in the history of time.

"Why didn't your family come to your wedding?" I'm stalling but I also want to know.

She rocks as though struck. "Who told you that?"

"Annette. Nicholas told me that they're religious."

"That busybody bitch." She takes another swig.

"I can't imagine that you'd let fanaticism stop you." Her anger is directed at Annette. Nicholas gets a pass.

She takes a deep breath. "I was a child. I was growing into power. I didn't know how to hide."

I wait.

"They tried to exorcise me when I was ten."

"Catholic?"

She snorts. "No. Backwoods Baptist. No one in those churches has ever been formally trained. Most of them haven't even been to college."

"I can't imagine you in a church."

She rolls her eyes. "I haven't been in one in a long time. As a child, they scared me."

"That must have been awful." It certainly explains her arrogance, her narcissism. She'd had to develop survival techniques.

"It was. They kept me chained to a bed for almost a week." Her eyes drop. "That's when I figured out how to change people's perceptions of me."

"You figured out how to hide."

She nods. "But it's exhausting. Constantly monitoring what others are thinking and feeling. I left as soon as I could."

"I'd love to see you in a church now."

She looks up, her eyes boring into mine. "Are you trying to distract me?" She sets her glass on the counter and comes toward me on silent, bare feet. She has ahold of my thoughts, though I feel certain she can't see everything. But her suspicions are roused and she stalks toward me, chin lowered, a dangerous glint in her eyes. I brace myself to meet her as she reaches for me, her fingertips dancing heat over my flesh through the long sleeves of my shirt. She has no idea how difficult it is to remain close to her when the magic comes up in her blood, how her power scorches me like the sun.

"You think she's angry at you." Her fingers trace over my jaw and toward my temples and I flinch. For the first time since meeting her, I flinch.

Her eyes flash and she withdraws her touch and reaches for the wine glass "You afraid of little old me?"

"Well." I lean back against the counter and pick up the bottle. Drawing deep, I watch her over the curved rim of glass. "It is true that I have never met anyone quite like you."

"How so?" She searches my face hungrily.

I have the sense that she is trying to figure herself out just as much as I am. Alex had been researching witchcraft, they had opened a shop dedicated to magic. She doesn't know what she is either.

I set the wine bottle on the counter. "I have been alive a long time..."

"How long?" She cuts me off.

I'm not ready for that conversation yet. "A long time," I repeat. "And there are things about this vampire life that I haven't been able to figure out."

"Like what?"

"Faith or magic or witchcraft or whatever you want to call it: it's real. Belief is a powerful force. It works as a sort of psychic protection. The belief of any person works to create a shield or force field, but some are weak and some are strong. Yours is amazingly strong and you use it with intention. I've never encountered that before." I hesitate and her brows lift inquisitively. "I mean, I've certainly met people – occultists, shamans, priests, even people who called themselves witches – who try to use this force with intention. And some of them were even successful. To a point. They manifest good fortune in their lives, they curse people, they shape their reality to their wills." I smile at her. "But you, you can blow holes in walls."

"And you've never seen that."

"No. But you were not able to bring Alex back from the dead." I ignore her wince as I say his name. I'm guessing but of course she had tried to bring him back. "What makes you think you can raise Yrsa?"

"I thought you forgot her name."

"I lied." She isn't denying it and I know that I'm right: she'd tried to bring Alex back from the dead and she'd failed.

I watch her lips thin. "Why?" she asks.

To tell the truth or lie again? I take another pull on the bottle to buy myself time and decide to tell the truth. "Because Yrsa is mine. My memory, my past, my failure."

"Your failure?"

"I tried to make her a vampire and she died."

"In fiction vampires just give humans their blood and viola! Vampire."

"It's a bit more difficult," I tell her. "Almost everyone dies." I drain the bottle and toss it in the bin. "Which is probably a good thing. Thousands of vampires would mow through the mammal population pretty fast."

"Nature does have a tendency to self correct," she muses.

I recognize that her wish to raise Yrsa is her way of testing the power she had once taken for granted and I feel a strong curiosity to see if she can do it. I have mixed feelings about facing my wife, dead for almost a millennium. But I want to have an idea of what Zorah can do if given the chance. She seems to think that her inability to raise Alex is an anomaly, and I feel a powerful interest to see the extent of her abilities.

"Okay, try it."

"Stay there." She spins in a circle in the grass, the hem of her dress floating up as she whirls. Her backyard is verdant and private, surrounded by a stone wall almost obscured behind hedges and grasses and bushes and flowers, encircled by tall trees. Four boulders mark the cardinal directions. There is a fire pit between them. This is not the first time Zorah has done magic in her secret garden.

Lantern light sends shadows leaping across the grass, her silhouette huge against the trees. I feel power gathering around her, like lightning energy. She places torches into the ground before the compass boulders.

"Why do witches draw circles?"

"Because it contains the power. And keeps anything I conjure on the outside where it can't hurt me."

"Why does it work?"

She grins at me. "Because I believe it will, I suppose." She sets four items in a row before the North torch: a jar of salt, a black bowl filled with water, a flask of whiskey, a dagger of polished steel.

Next door a dog barks and Zorah lifts her head, listening, annoyance flickering in her expression. I sense some directing of energy that makes the hair on the back of my neck stand up, and the dog falls silent.

"What did you do?" I ask.

"Made it sleep." She shoots me a smile without humor. "It sleeps a lot."

"Every neighborhood needs a witch," I say. "Cut down on the noise complaints."

She laughs. "Come in and sit in the East," she instructs and I walk to where she points to sit cross-legged, feeling the dew through the thin fabric of my trousers. The lantern warms my thigh pleasantly.

She turns and faces the North. Reaching up, she removes the clip in her hair and it tumbles down, white in the amorphous light.

"Put it out," she says and I blow out the lantern.

Darkness descends but I see her easily with my vampire vision. She exudes energy, the magic pouring off her in waves invisible to the human eye but almost blinding to me. I feel the heat of her in my retinas, on the tender flesh of my lips.

She stays motionless, the epicenter of a hurricane, gathering unimaginable strength. Kneeling, she calls out in a language I do not know. I feel myself sliding, the grass tugging at my slacks as I am shoved backward out of the circle.

She turns to face me, her vulpine features lit with radiance. I cower on the grass before her, exiled from the circle she has drawn. She steps to the edge, glancing at the torch, and fire leaps up. Reaching over the flame, she holds her hand out to me and I place my palm in hers without hesitation. From behind her back the dagger blade appears; quick as a prayer she draws it across my palm and my supernatural blood gushes forth, black in the ephemeral light. I feel a bright flash of pain, quickly fading as my blood goes to work healing me,

Zorah watches me heal for a moment and then turns to dip the blade in the black bowl. The fluid spreads across the surface of the water in a dark scrim.

"Why did you expel me from the circle?" I ask.

"I didn't." Her lips curve up. "I guess you're dangerous." She moves away, counterclockwise around the circle, the torches springing alight as she passes. She sprinkles salt as she goes. The salt glows as it drops from her fingers.

She faces the West and lifts her arms above her head, the dagger, washed of my blood, in one hand, the flask in the other. "Guardians of the West," she calls. "Guardians of the Land of the Dead, hear me!" She uncorks the flask and pours a large amount of the whiskey onto the ground, taking a large swallow for herself. "Hear me!" she calls again and suddenly the energy pours off of her in streams, vanishing toward the direction she faces.

The world falls silent. The city stills and I feel fear for the first time in centuries. I had wondered at the extent of her power but had never imagined anything like this. Blisters raise along my exposed forearms and I inch back, fearful of being burned alive.

"Set!" she cries. "Osirus, Dimmuzi, Tammuz, hear my call!" She pours the water containing my blood in a line before her, dissolving the salt. She's made a door.

"You will answer me!" A wind rips through the trees, branches cracking against one another. I hear the dog howl, but she takes no notice. "You will come to my call!"

The wind pushes against my back, gently at first and then with more force. It feels like it's blowing through me. I feel weakened.

Zorah throws her arms out and I have an impression of tremendous power.

Far away, over the horizon, something answers.

I hear the voice in my cells, in my vampire blood. I feel it as a vibration threatening to tear my atoms apart. There is a door in the West and it speaks in a tongue I refuse to understand. That language is meant only for the dead. To hear it is abomination.

Zorah hears it, too. For a moment her face fills with elation, and I understand the depths of her insanity in her smile. "Kali!" she renews her call. "Ereshkigal! Persephone!" She calls the gods of death by their names in every culture, the energy pouring off her the medium of exchange. I cannot imagine the reservoirs of power giving rise to such a display. "I need Yrsa, the one the vampire Zeke calls wife."

Again, I feel the voice, and see Zorah sway in its grasp.

"Give her to me. I would speak with her."

Such arrogance, to command the gods of the dead. I watch reality bend to her will. The West goes dark, the city lights extinguished, all sound except Zorah's voice silenced. I feel a deep shudder in the core of my being as the great door opens.

But what answers Zorah's call is not my dead wife. I catch a glimpse of something huge, black, and unimaginable, and then my vision splits. A terrible pain slices through my temples. My vision goes out like a lamp and cool liquid pours in a gush from my nose and ears. I feel my veins contract and the flesh on my lips split as the moisture leaves my body. It feels like the wind is blowing me away, toward that gaping maw Zorah has torn in reality. I am sure I have died. I cry out but the sound disappears under the rushing in my ears. All sounds fall out of the world. I lose consciousness.

I awake hungrier than I have been except maybe that first night I crawled from the ground, born anew into the shadows. I smell the rich tang of blood and lift my hands to my eyes. Gore has dried in rusty flakes over my skin. I see collapsed veins below the surface of my flesh. Struggling to remember, I see Zorah, crumpled on the grass.

I rise to my feet and run toward her, not fully aware of who she is or who I am in relation to her. All I can smell is her witch's blood, unlike anything I have ever tasted.

I am stopped in my tracks, halted by an invisible barrier that sends tingles and sparks across my exposed flesh. I push harder and my skin begins to smolder. I draw back, memory returning.

I shy away from the recollection of that black gate opening and walk around the invisible barrier until I see Zorah's face. She lies crumpled on her side, her silvery hair obscuring all but her mouth which drips a thin trickle of blood. She looks dead.

"Zorah!" I see the slow rise of her breath. "Zorah!" I call again but she does not move.

The hunger overwhelms me, a monstrous urge. I shake my head, distracted. I sense the daylight coming and run down the shaded walk of Zorah's house and onto the sidewalk. I look quickly up the street and then down, and into the startled face of a dog lifting its leg on the neighbor's gatepost. It wuffs in surprise.

The dog dies before it knows a thing, blood pumping down my throat until the body falls to dust, drained of all fluids. I am left holding a hide like an old rug. I shove it under the edge of the lilac hedgerow.

Life roars back into me, my veins expanding as liquid pumps through me. The stars have disappeared, and I feel the tingle of the coming sun.

I run back down the walk into the secluded yard. Zorah lies in the same position on the grass. Her circle of protection won't let me in and I beat my fist against the obstruction in frustration, sending shivers of warmth, similar to the coming sunlight, across my flesh.

I can't get to her and I am out of time. My skin will begin to smoke if I stay exposed, and so I retreat into the deep shadow of the deck where we'd spent that first delirious night. I pace up and down in the limited space and watch the sun rise. I cannot look directly at the brightness of the sky, but the shade from the large trees blocks most of the light's deadly rays.

The golden light of dawn creeps over Zorah, lighting her silver hair and pale skin with a rosy glow. I can do nothing but watch.

I watch her all morning. I see the sun's rays begin to tint her skin with red radiance, the pink darkening toward a burn. She never moves except for the slow rise and fall of her breath and the occasional stirring of her hair in the breeze.

At noon clouds begin to rise and by one it begins to rain, cool and refreshing in the summer sun. Zorah finally moves, rolling onto her back, opening her mouth to the water falling from the sky.

"Zorah!" Still nothing. I reach past the edge of the deck and grab a rock, the smoke rising from my skin even from limited exposure. Taking aim, I toss the pebble at Zorah. The stone passes easily through the barrier and bounces off her foot.

She blinks slowly and turns toward me, reaching sluggishly to move the wet shanks of hair that coat her face like a second skin. I stare into her eyes.

At first, I think that my mind is playing tricks. One eye looks perfectly clear, dark blue and shining in the light. But the other eye appears dark, the pupil grown huge, consuming the iris and the white. I realize that a blood vessel has burst, drowning her eye in dark blood.

"Zorah! Come to me." I hold out my hands and she blinks slowly.

Instead of moving toward me, she leans down as though to touch her toes and grasps the hem of her dress, drawing it up over her head, lifting her hips to let the fabric slide free.

She wears nothing beneath and I gasp at the gashes and welts along her skin. The dress appeared unmarred, but her skin has torn as though something buried beneath her flesh had broken free.

"Zorah," I call again, and she rolls over and crawls to me through the grass.

Up close, she looks worse. The eye is filled with blood and the blue iris peers at me through a haze of redness. The edges of the gashes look red and infected, seeping blood and clear fluid.

The scent of her blood makes me aware that I still hunger but I quell the thought. "What happened?"

Her eyes, the one blue, the other dark and alien, fill with tears. "I couldn't do it." The admission comes out in a soft wail. She buries her head in my lap, shoulders shaking. I rest a hand on her silvery hair, feeling the grief pour through her.

Gently, avoiding the gashes as much as possible, I gather her onto my lap where she huddles, trembling, the tears running from her eyes. I put one finger in my mouth and find the sharp incisors, biting down.

My mouth fills with the taste of my own blood. "Here." I tilt Zorah's face back and slip my bleeding finger between her lips. Her eyes slide closed, and she slumps against me, semiconscious, swallowing once and then again.

I watch the wheals on her flesh close, the frayed edges drawing together into red seams that lighten and vanish. Just a few drops of my vampire blood heals her in minutes. When I withdraw my finger from her mouth I have healed as well, not even a bruise marking the place I had punctured.

I shift her back against my knees so that I can look into her face. When her eyes remain closed. I shake her gently by the shoulders.

Both eyes have returned to normal and she looks at me from a face filled with light, illuminated from within by my magical blood. I watch a small chicken pox scar vanish from her forehead as the vampire inside her works.

"Zorah, what happened? I passed out."

She drops her face, a curtain of hair, tangled with grass and bits of debris, sliding forward. She brings her hands to her face.

"It didn't work." Her voice sounds muffled through her fingers.

"Zorah, I don't even know if raising the dead is possible. I don't know if the universe works that way."

"It has to!" She looks up at me, her eyes flashing though she still leaks tears in a slow river. "You are here. You can't exist. *Vampires*," she prods me sharply in the chest. "Vampires aren't real."

I take her hand so that she won't poke me again. "You lost me, love. Vampires shouldn't exist so you should be able to raise the dead? I'm not following."

She rubs the back of her hand over her eyes like a child and sighs. "You prove that the impossible is possible. If you're possible, anything is."

I shake my head. "Zorah, that's not logical. Just because the world doesn't know about us doesn't mean that vampires don't have a scientific explanation."

"What about me then? What about what I can do?"

"That has an explanation, too. You've said so yourself."

She stares out across the lawn, her brow furrowed. Though the signs of her trauma have faded, she remains wan, her blue eyes standing out of her pale face.

"So maybe raising the dead is impossible. That's why I can't do it."

This time I sigh.  "Maybe. But Zorah, you're going..." I redirect. "You're driving yourself crazy thinking about it."

She looks back at me, the line between her brows growing deeper. Then she pushes away from me and stands. She walks away into the sunlight, her skin almost too bright for me to look at. She holds her hands out over the circle she had created and I feel the crackle of her will. But nothing happens.

"I failed," she says. "I can't do it. I don't have enough power." She regards me solemnly. "I need more power."

# CHAPTER 7

# TURNING

"**I** WANT YOU TO make me a vampire." She lays her head against my arm and glances up at me with glittering eyes.

I do not move, but a chill works its rapid way down my spine. For a month I had wondered if this request would come and now here it is, making the space between us swell.

Though I betray no outward sign she senses my emotion and sits up, her silvery hair falling in a straight sheet over her bare shoulders and breasts, skin lighter than the curtain of hair.

It has been a month since she tried to raise the dead; the moon is dark again. A month in which I had become more accustomed to her home than mine. I am now able to pass freely over her doorsteps, no invitation required.

And I am falling for her. Not "in love," nothing so juvenile as that, but in fascination, definitely in lust, even into obsession. I have been wandering this world for centuries, thought I knew everything of its magical corners and enchanted places. But here is Zorah: impossible, tempestuous, suicidal, and more powerful than anything I have encountered.

"It seems, love, as though you of all people, have a vested interest in being mortal."

She looks away to where her hand rests against my arm, at the silver band on her left ring finger. A tiny line appears and vanishes between her brows.

"But vampires can die. You're not really immortal."

I sit up and rest against the headboard, resisting the urge to pull the sheet over my bare torso. The thought of turning her, seeing her as a vampire, is sweetly seductive, yet vampire blood kills almost all it enters. Though her strength is astounding I fear that the blood may be her undoing. It had killed Yrsa in a less than day and she'd been healthy and strong. Zorah is weakened by grief and alcohol and the power blazing through her.

I wonder about that power as well. Would the vampire blood enhance it? If so, what would she become? Or maybe vampirism is incompatible with whatever makes her a witch. In which case it would kill her.

"No," I say.

She gazes at me as though my refusal is beyond belief, her lips parted and glistening. "Why not?"

"Almost all of the people who ingest enough blood to turn die instead. I've told you this." I lift her hand to my mouth, turning the soft flesh of her wrist against my lips. "And the world is a much more interesting place with you in it."

"You think that I am mad with grief and rage at the world. You think this is my way of getting back at death. You think I'm not thinking clearly." She presses her wrist against my lips, preventing me from replying. I feel the pulse of her blood; I can smell the rich fragrance of it below her skin.

I nip at the tender skin pressed against me. She does not pull away and I bite harder, tasting the blood well into my mouth. The colors of her aura bloom before my eyes.

"I will just consume you completely and then I'll be able to do magic, too."

"It wouldn't last." She smiles. "Anyway, you'd miss me."

I reluctantly release her, swallowing the last vestiges of her essence, swiping my tongue over the two neat holes in her arm, my saliva causing the wounds to close.

She watches her arm heal with fascination. "How does it work? Why does a little bit of you heal me but more would kill me?"

I give in and pull the sheet up. "I think a little bit just provides healing. But a lot triggers a catastrophic immune response."

"Catastrophic," she repeats. "Some poisons work that way." She rubs a finger over the smooth skin of her wrist, skin that moments ago had wept blood. "Is that how Yrsa died? When you tried to turn her?"

I close my eyes briefly. I remember it like yesterday even though Yrsa is now bones in her grave. "Yes," I admit.

"And that's why you're worried that she's angry with you."

"No," I correct. "It was my choice. And hers. Neither of us knew what could happen. It was an accident."

"What happened when you turned? Did you almost die?"

"I think I did die."

"How did it happen?"

This memory is less clear but because of drunkenness, not time. "One night I met a man. He was urbane, charming, handsome, well-spoken. His Greek was much better than mine, though it was not his first language."

"Greek!" she says. "That's your accent."

I'm surprised. "I have an accent?"

She grins. "It's slight. But yes."

I file this piece of information away. When speaking English I try for a flat affect, shifting between American and British pronunciations depending on where I am in the world.

"You were telling me..." she prompts.

"He brought drinks. A lot of drinks. I don't remember leaving the bar. But I do remember a pain in my throat, drinking something rich and thick. Then I woke up." I don't tell her about the other flashes of memory, how his mouth tasted of honey, the feel of him inside me.

"That's it?"

"Yes. Yrsa told me I'd burned with fever and delirium for over a week. Then I died. Or appeared to. She was very surprised when I walked through the door." I smile, remembering how the bowl in her hand shattered when she'd dropped it, how she ran to me on bare feet through the shards of pottery.

"What happened to the one who made you?"

"I ate him." I laugh at her facial expression. It's clear this is the last answer she expects.

"You...what?"

"One thing none of the vampire stories talk about is how vampires prey on other vampires. There are some who love to hunt and kill the young. It's sport. And vampire blood is the best kind."

"So you're cannibals." She looks horrified.

"Some of us are. That's what I think my maker was. He turned people just to be able to feed on young vampires."

"Holy shit. That's crazy. So you got the better of him?"

"I did. Mostly luck. He came looking for me, but I happened to see him first. We fought. I won."

"Simple as that?"

"Basically. Then I tried to turn Yrsa. But she died. It took her about a day. She burned with fever, lost her mind, and then stopped breathing. I sat by her for three days to make sure she wouldn't wake up."

"She didn't."

"No. She started to rot." I push the covers back and stand up. Picking up my jeans off the floor I pull them on.

"Do you miss her?"

I look down into her pale face and smile softly. "Time heals all wounds. I've had almost a thousand years."

She gazes up at me, a small smile on her lips. "How can you ask me if I really want this? When you tell of it that way?"

I draw my finger along her fine jaw, tracing the small oval of her chin. "Zorah, I'm afraid I would kill you. And I'm worried that this may not be the best time for you to undergo a major transformation even if you do survive it."

She tilts her face away, peering at me from the corner of her eye. "Are you worried about my sanity?"

"Yes," I admit. "I think you need to heal more. I think we have all the time in the world."

She stands up abruptly. "*You* have all the time in the world. I could be hit by a bus tomorrow." She paces across the room, picking her dress from the floor and pulling it over her head. She grabs the bottle on the mantle and takes a pull, grimacing at the taste. The energy pouring off her is frenzied, corybantic. I can still see the fading colors of her aura, which darkens abruptly from blue to almost black.

I walk to her slowly and she watches me warily, taking another pull from the bottle. I gently take the whiskey from her and drink deeply, feeling the sugars and alcohol hit my bloodstream, deadening the hunger.

"I'll take my chances," I tell her. "You probably won't be killed by a bus. And you probably would be killed if I tried the transformation."

She narrows her eyes and takes the bottle back, pulling it from my hand when I try to resist. "Are you hungry, Zeke?" She holds out her wrist. "Take your fill."

"Don't tempt me."

She dangles her hand back and forth, taunting.

I yank the bottle away from her and drink. I feel my skin warm as my metabolism gears up. "I think I'm in the mood for a brunette tonight."

She scowls at me. "You kill a lot of humans for someone who's gone all moral."

"You're assuming that killing humans is wrong."

She reaches for the bottle, but I upend the last of it into my mouth and set it back on the mantle instead of giving it to her. Her eyes narrow dangerously.

"It's just like everything else, pet," I tell her, suppressing a grin at the way her eyes flare at the endearment. "Nature is set up in an endless cycle of prey and predator. Vampires are engineered to capture victims." I hold my arms out, palms up, and let the grin loose. "And who am I to defy nature?"

"That's an excuse and you know it. You just told me that you're more like cannibals than anything."

"Okay, fair enough. So maybe I just like the taste of human blood. Just like when folks want to eat a steak and murder a cow."

"Cows are not like humans."

"Bollocks!" I point a finger at her and wave it reprovingly. "Now who's succumbing to faulty logic? The vast majority of human beings have about the same amount of common sense, reason, and intellectual ability as a really intelligent Jersey." I turn her phrase back on her. "And *you* know it."

She crosses her arms and looks away, her jaw set. "You're trying to distract me."

I lower my tone suggestively. "I know another way to distract you."

Her face whips back toward me, her lips narrowing. "Don't you dare change the subject."

I step toward her, bringing my hands down the bare flesh of her arms, gentle, using all of my vampire charm. The charm that my kind uses to seduce our prey. "What's the subject again?"

She shoves me away, her hands warm against the naked skin of my chest. I take a quick step back to keep my balance and she flounces past me, yanking open the door to the hallway. Sunlight pools at the opposite end of the short corridor, pouring through the living room windows. My eyes water.

She turns, stepping slowly backward, away from me. "Forget that it's daylight, Zeke?"

I stalk after her, safe in the shadows. "Never."

"Daylight. And you can't have me."

"I've had you three times in the last twenty-four hours," I remind her, grinning.

She scowls, a flush lighting her cheekbones. "Fine. If you won't do it, I'll find someone who can."

I catch her before she can blink, pulling her body roughly against me. "Don't you dare. You have no idea what you're saying." I shake her none too gently and she pushes away but I hold her, fingers digging into her flesh.

She slaps me hard, her fingers curled under, a stinging blow across my face. A star bursts in my left eye and I growl, releasing her so abruptly that she almost falls. Her pupils are dilated, her face flushed, her breath coming hard. I see the telltale signs of bruises bloom on her upper arms.

"What's this, Zeke?" She pushes her hair out of her face, her chin lifting defiantly. "Are you afraid for me?"

She is so beautiful that I want to drain her on the spot and the depth of my hunger for her frightens me. In that moment I almost did it. I almost took her. "Fine," I say instead. "Do whatever the hell you want."

Her chest heaves with rapid breath. "You should remember that I am not yours to command."

"Yeah, just mine to fu..."

Her eyes widen. "What?"

I linger over the words in my mouth, childishly pleased to see the fury on her face. "Mine to fuck." I say it slowly, deliberately.

Her words tangle and she splutters, her blush darkening a shade.

I laugh without humor, the sound harsh to my ears. "You called me, love." I point at her again. "And don't you forget it."

She spins on her heel and stalks away into the sun, into the light where I cannot follow. For a moment her body is silhouetted against the light, deliquesce, almost too bright to bear. And then she is gone.

# CHAPTER 8

# MALACHI

T HE PAVEMENT GLIMMERED UNDER the streetlamps, wet with rain that fell in a thin mist, catching the light in crystalline shimmers that clung to my eyelashes. Past midnight, the crowds that swarmed the wharf have long departed save for the homeless and the college drunks leaving the bars, laughing and holding one another for support.

I sat in the doorway of a shipping office, listening to the waves, watching the cold rain fall. I pulled my fleece jacket closer. Alone and unseen, I allowed the mental barriers I erected before my vulnerable mind to slip. The colors came rushing in, imbuing the world with Technicolor, almost too beautiful to bear.

The auras of the trees breathed a deep green, pulsing with the rhythm of the universe, the faint respiration of all living things. The sky glowed, deep purples shot through with the unhealthy olive of air pollution. The rain fell silver, coating everything with cold light, each drop a swarm of living molecules. Bats swept through the lights high above, and the bugs that clustered around the warmth even in the rain. The bats glowed red and they darted, too fast for my eyes to follow. Zeke's aura was the same color red but bigger, predatory, hungry. Each time the bats took a bug a tiny burst of white light flashed, a living being consumed.

I had left Zeke more than seven hours ago, running into the sunlight where he could not follow. I wondered if he still waited in my house or if he had left, returning to wherever he lived when he wasn't in my bed.

I closed my eyes, taking a deep breath. My mind raged, as it had since Alex died, tugging at the corners of possibility, searching for a way out, a way to roll back time, a way to erase his death. I reached into myself, searching for the quiet center.

I felt him manifest before me, the breeze on my face his breath, the tapping of raindrops his soft laugh. I opened my eyes and looked into Alex's face formed of the mist and rain. He smiled and evaporated. My focus blew away on his wind.

I sighed. Before I had found working my will easy, like breathing. Now it felt like my magical muscles had atrophied. Everything took more effort.

I closed my eyes and reached out with my mind, looking for those red, predator auras. Color bloomed in my consciousness and I reached for them, glowing bloody among the sparks of life inhabiting reality like stars, like galaxies. Distance was impossible to gauge in this other world. I sank my mental claws into one of those crimson auras and pulled. When I demanded of the universe, I always got what I wanted. If Zeke denied me, I would find another way. I was tired of waiting.

I pulled. The red aura resisted and then turned toward me. I felt a draw, deep in my being, rising exhaustion. My focus faltered and I let it go. Zeke would turn me, he had to. I just had to convince him that it was the only way I would survive. I couldn't keep going like this.

Then I saw him.

He stepped into a circle of yellow halogen light on the far side of the four lanes and lifted his face into the rain. The glowing droplets coated his face in liquid silver, and I watched the mist flow into his nostrils as he inhaled. He looked like a

Botticelli angel in leather and flesh, hair the color of oil coating his shoulders and streaming down his back. He wore a long vinyl coat and the rain flooded down him, turning him into a statue of living metal. But his splendor was not what made me shiver.

His aura is what made my breath catch. It surrounded his body in a blood red cloud, shot through with darker maroons and blacks, like blood in moonlight. And I knew him.

Vampire.

It had worked. I had summoned another.

He dropped his face and opened his eyes, looking across the street almost straight at where I stood in the shadows. I brought my mental barriers back up and the colors faded from reality. Now I could see him clearly, devoid of the cloaking luminescence of the silver rain. Now he was just wet.

He was dressed all in black: leather pants, black shirt, and the vinyl coat. Some sort of silver belt buckle caught the light; otherwise, his white skin was the only thing light about him. That and his eyes. I thought they might be green.

He glanced up and down for traffic and then trotted across the street, his coat billowing behind him. As he drew closer, I saw the rings in his eyebrow and nose and the silver stud in his lip. The belt buckle was a longhorn skull. He looked young, a lovely androgynous face with a sharp narrow little chin below gently rounded cheeks. And he was not human.

He took a last long step onto the sidewalk fewer than ten feet from where I stood and glanced around. His eyes were the color of seawater in sunlight, contrasting beautifully with his white skin and black hair. The stud in the middle of his full lower lip glinted with the tiny sparkle of a gemstone like the droplets of water that coated his skin, giving him a crystalline shimmer.

I looked past his surface at his aura and the redness swarmed out from him, enveloping him in a cloud like a mist of blood. And he saw me.

I knew his vision would be sharp. I knew how Zeke saw in the dark even better than I did. And this boy looked immediately into the shadows where I stood as though I had called his name.

He smiled and I almost laughed, it was such an innocent expression. When Zeke got hungry, his chin dropped and his eyelids lowered, transforming him immediately into a predator. This boy was still the angel, even with prey in his sights.

I stepped toward him into the light and his lips halted their upward ascent as my eyes met his. I did not look away and he smiled wider, biting his lower lip.

I grinned and he looked startled. "I know what you are," I said.

"Oh, yeah?" His voice was pure Texas twang and I did laugh this time.

Fucking players. All of them. He used his beauty to disarm his victims—I could tell this without reading his mind.

"Yeah. Hollywood makes movies about monsters like you."

"I'm no monster. Can't a guy take a walk in this town without being accused of villainy by some girl lurking in a doorway?"

"You're no guy."

"How do you know that?" He stepped closer, into the overhang of the doorway, now fewer than six feet away. His eyes glinted in the white of the streetlights.

"I can see you." I reached out and trailed my fingertips along the surface of his aura. The red mist parted, and I watched the blue of my essence disrupt his energy.

He stiffened and shivered slightly, the motion almost undetectable except for the rain water that fell from his coat in a gentle patter. "Monsters don't exist, didn't anyone ever teach you that?" He took a half step back away from me.

"I guess not." I leaned back against the wall behind me.

He looked at me appraisingly, then pulled a rumpled pack of Camels from his coat pocket. Seating one in the corner of his mouth, he held the pack out to me.

Fuck cancer. I planned to either die or be a vampire, so what the hell? I stepped forward and wrapped my lips around a cigarette protruding from the pack. When he held the lighter for me, I cupped my hand around the flame and, quick as lightning, drew a finger across the back of his hand holding the lighter. My finger left a red welt, like sunlight across vampire skin.

He jumped, a cry escaping his mouth, the cigarette flipping out of his fingers, sizzling out in the damp at his feet.

"What the FUCK!" He looked disbelievingly at the weal on his skin. "What did you do?"

He was on me like lightning, like death, like a sudden heart attack, shoving me backward into the wall, and all I could do was laugh.

Laugh into his beautiful face, laugh into his seawater eyes, laugh against his pale skin as I raised blisters along his lips like lava, like venom.

He sprang off, flinging himself into the rain, hair across his face in Medusa snakes, his mouth curving up over fangs. "What the FUCK are you?"

His skin healed over the wounds and he straightened up, the angelic countenance finally slipping, the predator shining forth from beneath.

"I am Zorah." I stepped into the light and the rain came down on my hair. "And I've been waiting for you."

He held his ground but flinched as I smiled. I loved to make vampires flinch.

"What are you called?" I asked him.

He dropped his face, his eyes falling into shadow. "Malachi. What *are* you, Zorah?"

I reached into my pocket. "Some call me a witch. That's as good a term as any." I had a pink Swiss Army knife on my keychain, and I unfolded the blade, a whole inch in length. But I kept it sharp, and I drew it across my palm, letting my blood well. I saw his nostrils flare as he caught the scent, but he didn't move. I had him scared.

"Want this?" I held my palm out and the blood pooled in the cup of my hand, diluted by the falling rain. I flattened my hand and the liquid poured off. More blood welled; I had cut deep.

I flashed him a grin and his eyes narrowed slightly. "You could help me with this," I said. "One drop of your vampire saliva would fix this right up."

He took a step toward me, then stopped. "Vampires aren't real."

I didn't bother acknowledging that. "I won't hurt you unless you try to hurt me," I promised.

Still, he hesitated.

"You're the monster, Malachi. Remember? You scared of little, old me?"

He approached with caution and took my hand, bringing the slash in my palm close to his face. He licked across my skin and I giggled at the tickle.

His eyes widened and I watched his pupils dilate. He looked up at me, a smear of my blood darkening his lower lip.

"You taste like..."

I pulled my hand away from him and watched in fascination as the cut healed, the sliced edges of my skin drawing together like a zipper.

He straightened and looked at me appraisingly. "Alright. You have my attention. I want to know what you are."

"I'm Zorah." I smiled.

"Right. And I'm Malachi. But what are you?" He gestured at my hand, now hanging by my side. "You taste human but different somehow. Like I remember sunlight feeling. And...why can I see colors?" He touched his hand where I had burned him. "I've never met a human who could do that."

"I'm a witch," I said again and his eyebrows lifted.

"So you said." He ran his tongue over his lip. "Like the little pagan goth chicks who hang out down on the docks on full moon nights?"

"Not exactly."

I remembered the look on Zeke's face when I left him, walking into the last sunlight of the dying day. I had run away from him, rebuffed by his refusal to make me a vampire. I had told him that I would find another of his kind. And Malachi had appeared. I could call every vampire in the world if I wanted. Call until I found one who would work my will.

Malachi cautiously stepped back under the overhang. "A witch. So...prove it."

"The welt I raised on your hand isn't proof enough? I could burn you alive with a thought."

He shrugged. "Do something without touching me." He lifted his wet hair. "Dry me off."

"You gonna ask me to conjure an umbrella next?"

"Can you?"

I considered. "Translocation is difficult. But drying you off? That's easy."

It was a simple matter of focusing on the water molecules, breaking them with a gentle touch of my mind. Steam puffed up and we were both dry.

"My god." Malachi twisted a length of his black hair around his hand and looked at it disbelievingly. The fine strands curled at the tips in the breeze. "Well, thank you, I guess."

"Do you drink, Malachi?"

He chuckled, his cherub mouth opening over tiny, even teeth. His white incisors were slightly longer and sharp, as though filed. Zeke had the same teeth, too discreet to notice but sharp as razors.

"Hell, yes, I drink. But what about that umbrella?"

"This is easier." I held my hand into the rain and the droplets ceased as though turned off.

Malachi stepped out into the damp and looked up into the rainless clouds. "That is a neat little trick."

I stepped out beside him, pulling up my hood against the humid air. "Let's go to Old Joe's." I remembered the first victim I had found there for Zeke, the man's polluted aura and the way his wallet had fallen to the pavement as his body blew to dust, all his juices pouring into Zeke's hungry throat.

Regulars still crowded the tavern at this late hour and I slid between two huge bikers to the bar, ignoring the eyes on me. I disregarded my reflection in the mirror behind the bottles; I looked all tired eyes and chalky skin that no amount of concealer and eyeliner could hide. I saw Malachi behind me, pressed into me by the throngs.

"Vampires can be seen in mirrors," I said, mostly to myself.

Malachi heard of course; vampires have sharp senses. "We're physical. All that myth and nonsense is superstitious bullshit." His fingers rested lightly on my shoulder and I felt the coolness of his skin through my coat.

The cooler a vampire's skin, the longer it has been since feeding. I wanted Malachi hungry. "Whiskey," I ordered. "And a glass of your house red."

"How do you know what vampires drink?" I felt Malachi's breath stir the hair on my neck.

"Strong liquor keeps the hunger at bay, right?" When I turned to face him, he stood closer than I expected, and I saw tiny freckles over his nose, slightly darker than his skin.

"You know a lot about us." I felt his cool breath on my face and smelled a light scent, like flowers. Zeke smelled of sunlight on sand, the smell of the desert after the rain. This one exuded the delicate scent of jasmine.

I handed him the whiskey and watched him drink, the tilt of his elfin chin, the way the skin rippled along his throat as he swallowed. He set the glass on the bar and turned to me, leaning in, his scent enveloping me.

"Tell me, Zorah. How you know so much about vampires."

I saw the flecks of darker green in his ocean eyes and the sheen of moisture on his mouth.

"How long have you been a vampire?"

"I asked a question first."

"So you answer first."

He tilted his head back and contemplated me from under lowered lids. "Eighty years."

I almost smiled. I didn't know exactly how long Zeke had been a vampire, but he predated this baby by centuries.

"So, Zorah." Malachi drew one finger along the back of my hand resting on the bar. "How do you know so much about vampires?"

"Are you still hungry?"

This distracted him. His lips curled up over sharp teeth and he glanced around the pool hall.

I leaned into him and his eyes came back to me. "Because I am excellent bait."

"Are you for real?" he whispered.

He was lovely, much more delicate than Zeke. He couldn't have been out of his teens when he had been turned.

"No," I replied. "I am not real." I dropped the shield from my mind and color flooded in, almost too bright, and I narrowed my eyes against it as though that would help. Prey caught my attention immediately, a man with an aura the color of air pollution, it coated his body like oil, shot through with a blood red streak emanating from his groin. I knew this aura: rapist.

"I bet I can get him outside in under five minutes," I said, gesturing.

Malachi appraised the man, bent over one of the pool tables to take a difficult bank shot. "Okay," he said.

I heard him laugh as I sauntered away, rolling my hips more than usual, unbuttoning the top buttons of my blouse.

I knew what I looked like. I looked like a victim, frail and pale with my Norse features. I heightened my pallor with black clothes, the shimmering blouse, the tight jeans, the fleece jacket hanging in artful tatters. Grief, alcohol, and the absence of sunlight had given my face a new angularity, shadows swarmed under my cheekbones and beneath my eyes. Tonight, I'd heightened this effect with black eyeliner smeared over my lids.

I stopped at the pool table and glanced around the bar as though looking for someone, reaching out with my powerful mind. I caught the man's eye as though by accident and looked quickly away, sliding between the people toward the back door.

Pool Player dropped his cue and followed me. The other player gaped after him. Malachi swallowed the last of his whiskey and moved away from the bar.

I stepped into the shadows of the dark alley, lit only by orange storm light. I glanced over my shoulder, startled by the proximity of the man behind me; he took a long step and was on me.

"Hey, baby," he slurred and I heard a lifetime of alcoholism in his voice. He grabbed my arm and I let him, pulling away, not hiding my revulsion. I felt happy that he was about to die.

The door opened behind him silently and Malachi stepped into the darkness, black against black.

I let the man pull me in, putting forth minimum effort. He was strong but drunk and I resisted enough to keep the illusion of victimization. "Get your hands off me!"

He swiped a clumsy hand across my chest, grabbing the collar of my blouse and ripping. I heard buttons patter across the pavement, and I shoved him back.

Malachi reached into his jacket and extracted the rumpled pack of Camels. Tipping his head into the small flame from his lighter, his eyes flashed green. Drawing the smoke into his lungs, he leaned back against the door.

I shoved the man again. "You could step in any time," I said and Malachi grinned.

Pool Player did not realize that I spoke to the vampire lurking behind him. "I'll step in, baby. Girl like you asks for it when she comes to a place like this." The man tried to kiss me and I spat in his face.

Before I saw it coming Pool Player backhanded me. I felt my lip split against my bottom teeth, and a meteor shower flashed across my vision. I cried out, my hands flying to my face. I found myself on my knees and then shoved down against the pavement. I smelled the musty scent of old alcohol, fermented and mixed with the fish smell of ocean salt. Distantly, I felt the man tug on my jeans. Squinting through eyes gone blurry, I found Malachi, still standing in the doorway, still smoking, his smooth brow slightly furrowed, quizzical and half amused. He waggled his fingers, nails painted black, in a wave.

I realized that not all vampires are like Zeke.

The rage boiled up as I felt a knife slice through my belt and jeans. Pool Player gave my pants a sharp pull and they caught on my hips. This asshole planned to rape me in an alley, and apparently Malachi planned to watch.

The power didn't feel tired now. It surged into me like God.

I kicked out with inhuman strength, feeling my foot connect with yielding flesh. The weight rolled off me and I leapt to my feet, almost levitating with fury. Reaching down, beyond thought, I grabbed the man by the chin and the back of the head and wrenched my hands in opposite directions, just like I had seen in the movies, putting considerably magical force into the twist. And just like in the movies, his neck snapped cleanly with a sound like a boot heel crunching through ice.

I stood up and pulled my jeans back up, sliding the ruined belt out and letting it fall with a clatter of buckle. My shirt was ruined too, the buttons torn away, the edges flapping over my black bra.

Malachi pushed away from the door, casting his cigarette to the ground and grinding it out under his heel. I stepped forward and slapped him with all my strength, leaving a white handprint on his pale skin.

He grinned at me through sharp teeth. "Didn't you hear the man, pretty Zorah? Girls like you ask for it."

I loosed the power of my being, raising blisters across his skin like a brand. His hair and eyelashes caught fire and his skin began to smoke. His eyes widened and he stumbled away from me, tripping over his own feet. I stopped him with a thought and pulled him toward me until he was close enough to slap again. His burning skin flaked off on my hand.

I relented. I needed him. I watched the burns heal and became aware of my jaw throbbing.

Impossibly, Malachi smirked. "I knew you could take care of yourself."

I slapped him again for his insolence, his skin so cold under my hand that he felt carved from stone. "Rape," I said, poking my finger into his face, "is wrong."

His eyes narrowed. "So?"

I was stymied. "How can you not care?"

He shrugged. "You know vampires. So you should know ethics don't apply to us."

And I finally saw past the glamour, saw him for who he really was. A predator, driven by hunger and malice and not much more. I had been fooled by the beautiful elfin face, fooled by the green eyes. So stupid. I laughed.

Malachi took an uncertain step back, his cupid's lips parting. For all his bravado, I did frighten him a little.

I pointed at him and he flinched. "You. You will stay in the city. I have need of you." I held out my hand, palm up. The heel of my hand was abraded from the pavement, beads of blood on the surface of my skin. "Taste."

Too hungry to be asked twice, he grabbed me by the wrist, but I stopped him from biting into the blue veins pulsing there. His face froze an inch from my flesh.

"Lick."

His tongue, as pink and perfect as the rest of him, lapped across the blood and he looked up, pupils dilating. "My god."

"Goddess," I corrected him and pulled my hand away. I had mental hooks in his head and I twisted them. He gaped at me.

"Stay in town." I turned and walked away from him, pulling my coat closed over my torn shirt, zipping it against the cold.

"I'll be around," he called after me. "Anytime you want me."

# CHAPTER 9

# CHALMECATECUHTLI

I CLIMBED, THE ROCKS smooth and cool beneath my hands and bare feet. I pushed away the thorny fronds of the juniper bush and tucked myself in beneath the trees, sitting on top of the stone wall that surrounded my house. Reaching in my back pocket I extracted the silver flask and drank, the strong brandy sending shivers of warmth through my chest.

The last light of the red sunset streaked the sky with brilliant hues. Still light enough to see clearly but darkening rapidly.

I heard him several blocks away, the roar of the motorcycle as it topped the hill at the end of my street. He pulled in fast, the bike rocking as he brought it to an abrupt halt, using both brakes and his foot against the curb to stop the forward momentum. I had a delicious moment before he saw me when I could just watch.

Zeke put down the kickstand and swung off the bike, pocketing the key, running a hand through his spiky hair, making it stand up in a flaming halo. The red roots were longer, the bleached tips glowing in the dying light as though he had been dipped in gold. He looked up the walk toward my house, a faint line appearing between his dark red brows, his chin dropping so that the shadows filled the caverns beneath his cheekbones.

He looked dangerous in the best possible way, romantic and fantastical.

He saw me, his predator vision far superior to mine. He grinned over sharp teeth and leaned back against the bike, pulling a flask from his shirt pocket. "Pretty little Zorah, sitting in a tree," he crooned softly. "I smell brandy."

"You have your own flask."

He grinned. "Mine doesn't have alcohol in it." He set it on the seat.

I held out the flask and he walked to me, reaching up through the fronds of the tree. I handed him the flask, but he shoved it in his back pocket and found my bare foot against the stones. He brought my toes to his lips and nibbled along them, making me giggle.

"Am I forgiven?" My foot rested against his lips and he looked up at me over it, silver eyes in the dying light.

I put my feet on his shoulders and stood up, holding the limbs for balance. He supported my weight easily, running his hands up my legs, grasping me behind the knees. He let me slide down, his hands gliding up to my thighs so my knees came to rest on his shoulders. He put his nose into the V between my legs and inhaled. A tingle worked its way through my groin, but I pushed him away and he let me slide down the length of his body. I smelled him, desert after the rain.

"No." My lips were even with his, his breath on my face. "You're not forgiven."

"Forgive me." He breathed the words, his lips brushing mine.

I shoved against him, my feet still an inch off the ground but he held me easily, shoving me back against the wall, his knee between my legs, his booted foot against the stones for balance. I kept my hands braced against his chest, holding him away, the stones rough and uneven against my back.

His chin dropped suddenly, his grey eyes narrowing. "You smell different."

I laughed. "Really? How?"

He put his nose into my hair and breathed deep. "Have you seen another vampire?"

The question was so unexpected that I didn't have to feign surprise. I had showered, my torn clothes buried deep in the trash. Almost twenty-four hours had passed, but still he smelled Malachi.

"What?" My voice cracked, adding to my surprised act.

"I can smell..." His words drifted.

"If I have seen another vampire, I wasn't aware of it," I said, my tone light.

He breathed deep again.

"Have you changed your mind?" I asked, hoping to distract him.

Instead of answering his lips closed over mine, taste like rain on my tongue.

He finally let me up for air, and I breathed deep of his delicate scent. "Have you changed your mind?" I asked again.

He sighed and stepped back, letting me gently to the ground. "Zorah...look." He looked down at me. "Give me a month."

"A month?"

"Yes. Let's have this discussion again in a month."

"Why a month?"

His lush mouth tightened. "Just give it a month."

Last year, I would have said that was nothing, but time had become funny since Alex died. It had been five months and I felt as though I had lived lifetimes, each day a millennium, each week an age.

I walked to him, into his arms, my face tilting up to his. "I'm ready now, Zeke."

To my surprise he held me away, his hands firm on my bare arms. "I'm not. I have to think this through, Zorah. I need time."

"I thought you said that it was me who needed time."

"Maybe both of us do." He pulled the flask from his pocket and drank deep.

I couldn't stop the tears, burning in my eyes. "I *can't*, don't you see that? I cannot live this life anymore!"

He took a step back from me, mouth hardening, chin jutting.

"Zeke, before you came, I was killing myself. Slowly but surely, drinking too much, not eating. I was looking for death, ready to take matters into my own hands. And you found me. And I knew you from the moment I saw you. So why can't you trust me? Trust this?"

His eyes darkened. "Zorah, no offense but your experience with death? It's minimal."

I flinched but he pressed on, his breath coming harder.

"I deal in it. I take life. I drink people's futures." The killer in him burned, a hard and hungry thing. "You cannot imagine the things I've done. I have helped and harmed, offered salvation and damnation. I have tortured, maimed. Just to see if something would stop me. Just to see if some divinity or devil would intervene. And all I have learned is that I am a killer. Designed for one thing. You need to think very carefully about whether you want to enter my world."

His breathing came ragged. "Alex died on the highway while you lay dreaming."

The tears I held spilled, burning down my cheeks but he did not relent.

"And I would have killed him if he had caught my eye. I would have licked his blood off the pavement and off of his broken skin." He enunciated each word carefully, driving them like nails.

The images I tried to hide flooded in, impressions of things that I had not seen but imagined, nonetheless. I saw Alex, his body broken and torn, blood matting his dark curls. I saw the glass embedded in his flesh and I fell to my knees, gasping for breath.

Zeke sank to a crouch, his face level with mine. His dark eyes bored into me. "I have tried to make companions, Zorah. I have watched others try. And they have all died in screaming agony with their skin on fire." His face became harder than I had ever seen it. He was a god of death and blood, of the underworld and still beating hearts.

"This is no small thing that you ask of me." His voice dropped, quivering with passion or fury. "A month. Take it or leave it." He stood up looked down at me, his lips curled. "Sunset. In thirty days." He turned and walked away. I heard the roar of the bike, and he was gone.

I was drunk. Not falling over drunk but good and buzzed, the gin roaring in my veins. I sat at the bar in some tourist dive downtown, watching the auras of the other patrons.

I had forced myself to endure seven full days and nights, convinced that Zeke would return but he had not. I could not sense him or find him in the vast city and so here I sat. Intoxication showed up on a person's aura as a green film, darkening as more alcohol entered the bloodstream. I checked out my own aura, the olive over the blue glow.

I drained the last of my drink and pushed back from the bar. The night air hit my skin and I turned left, heading in the general direction of home, fifteen blocks away. The death wish felt strong tonight, fueled by gin. The desire to end it washed over me, and I saw my aura darken toward black. I could not wait any longer.

"Malachi," I whispered.

I felt him in my head as he heard me. I caught a quick glimpse of streetlights, people standing outside to smoke, heard a quick clash of music. Then he closed his eyes to hear me.

"Come to me," I whispered. I felt his cool amusement. I stepped into the shadows to wait, sinking down on a convenient bench.

I didn't have to wait long. I saw his aura before I saw him, blood red against the pale green of the trees lining the pavement.

"You know," he tilted his face down to appraise me, eyes shining pale in the streetlights. "That's a neat little trick. Calling like that." His voice was deeper than I remembered, velvety and rich.

"Telepathy's the new thing, hadn't you heard? Better than texting." I had to concentrate to keep the words from slurring.

He smiled. "Can you read my thoughts, too?"

"Thoughts are difficult," I admitted. "I catch surface stuff, but most people are thinking several different things at the same time. It comes through as a jumble."

He said nothing to that, only looked around, his black hair rippling. The tips brushed his belt, today a strip of leather decorated with a row of machine gun rounds.

"Is punk rock the vampire look this year?" I asked.

He looked back at me, his glance speculative. "How many vampires do you know, exactly?"

I smiled and shook my head.

He chewed his full lower lip. "Your secrets." He sank gracefully down on the bench and pulled a pint of whiskey from an inside pocket, unscrewing the cap and drinking deep. "So why did you call me, pretty Zorah?"

I wondered why they called me the same thing. I wondered what I was doing here with Malachi and, most of all, I wondered where Zeke was, how he could have left me, how he could be letting this happen.

I took the bottle from Malachi, the alcohol howling through me. "I want you to make me a vampire," I said.

His dark brows lifted. "Do you know how difficult it is to make a vampire?"

"Yes, almost everyone dies. I'm willing to take that chance."

"Now what could have possibly happened to make you want to throw away your life?"

"That's really none of your business."

The corners of his cherub's mouth curved up. "I'll find out anyway. When I drink."

"Does that mean you'll do it?"

He gazed at me thoughtfully. "I have always wanted to make another."

"You haven't tried?"

He shook his head, deflecting. "What makes you think I won't just drink you to dust?"

"I can stop you, remember?" I extended one hand and drew it through his aura, watching the red mist swirl around my fingertips. His eyes narrowed.

"Maybe so." He held out his hand for the whiskey and I passed him the bottle, considerably lighter now. "What's in it for me?"

"My blood's not enough?"

He ran his tongue over his lower lip as though already tasting me. It made me feel adulterous, watching him, and I wondered if the pleasure would burn as brightly as it had with Zeke.

"You tell me why you want this, and I'll tell you if I'll do it."

I swallowed more whiskey and then reluctantly said, "I lost someone."

"And you don't want to join them?"

I didn't answer but he just looked at me, an angel in ice and moonlight. And so I was forced to say, "I think I can figure out how to bring him back. But I need more...time." I almost said "power."

Malachi's brows rose again. "You can raise the dead?"

"I don't know. I haven't been able to do it so far. But I want to keep trying."

He didn't say anything but eyed me speculatively. I couldn't read his thoughts, but I felt his curiosity.

"Fine." I took the bottle back and drank irritably. "Maybe I'm just sick of this life."

He nodded at that. "Fair enough."

"So will you do it?"

He grinned over sharp teeth. "Yes, I'll do it. I want to see if it works."

The anticipation drowned in the wave of fear that swept me and I took another drink, annoyed to see my hand shake. "How long will it take?" The tremor did not reach my voice.

"Well," Malachi shifted slightly. "I have heard that doing it slowly can increase the survival rate."

"The trick is to wear down the immune system," I said.

"You got it. I drink a bit and then you drink a bit. Never enough to kill you and never too much of my blood at the same time."

"How long will it take?" I repeated my question and took yet another sip of whiskey.

"A week?" Malachi shrugged. "Maybe two."

"Where? If it takes that long, where do you want to do it?"

He studied me for a moment. "I have a place." He stood up and held out a hand. I placed my hand in his and his warm fingers closed over mine.

"Here we are," he said, unlocking the steel door.

I looked around doubtfully. He had brought me deep into a warehouse district where I'd never been and down a set of steps to a basement door.

Malachi saw my glance. "You can scream as loud as you want here and no one will hear."

"I'll be screaming?"

He shrugged. "Maybe."

I hesitated, and he made an impatient gesture. "You coming or not?"

It was the last moment to turn back, my last instant of choice. I could walk away now and wait for Zeke. Keep living my life. Try to learn to be human without Alex.

When I walked into the dark opening, it was without a backwards glance. Malachi laughed softly and followed me.

When the door closed total blackness descended until Malachi held his lighter to a huge candle fixed in its own wax on a square pillar at the bottom of concrete steps. Our shadows jumped and danced in an immense space.

Malachi lit a taper from a small stack of them piled next to the steps and led the way into a big, open room, concrete floor beneath low rafters, festooned with cobwebs and dust. Gradually a shape loomed in the darkness, and I made out a huge four poster bed heaped with quilts and blankets. It appeared to be the only object in the room.

"Have a seat."

I sat on the bed. The blankets felt clammy under my hands.

Malachi set the candle in a sconce attached to a post and rummaged beneath the bed, surfacing with a bottle of whiskey. The label had peeled away but the smell was unmistakable as he cracked the top. The liquor felt velvety and very strong sliding down my throat.

"This is a nice vampy hideout you have here."

He smirked, his hair slipping forward across his cheek.

I drank again and stared away into the darkness, wondering about the next move.

Malachi crawled onto the bed, and I laid back against the pillows. His warm hands wrapped around my wrists, pushing me down into quilts that smelled of damp. I tilted my head back.

Pain, shocking and enormous, pierced my throat and I screamed. It was so sudden that at first I could not repel him and then I pushed with all my psychic power, sending him flying off the bed.

I sat up, my hands searching my burning throat. My heart beat very loud. Warmth pulsed down my dress and I looked down, dizzy, at the dark stain spreading over the white cloth.

"You should let me do something about that," Malachi said. His voice came from a great distance. I looked up to see him crouching ten feet away. Red pulsed in my vision. Automatically I pushed the auras away, but the pulse did not stop.

"You're going to bleed to death in another minute if you don't let me back in," he said, and I realized that blood poured from my severed jugular, covering my body and the bed in gore. I smelled blood, my blood.

Malachi stood and moved quickly toward me. I flinched as he ran his hands into my hair and pulled my neck to his mouth, but he only placed his lips over the wound, his tongue gently massaging my skin. Darkness swirled the world away.

When I awakened, he was the first thing I saw. He sat on the foot of the bed watching me, his hair covering the side of his face, flowing over his white chest in shimmering strands, catching the flickering candlelight. His nipples were pierced with heavy gauge silver hoops.

I sat up, dizzy and nauseated. "What happened?"

His black brows lifted slightly.

"I mean..." I lifted a hand to my throat and explored the two punctures there. Dried blood coated my dress and matted in my hair. "Why did it hurt like that?"

He grinned and the demon danced under his features, capering between his gleaming teeth, behind his storm water eyes. He was so unlike Zeke, my god of fire. The predator was always in Zeke, lurking just beneath his frosty skin, surfacing in his twisting lips and silvery eyes. It hid behind Malachi's pretty face.

"Did you expect it not to hurt?" He grinned.

"I thought..." I hesitated. "Vampires can make it feel like good. You know. Like sex."

He leaned toward me, the curtain of hair slipping forward, blocking his features in shadow. "Now, why would you think that?"

I swallowed the bile that burned in the back of my throat. I had walked into every girl's nightmare, the beautiful boy in the torture basement. Had I lured him? Or had he trapped me?

"You know another vampire." He flipped the hair back and I watched his lips twist into a snarl. "Pretty little Zorah got seduced by the sexy vampire." He laughed.

He leaped forward, faster than imagination, and grabbed me by the ankles, pulling me down the bed, his body between my legs, the roughness of his jeans against the thin fabric of my underwear. He wrapped a hand around my neck and hauled my face up toward his. His breath smelled of jasmine and blood.

"It hurts because I want it to hurt." His lips parted and I saw his pretty, pink tongue between white teeth. He bit down and black blood welled, dripping into my upturned face. He pulled my head back, the blood splattering across my lips. "Drink if you don't want to die."

And I did. I did not know the price and yet I was willing to pay anything, willing to sacrifice it all.

The blood bloomed on my tongue like flowers. I swallowed and swallowed again. It heated me like the whiskey and the pain faded.

He lowered his mouth to mine, his lips soft. I felt his magic pour over me. I let it, swallowing more of his blood.

His hand tightened around my throat and he pressed his body down on me. I gasped for air, but he tightened his grip. I beat against his chest, making him laugh. Spots began to swim before my eyes. I drew my nails sharply down his arm, peeling away skin.

"How far are you willing to go, pretty Zorah?" He bit down on my lip and I felt his teeth piece through my flesh. I cried out. I had never felt pain like this, so intentionally inflicted.

He licked along my mouth, lapping my blood. "You asked why it hurts? Because it's not worth it if it doesn't."

I couldn't breathe, on the verge of passing out again. He relented, allowing me a quick sip of air.

"I can stop you," I whispered.

"Before I snap your neck?" His grip cut off my air again. "That might be interesting. Why don't you give it a go?"

I lifted a hand to his chest and rested it against his warm skin. He pulled his face back a bit, his brows lifted, curious. And I relented, my arm falling to the bed. I could not turn back now. No matter the cost.

He laughed in my ear. When the pain came again, it was bigger and I screamed as the darkness took me.

# CHAPTER 10

# FAIRY TALES

I WILL BE WAITING for him when he comes, like in a fairy tale. The edge of night will bring him. He will come up my walk with the vanishing sun glowing in the tips of his hair. His chin will drop in that way it does, his lips curving up in that smile I know is only for me. Beautiful death in the dying day on the edge of endless night. I am the princess and he is the dark prince. He will awaken me with his touch and his kiss will be for all time.

Then the pain. It ripped through my abdomen and I wept, weaker than before, my voice cracking and hoarse. I froze and shivered, dripping sweat. My teeth chattered and Zeke's image blew away on the wind. I cried feebly.

Darkness pressed in and the floor beneath me felt cold and damp. The only light came from a guttering candle on the floor twenty feet away, casting shadows on the huge four poster bed that loomed alien in the dark behind me, an ancient relic of eras bygone, the mattress stained and unspeakable. The shadows twirled and danced in ecstasy over my agony.

The pain cut through me, glass in my veins. I writhed. My stomach cramped, and I brought my knees to my chest, though the muscles in my back screamed in protest. Everywhere hurt, kidneys throbbing, muscles strained and protesting. My flesh was mottled with bruises and abrasions, a neat row of puncture marks up my arms from his teeth. He drank again and again, until I felt my heart fall into rhythm with his.

All at once I burned with heat and pushed the filthy quilt off with a groan. He had left me naked, drying blood flaking off my chest and thighs, bites and scratches scabbing over. More blood, my blood, dried on the cracked floor in a dark and muddy pool.

Shuddering with effort, I rolled to my knees and knelt on the quilt, the cold of the concrete seeping through the fabric. I was too weak to stand and I dropped my head, sobbing, pain in every shaky breath. I wondered if he'd broken ribs. I retched, but only brought up bile that burned the back of my throat.

I will be waiting for him when he comes but it will not be Zeke. Not Zeke glowing in the last light of the dying day with his red and gold hair. Not Zeke with his perfect face, the shadows swarming beneath his cheekbones and shifting in his silver eyes. I will be here when he comes, there is no avoiding it.

A shadow moved across the room, darkness against the dark, and I gritted my teeth against the screams I knew he would tear from me. All of my mental defenses had fallen and his aura poured off him in wild red waves, burning against the dark. My own aura, normally deep and vibrant, had taken on a sickly greenish cast. My blood on the floor shone with the same glow but fading. My blood was losing life both inside and outside of me.

Malachi wore only jeans and his white skin rippled across his stomach and arms, his black hair coating his shoulders like oil. The reason that all vampires are beautiful in the movies is because who would want to spend eternity with the plain, the homely? Of course they are beautiful. The vampire virus takes the raw material and transforms it into the perfect predator, designed to attract with every sense. Physically perfect, they emit pheromones designed to heighten the desire of their prey. Zeke smells of the desert after the rain, Malachi like night blooming jasmine.

Only I could see their secret, hidden in the auras that poured from their essence. I had seen that same red only on the great cats, the tiny darting bats of the sky, crocodiles in their watery beds. That aura brightened every time he hurt me.

I saw the glitter of a glass in his hand. "Here." He held it out and I saw dark amber liquid. "It will help with the pain."

I took it and drank, the whiskey scorching my raw throat. I gagged as the heat hit my stomach but held it down, drinking it all, the warmth bursting in my belly. Malachi watched me choke, a small smile playing on his mouth.

"It's time for more of this, too." He produced a switchblade and clicked it open, the blade appearing like a magic trick. Holding out his wrist, he drew the knife across the blue veins. His blood seeped from his flesh and I smelled it, rust and jasmine. Already the flesh began to close across the wound.

My stomach roiled but it was too late to turn back now. I could give up and die or I could continue to fight.

And still probably die. I would see Alex in this world or the next. I wanted it on my terms, but nothing I had done worked: I couldn't bring him back. Dying myself brought no certainty. All I could do was keep going. I didn't care how it turned out as long as it was finally over. As long as it made the pain stop.

I took his hand and brought his flesh to my mouth, swallowing the viscous liquid that blossomed on my tongue. The scent of jasmine filled my throat, sickly sweet and cloying. I caught flashes of memory and each one made me shudder. A girl, mascara streaked down her face as she screamed, a raw and tortured sound. A boy, no older than ten, running, his terrified face over his shoulder and then he stumbled.

Malachi pulled away and I curled inward, freezing again. I *wanted this*, I reminded myself. I *asked for this*. If only I had known the price.

"Sweet little Zorah," he crooned. "Sweet little angel. So lost. So alone."

"You forget yourself," I hissed, looking up at him through tangled hair. He glowed, Cupid deranged, his perfect mouth a pink bow beneath seawater eyes. The rings in his eyebrow glinted in the light and he opened his jeans with a rip of buttons. I moaned. He was pierced below as well, three deadly spikes.

I will be waiting for him when he comes. I will wait for him in the shadows, Sleeping Beauty awakened from the dead by the kiss of the dark prince. I will run to him and he will take me into his arms, he will consume me, his aura enveloping mine, red on red for all time. He will be my lover who cannot die. My Zeke of the innumerable ages, with his fleeting smile of sharp teeth. He will carry me away into the magic night, his mouth coming down on my lips, and I will kiss him forever.

It should have been him who turned me.

I screamed, though I no longer had the strength for it. My insides leaked out through my pores, my ovaries liquefied and consuming my womb. So hot, burning, my skin suppurating, howling with agony.

The vampire virus kills almost everyone it enters. Zeke had told me this and Malachi said it, too. They both told the same story: the spiking fever, the fall into coma, the final agonized breath.

He sat on his heels and watched, my angel of agony, my dakini of death. Naked now, the studs in his flesh glinted in the candlelight. He was coated with streaks of my blood, like brands on his silvery skin.

"He won't save you." He grinned over sharp teeth. "Fairy tales aren't real, pretty Zorah. In this world, the monster always wins."

I rolled onto my stomach, the lacerations in my skin shrieking and burning. I felt the fever in my body, raging through me, burning me up. I drew deep on the well of power inside me, the special hidden place he could never touch no matter how he dug into my flesh. The place my magic lived. "You will never understand, Malachi. You are the monster, but I am the myth. You can never have me."

His smile made angels burst into flame and fall smoldering from the sky.

"Just a body, Malachi. I am so much more than just a body. Now where's that whiskey?"

"You know," he handed the bottle to me. "I have never met anyone quite like you."

It burned, but I didn't care. I grinned at him through bloody teeth. "I live to impress."

One black brow arched. "That comeback isn't up to your usual standard."

I took another shot and curled myself up, fetal, conserving myself. "I sort of have a lot going on."

"Hmm. What with the dying and all?"

I shot him the most toxic glare I could manage.

He grinned. "What you say we ramp it up a bit?" The knife cut into my skin before I saw it coming, slicing down through the sinew of my thigh, my blood welling. His mouth against me, in me, devouring me, his aura lightening. My flesh healed and then he bit me again and I howled. The pain consumed everything. I reached inside myself, the power like a deep blue well in my mind, and drew it in. I brought my hand to his shoulder and focused my attention, pushing aside the pain. I elevated the temperature in my palm and he leapt back, a cry escaping him. My handprint stood out, a welt of red.

He glared at me, and then glanced down at the burn on his skin. His pink tongue lapped slowly at a drop of my blood on his lower lip, the gesture sensuous and obscene. "I leave you like this now and you die," he said.

"I'm dying anyway," I replied.

A slight shake of his head, imperceptible but for the ripple of his hair. "When I bite, you heal."

"What?" He was right. He had bitten me, and my flesh had drawn together over the wound. The pain prevented focus on this remarkable fact and I hesitated a moment too long. He leapt on top of me, pinning me to the abrasive concrete, his mouth up under my jaw. I felt him tear, his teeth sliding into me, and the agony overwhelmed. I tried to repel him but the cool blue well of power in my mind was inaccessible, overcome by the torment of flesh. The dancing shadows came for me. And their teeth were all sharp.

A fairy tale princess always needs a savior. Only in Disney movies do they actually come. In the real stories, the ones that began as folktales in the wild places of the earth, the princess gets swallowed by monsters or abducted by pirates. The strong women of these stories are always witches, evil and heartless. They don't need saving.

I thought of Alex, dying on the highway at night. He had not come to me here. I went into this darkness alone.

The tears came again, but not from the pain. I wept for the one I had lost, the death that had started it all. Alex was gone as though he had never been. If I survived this, became vampire, would I sacrifice ever seeing him again?

Closing my eyes, reaching deep, I felt for the earth under the concrete. The worms and tiny creatures moved there, each a spark of life. I felt the virus in me, an invasion trying to change the biology of my being. I felt the fever, the cellular ruptures as the virus forced its way in.

I thought of Zeke, but I refused to call him. This was mine alone. I am become vampire, destroyer of worlds.

I opened myself. I pictured my immune system as a tiny army on white horses and I envisioned the virus like a red cloud of poison, overwhelming, the miniature soldiers keeling off their horses, their swords falling into the moist swamp of my body. I became transformation in motion.

I called to death and he had answered. Not as a cloaked figure with a scythe but as a vampire with silver eyes, an impossible being who could not die. Death is not a step into liminal space but a transcendence into immortality. Not a sweet suicide oblivion but an eternity of everlasting. When Alex died, I fell into darkness, my forests laid waste, my verdant pastures drought-stricken. With all of my vast power, I could not raise him from the dead. I seduced death like a whore but then Zeke came, a shining star in the darkness. But he refused to give me his power, the power of immortality, the power over death.

Reaching out with mental fingers I found life all around and fastened to it with psychic teeth, pulling all that vitality into myself, using it to heal. I harnessed my will and focused, bringing all the considerable might of my determination to bear on my wounded and dying body.

I felt my temperature rise. The army of my immune system began to shriek and cook. My eyes were too dry to open and I pressed myself down against the cold concrete. If I survived this, I might be brain damaged, a witch vampire deranged. I did not care. My body became a funeral pyre.

When I awake, it is no longer dark. The door to the basement gapes open, letting in weak sunlight. The light is so shocking that I cry out and scuttle backwards over the floor to the bed, pulling the filthy quilt over me against the bright. My eyes feel pierced, lacerated. I lay beneath the filthy cover feeling my body burn.

I don't know where Malachi is, but I cannot sense him. Maybe he left me to die. Probably so. I have no idea how long it's been. I push the duvet down below my eyes. The light from the door is fading. Night comes on kitten feet.

I realize I can see the contours of the room, every surface covered with living organisms. The tiny microbes that coat stone and earth range in color from blue to green to gray, and the room lights before my eyes. I see the floor and walls, the tiny insects in the rough beams of the ceiling. The bed crawls with minuscule life and I flinch in automatic revulsion.

I push off the coverlet and stand, wincing at the streaks of filth on my body. I have never felt so dirty, so defiled. I rub my hand down my side but only smear the grime into my skin. A deep burning pain fills my middle. I look around for my clothes, struggling to remember what I had been wearing. It seems so long ago, not days but years, that I had come here, following Malachi, thinking I knew the danger.

There is a wad of fabric in the corner and I shake it out to reveal a black dress. It is not mine. A pair of panties, shredded almost beyond recognition, fall to the floor. Though it revolts me to think of where it had come from, I pull the dress over my head. My body is so weakened that my head spins and I have to lean over to catch my breath. Fever rages in my body.

This is a choice; I chose what to become. Walking across the floor toward the door takes every ounce of strength remaining. I have to pull myself up the steps. Even the soles of my feet hurt.

Letting myself out into the night I look up into the sky. The warehouse looms over me, still and dark. I fall to my knees, unable to stand. My palms on the pavement seek the energy under the concrete and I draw on it, feeding like the creature I wish to become. That bed must go. It all must burn.

I send thoughts of conflagration into the basement behind me. Fire leaps at my command and races across the floor toward that monster of a bed. The mattress blazes. I stumble into the arms of the welcoming night.

# Chapter 11

# Head Trips

Sunlight falls like honey across the fine hairs on my arms. There is no hunger, no blood, only heat and sweat that runs down my face, salty on my lips and tongue. This is a world of fire and colors so bright that I squint against them, flashing off blue water and green grass. This is a world of dreams where there is no pain, no loss, no fear. In this world Zorah lies soft and somnambulant in my arms, her hair the color of sand across my tanned skin.

This is only a fantasy. It has been nine hundred years since I have seen the sun.

I have been in this room for a week. It is the basement of one of the apartment buildings downtown, a building I own. I had converted this space into living quarters – it has everything a vampire needs. No windows, access to the sewers for daylight excursions, thick concrete walls. I had covered the floor with a wool Persian rug and hung the walls with Japanese prints – tiny human figures amidst mountains and clouds. There is no kitchen, no toilet, only my bed in the middle of the opulent rug, a black industrial size refrigerator, a flat screen television, claw foot tub, and a hulking mahogany wardrobe.

Zorah's gift of sight would come in handy; I would give anything to know where she is. But she's been silent. My phone has not rung and her voice has not spoken in my head.

I toss the sheets back and walk nude across to the wardrobe. From its Narnian depths I pull a pair of black jeans and put them on. I wonder what day it is. I have lost track.

Then I am on the floor, my hands clapped to my temples, fingers digging into my face as she screams inside my head. I cannot think, I cannot see. She consumes everything.

Blundering toward the door I step into sunlight, weak and diffuse, falling through the garden level window at the end of the hall. My skin smokes and I recoil, slamming the door against the lethal light.

Her voice is so loud inside my brain that I feel warmth gush down my face. Her psychic invasion ruptures me. I retch, an unfamiliar human gesture, and watch blood drip from my nose and pool on the concrete, seeping into the porous stone. Can vampires have aneurysms?

*Zeke! Come to me! Zeke! I need you! Save me! I'm dying.*

I sprint across the room and sweep back the rug, hauling up the concrete cover over the sewers. I hoist the block above my head and drop into the blackness, closing the door to my lair behind me, hanging for a moment from the metal handle before dropping ten feet into cold water. I remember too late that I never put on shoes.

In total darkness, a vampire navigates with something more than sight, something like intuition. I head east at a dead run, feeling more blood seep down my face. The shriek in my head is constant and I obey its call because I have no other choice. For Zorah, I come at her command.

I burst through a locked door, the metal giving before me like paper. The light is shocking, and for a moment I think I've come out into the sun. But I do not burn.

Looking around, I discover myself in a parking garage, lit with fluorescent lights. The portal into the sewer yawns behind me, and I close the door out of habit.

I smell her scent, faint on the air, mixing with exhaust and oil and a million other human scents. Her voice has faded again, the screams dying to a low troubled murmur worrying the back of my mind.

I hear the ping of elevator doors and I head toward the sound at a trot, ignoring a woman with a stroller who jumps and gapes at me as I hurry past. Her toddler gapes at me too, comically imitating her mother.

In the elevator I study the buttons and select "Admissions." When the doors slide open, I recognize the lobby of the general hospital. I bribe an intern here for human blood from the blood bank. The aroma assaults me: cleaning chemicals, a thousand medicines, rot, necrosis, and the overpowering scent of blood. Unlike humans, I cannot acclimate to smells. Luckily, I don't really have to breathe. Vampires have to expel air to speak, of course, but we don't need it to live.

Approaching the nurses' station, I catch a glimpse of my reflection in the floor-to-ceiling windows. It is dark now, and I see myself clearly in the glass, a white skinned wraith in black jeans, shirtless and dripping unthinkable gunk. I can smell myself and I know that they can too, the patrons with their variety of human ills who shrink at my appearance.

The nurse does not flinch, only looks at me sharply over half-moon glasses, her brows lifting over a professionally blank stare.

"Are you injured, sir?" she asks.

I brace myself and suck in air. "A friend," I stammer. Zorah's voice has faded. "My friend was brought in."

"Her name?"

"Zorah. Her name is Zorah."

"Last name?" The eyes regard me coolly.

I hesitate. Do I know Zorah's last name? "I…" I grin self-consciously, dipping my chin and running my hand through my hair, newly bleached and platinum. "I don't…I don't know her last name."

The nurse shows no sign of surprise. "Were you in an accident?"

"Me? No. She was."

"When was she admitted?"

All these questions I cannot answer. I place my hands lightly on the counter and lean forward, looking into her experienced and skeptical eyes. "Look, I don't know exactly. I just know that she's here."

"Are you family?"

This one I can answer. "The closest she's got." I give her my best smile and see her eyes soften around the edges.

"Sir, without a last name I don't know how much I can do. But let me speak with the ER. Can you give me a description?"

"Tall. Late twenties. Light hair, blue eyes. Her name is Zorah."

"So you said. I'll see what I can do. In the meantime, there's a restroom down the hall. Let me get you a towel and you can clean up." She bustles around a corner and reappears with two white towels which she hands to me.

"Thank you." She gives me a small, guarded smile before disappearing behind a door. I walk to the bathroom and lock it behind me, going to the sink and running a bowl full of water. Wetting one of the towels I begin cleaning the sludge and dripping ooze from my skin and jeans.

A few minutes later, tolerably clean, I let myself out into the hallway and walk back into the waiting room, ignoring the stares at my bare feet and torso.

A vampire almost glows under fluorescent light – our skin is so pale and translucent that bright light almost shows us for what we are. I sit in a chair as far away from the other patients as I can and examine the blue veins in my hands, knowing that most eyes are on me.

"Zeke?"

I start and look up to see a silver haired man. His name comes to me and I stand. "Nicholas."

"How did you know she was here?"

"That's a complicated question." I laugh to myself and hold out my hand.

He shakes it, taking in my nearly naked form, still damp and slightly fragrant. "Are you okay?"

"Another complicated question. Where is she?"

His face drops, and he rubs his hands together in a nervous gesture. "They're evaluating her."

I reach for his restless hands and draw him down into the chair next to me. "Nicholas." I focus on his eyes until he meets my gaze. "What happened?"

The older man shrugs, shaking his head. "I don't have all the details. I just arrived a few minutes ago. I got a call."

The double doors at the end of the waiting room open and a young and tired looking man in medical scrubs emerges. Nicholas jumps to his feet and I rise as well as the man turns to us, taking in my disheveled appearance with only the slightest lift of his eyebrows.

"Zeke, this is Doctor Chavez."

I hold out my hand, appraising the other man. His eyes look gentle and weary, ringed with dark circles, and he smiles slightly. "I'm Zeke."

If he notices the absence of a last name he does not comment, only asks, "Are you a relative?"

"Zeke is a close friend and here at my invitation," Nicholas responds smoothly, and I feel a surge of gratitude. "Tell me, what's wrong with our Zorah?"

Chavez takes Nicholas lightly by the elbow and gestures toward the double doors. "Please, let's go to a private room."

A shiver of trepidation runs down my spine, and I follow the two men into a bland room with a table and several chairs, hotel art gracing plaster walls. We sit, Nicholas and I next to one another across the table from Chavez.

"Gentlemen, the prognosis is not great."

The shiver transforms into a ball of ice that settles into the pit of my stomach.

Chavez leans forward and looks at us solemnly. "She has a severe concussion and swelling of the brain. Her white blood cell count is off the charts. She was unconscious by the time she arrived in ER and delirious before. She has two cracked ribs and bleeding in her left lung. She has been beaten severely. There are signs of forcible sexual intercourse. She has bite marks on her breasts, throat, and thighs. Do either of you have any idea if she's been exposed to..." he hesitates. "I don't even know what I'm asking. A biological agent? Has she traveled out of the country recently?"

"No," Nicholas says. "She's been here."

I cannot control the breath expelled in a rush. "How...?" The question trails off as a new one forms. "But no one could rape Zorah."

Both of the men look at me, and Chavez places a cool and professional hand on my forearm where it rests on the table. "I'm afraid that there's always a way for a man to inflict damage on a woman," he says softly.

I shake my head in disbelief. "You don't know Zorah. There's got to be more to the story."

"There always is," Chavez responds. "Tell me, when did you see her last?"

What he's really asking is obvious, and I glower at him with enough heat that he removes his hand from my arm. "The last time I saw Zorah was more than two weeks ago. And I would never..."

Nicholas places a restraining hand against my shoulder. "Zeke would never do this," he says.

Chavez relaxes and shrugs. "Actually, I believe you. She's been asking for you."

I stand up too fast, unnaturally swift, and watch as both men blink at me and glance at one another uncertainly. I ignore them. "I want to see her."

"I thought you said that she's unconscious?" Nicholas looks at the doctor, perplexed.

"Restless. She cries out. She was calling for him when they brought her in."

"May we see her?"

Chavez rises smoothly. "Of course. This way please."

We traverse the halls to a door like any other. Chavez pauses. "Remember that she has been beaten. Her appearance is rather..." he pauses. "Shocking."

"I want to see her. Now." I reach for the knob and no one stops me so I enter, moving swiftly past a drawn curtain and into low light cast by a lamp on a small round table beneath a window, mirrored and dark.

She lies still and small beneath white sheets, her hair hiding her face in a silvery curtain. There are wires everywhere and I smell her blood, intoxicating even through the astringent scent of the hospital. There is another aroma as well, jasmine, but I ignore it and go to her.

I gently pull her hair back from her cheek, revealing her face in profile against the pillow. Warned by Chavez, I am surprised that the damage is not more extensive. Her upper lip is cut and swollen, and a bruise blooms on her cheekbone. Two black stitches bind a laceration over her eyebrow, but her forehead is smooth and unmarred, her full lower lip inviting and relaxed. I slide my hand under her face and turn it toward me. There is a bruise on that side as well, faded and yellowing over her jaw.

So suddenly that I jump, her eyes fly open. The right is red and shocking, full of blood, her iris clouded with burst vessels.

"Zorah?"

"Flowers bloom in the dark of the moon," she says clearly and it seems as though her eyes focus on me. Then, when she screams in my face, I hear it in my ears and in my head, so loud that my vision dims.

"VAMPIRE!" she screams. "Vampires in my SKIN. Vampires in my EYES!"

I see more blood blossom in her torrid right eye and watch the veins in her temples surge. I hear her heartbeat, fast and fluttery, filled with fluid.

Heat pours off her skin, shoving me back. I see Nicholas and Doctor Chavez, frozen in shock, as I fly backward off the narrow hospital bed.

My reflexes save me and I land on my feet. She sits straight up and I have an eerie premonition that her head is about to spin around on the narrow stalk of her neck like *The Exorcist*. Instead, the bulb in the lamp bursts, sending tiny shards of glass tinkling across the floor.

I clearly hear Chavez say "Shit" in a tiny, surprised voice, and see him move across the room in the dark. In seconds the overhead light flashes on.

Zorah convulses, her back arching to a painful and impossible degree, her head flipping back like a flower blown by the wind as she stares up at the light with her wild, mismatched eyes. I see livid bruises on her arms and deep bite marks, ringed with furious stains of blood. She screams wordlessly, and I feel warmth gush from my nose again.

"LIGHT TOO BRIGHT!" she howls and the IV in her hand flies out of her skin and embeds itself in the wall. The overhead light shatters with a low pop and the room again descends into darkness.

I am dimly aware of the door opening and Nicholas running across the room. I launch myself at Zorah, wrapping my hands around her shoulders. The magical heat pouring off her raises blisters along every exposed inch of my skin as I press her down into the mattress, covering her with my body.

"Zorah, Zorah, pretty Zorah," I whisper frantically in her ear. Enormous energy gathers inside her, and my flesh begins to boil and smoke. "Zorah, I am here. Zorah, I will never leave you." I press my burning lips against the tender flesh beneath her ear. "Zorah, I will die here with you. Zorah, please don't kill me." Beneath me, I feel her body tense, and then I fly off the bed and into the wall. My skull smacks against the plaster, and everything goes dim around the edges.

# CHAPTER 12

# OVER THE EDGE

THERE IS A FLASHLIGHT in my face, blinding me, and hands pull me to my feet and roughly toward the door. Disoriented, I allow myself to be pulled, then, coming to myself, resist. No human power can move an unwilling vampire. The hands scrabble over my arms, and the light shines back into my face. Irritated, I take the light and direct it at the floor. In the dim light I see that my arms are cracked and flaking. I look as though I have been stranded in Death Valley for a week. But I heal fast. I just need to keep these humans from seeing me clearly for a few more moments. I cover the flashlight with a palm.

"What happened?" Nicholas asks me. I can see him in the dark, but he can't see me. His pupils are dilated and huge.

Looking toward the bed, I see Zorah lying motionless, her head twisted at a painful angle. Her eyes gaze sightlessly up at the ceiling. For a second, I think she's dead and then I hear her heartbeat, faster than Nicholas's, and I take a deep breath, forgetting the stench of the hospital. I cough out the smell of bleach.

"I did this," I say without thinking.

Nicholas grabs my arm. His fingers against my burned flesh sting and I swat him away. "What do you mean, you did this?" he barks.

I see where he's gone wrong. "I mean, I didn't do *this*." I gesture at the bed. "I didn't do this to her. But she's here because of me." I lean over, pulling away from Nicholas, my hands on my knees. If I hadn't turned her down...but where the hell had she found another vampire? I inhale, finally paying attention to that jasmine scent. It fills the room, cloying and unmistakable. I should have recognized it before for what it is: the powerful pheromones of vampiric blood.

I should have known. She knows we exist. She'd warned me that she could call another. I've underestimated her. Refusing her hasn't slowed her down at all.

Nicholas grabs me by the shoulders and I let him pull me upright. "What the hell are you talking about? Zeke, what is happening?" He yells the last words, and I feel the mist of his breath against my face.

I shove him away. "I don't know," I snarl at him.

The door slams open, and Chavez runs in carrying another light. Luckily, my skin has healed, but my body temperature is dropping. I'm expending tremendous energy. I will need to feed soon.

Other forms appear behind Chavez, and more flashlights light the gloom. I can smell each individual, their unique bouquet. Vampiric hunger is not overwhelming the way it's depicted in some fiction, but they sure do smell tasty. It makes the odors of the hospital easier to ignore.

"Check her," I hear the doctor bark. "I think her IV dislodged."

I bite back a bray of laughter at that.

The doctor's face, wan and pinched, appears out of the dark. "You two. I'm sorry but you'll have to step out."

"I'm not going anywhere," I say.

"I appreciate your concern, Zeke. But we've just had a bit of an event, and we need to take care of her."

This time I do not hold back my laughter. "'A bit of an event'? What do you think happened? An electrical surge?"

This time, it's the doctor who shines his light in my face. I shove it down. "You have no idea what you're up against. Trust me, doctor. You want me here. I'm the only one who stands a chance of stopping her if it happens again." I hope I won't have to go through him. He's trying to help the human in Zorah, something I don't know how to do. I need him alive.

Chavez looks at me hard, his dark eyes probing my face. He swings the light to the IV needle buried two inches deep in the wall. I hear one of the people in the doorway gasp.

The doctor sets his flashlight gently on the tray table at the foot of Zorah's bed and walks to the door. "Give us a moment, please," he says in his soft and artfully professional voice. The people file out, and he shuts the door.

He walks swiftly back across the room and glares at me, crossing his arms across his chest. "Okay. Let's hear it."

Nicholas looks at me inquiringly.

I falter. What is there to say?

"It was no electrical surge and my eyes are not fooling me." Chavez points at the IV. "I'm not stupid. So don't treat me like I am."

"Zorah is..." I hesitate. "Special."

The doctor looks at me steadily. "Special like telekinetic?"

"What do you know about telekinesis?"

His dark eyes narrow. "I read Stephen King."

I glance at Zorah, lying limp beneath the sheets. "That's it, more or less."

"Okay, listen." The doctor points his finger at my nose. "I don't care what she is. She's hurt, and she needs help, and my world is bigger than Western medicine. So tell me what to do."

I cannot help but admire him in this moment. He is faced with something unlike anything he has seen, and yet his mind cuts to the heart of the matter, and he is willing to help in the best way he is able.

"You have to let me stay because I'm not certain what's happening, but I do stand the best chance of stopping her if she wakes up again. She's stronger than you think. Right now, try to get her stable. Try to find out what's happening to her body."

Chavez digests this in silence for a moment, and then gives a terse nod.

"And I don't recommend turning on the lights."

He grins a bit at that as he goes to the door and summons the crew back in. "Nurse," He addresses one of them. "Get this man something to wear." He gestures toward me, and the nurse disappears back out the door.

I watch them work by the glow of flashlights, reinserting the IV, taping a stitch that has pulled loose on Zorah's brow. The machines monitoring her vitals blink, casting a pallid green radiance over the room. Zorah lies limp and still, her breathing harsh and labored. The nurse returns with a stack of blue fabric that she shoves at me and a nightlight that she plugs into the wall. It casts a small glow over the grim proceedings.

I step into the adjoining bathroom and shut the door. Peeling off my rank jeans, I fold them tightly and jam them into the small garbage bin. The blue fabric proves to be clean scrubs, and I pull them on gratefully. There are even socks and a pair of foam clogs that fit my feet. It feels good to be clothed.

Letting myself back into the dim room I see that everyone but Chavez is gone. Even Nicholas has disappeared. Zorah lies still and quiet in the bed.

The doctor looks at me with his serious dark eyes. "Zeke, I have no idea what's going on here and I don't know if I can make an accurate diagnosis. But she's slipping. I think it's a virus. There are antigens in her blood that I haven't seen before."

I wonder what will happen when the lab is unable to identify vampire antigens. But I can only worry about one thing at a time.

He swipes a weary hand across his face. "Her vitals are weakening; her kidneys are shutting down. I think there's internal bleeding. The swelling of her brain is going to start neurological damage."

"Are you telling me that she's dying?"

The other man sighs. "I don't know what I'm telling you. If it was anyone else then yes, I would be telling you that she's dying. But with her I don't know what to think." He gets up and walks to the bed, shining his flashlight along Zorah's jaw, careful to keep the light out of her eyes. "Look at that."

I don't have to ask, I can see it, too. The bruising fades before our eyes, revealing pale skin, flawless and perfect in the low light.

"Her external injuries are healing at an accelerated rate. But her internal injuries are so severe that I don't know..." He trails off. "I just don't know." He gives a helpless little shrug.

Zorah shifts restlessly and makes a soft sound. Chavez clicks off the light and she quiets.

"What should we do?"

He expels air in an exasperated little puff. "What we're doing, I guess. I have her on medication to hopefully control the swelling in her brain, and enough tranquilizers to down an elephant. She shouldn't wake up again."

"What's her brain activity like?"

"Off the charts. It's a full-scale symphony with Technicolor surround sound in there."

I am comforted by this. I have no idea if Zorah is capable of healing herself, but the hyper brain activity makes me think she's trying.

"I have other patients," he says. He looks genuinely sorry, and I feel bad for him. His fragile human mind is trying to grapple with what he's seen, and he has no way of understanding or reconciling his experience.

"I'm sorry. I have to go."

"Of course you do. It's okay. I'm not going anywhere."

"Ring the nurse if you need me. I can be here in three minutes from anywhere in the hospital."

"Okay."

He stares at me a moment longer. "I've never seen anything like this."

I smile ruefully. "Neither have I."

"It's interesting."

I snort laughter. "Yes," I agree. "Zorah is very interesting."

"I'm glad I was on duty tonight."

I give him a nod. "Me, too."

With a last backward glance he leaves, and I walk to the bed and sit carefully next to Zorah. She is burning up, the heat pouring off her skin, but nothing like the oven she'd become before. This is just fever. Sweat droplets form on her skin though she shivers. I smooth damp hair back from her brow and pull the sheets up around her. Her eyelashes flutter, but there is no recognition in her wild and glittering gaze. She stares sightlessly past me and murmurs, "They are all growing so *fast*," in an amazed tone.

"Who is growing so fast, Zorah?" I ask and she shifts, her eyes slipping closed.

I don't think that she's going to answer and then she says, "The babies."

I lay my cool cheek against her hot one. "Who did this to you?" I whisper the words into her ear. There is a bite mark on it.

She murmurs again but without words and then quiets. The machines beep and blink.

The door opens softly and Nicholas enters. "How is she?"

I shift so that I can slip my arm beneath her. "Dying, apparently."

He flinches when I say it. "I ran into Doctor Chavez in the hall. He told me that she's difficult to diagnose." He walks into the room and sets two cups of coffee on the table. Sitting, he removes packets of creamer and sugar from his pocket and lines them up in careful rows. "Zeke, I have to ask you a question."

"What's that?"

"Can you save her?"

I pull Zorah's hair across my face, hiding behind its silver veil. I hear the blood moving sluggishly through her veins, driven by her erratic heart. I can smell her, too, sweaty musk over the clean scent of her skin. Jasmine hangs heavy in her hair.

"What are you asking me?" I say.

"I saw the state of you when she burned you, Zeke."

I close my eyes. I work so hard to ensure that no human ever knows what I am. I am strong, but I am not invincible. If people knew about vampires, if the military industrial complex ever found out about vampires....

"I am not her savior, Nicholas," I say against the soft skin of her throat. "I am not a white knight."

"But you are something," he says. "Something like her."

I sigh in relief. Of course. He knows a bit about her power, and I can just let him think that I am a witch, too.

"She's much more powerful than I am," I say. "She has to save herself." In my arms, Zorah stirs.

# CHAPTER 13

# IN THE CLOUDS

I SEE THEM GROWING but they are not in wombs. They grow like flowers with their roots in clouds. They are the new ones and they break my heart. I know what pain awaits them: disease, loss, madness.

The ceiling above me is white and pristine. Nothing grows there, no auras, no nothing. I drift in the white.

"I am not her savior," I hear him say.

But he is.

The electricity floods my brain and lightning flashes down from the ceiling, from the sky, from the clouds full of babies.

# CHAPTER 14

# INTO THE BLACK

Z ORAH STIFFENS IN MY arms. I alert instantly, pulling her hair back. Her eyes are open, the right still full of blood, black in the gloom, her other eye dilated and wild. She makes an inarticulate sound and points up at the ceiling. Her fingers stiffen and her hands become claws. Her back arches and every muscle in her body tightens.

I slide my arm from beneath her and sit up, uncertain as to what this new development means. Then she begins to shake, her feet beating a rapid rhythm on the mattress. Her teeth snap together and tendons stand out in her neck.

Nicholas appears and presses the call button over the bed. "Hold her down," he orders. "She's seizing."

It is like grabbing live wires, humming with tension. Her head jitters back and forth, thin foam working between her teeth and running across her chin. I do the only thing I can, covering her body with mine, wrapping my legs around her legs, pulling her into my chest, my arms over her head, cushioning her and holding her tight.

A nurse appears at my side and moves one of my arms to peer into Zorah's clear eye with a tiny light. "Let her go," she orders.

I look at her doubtfully.

"We haven't restrained seizing patients since the 90s. Let her go, honey," she tells me. "Just slide against the rails and cushion her. I'll get this side."

I do as she says, and she quickly slips pillows along the other side. Zorah thrashes, and I cover my face with my arms.

"Where's Doctor Chavez?" Nicholas asks.

"On his way," the nurse responds tersely. She places what looks like an inhaler in Zorah's nose and depresses the trigger. Zorah stops thrashing and arches up off the bed. I wrap my arms around her from behind, her body twisting away from me. Then she collapses.

"Well done," the nurse says as Doctor Chavez appears over her shoulder.

At that moment Zorah bites down on my arm. I feel her teeth slide into my flesh and I howl.

Doctor Chavez's eyes widen, and he clamps a hand down on Zorah's jaw, trying to dislodge her, but she doesn't flinch. I can't see her face from my new position, but I feel her tongue rasp across my skin as blood wells. She swallows.

The nurse hands Chavez a hypodermic needle which he inserts into the IV tube still connected to Zorah's hand. In less than a minute I feel her relax, and her teeth loosen from my arm. I gingerly release her so that I can examine the damage.

Blood trickles from two crescent shaped wounds several millimeters deep. In another moment she would have torn off a chunk of me and probably swallowed it whole. The wound throbs sullenly in time with my heart.

"That is nasty," Doctor Chavez says with something close to admiration. "Why don't you go with Nurse Adderly and we'll get it cleaned up? I think some stitches are in order."

"I'm not moving," I tell him. "And no stitches. Just a bandage."

"You heard the man," he tells the nurse. His fingers are beneath Zorah's throat, though I notice that he's careful not to get too close to her mouth. He shines a small light into her eyes and listens to her breathing.

The nurse comes to the other side of the bed, and I allow her to clean the wound, pulling the frayed edges of my flesh together and holding it with tape. "You really should have stitches," she says but I ignore her, and she wraps gauze tightly around my arm, her brow furrowed. I begin to heal.

"Zeke, I'm going to need you to move," the doctor says. "I need to examine her."

I slide away and off the bed, favoring my injured arm. I'm healing slowly. I need blood.

Chavez rolls Zorah onto her back, tugging the sheets away from her and pulling up the hospital gown. I wince at the exposed damage. There is a deep cut down her thigh that has been stitched together with more of the black thread, and a thousand other cuts and lacerations mar her white skin. Her face is slack and disturbing, her eyes open but vacant. My blood coats her lips and chin, and I can see bloody teeth between her drooping lips.

"This is so fucking weird," Chavez says to himself, and I laugh before I can stop it.

"Isn't it though?" I say.

His dark eyes rest on me, and he snorts without humor as his hands move gently across Zorah's abdomen.

"Hospitals have stories, you know," he tells me. "We get the weirdest of the weird. I've met people who swear that they have seen ghosts, cut people open just to find alien innards, met werewolves, seen shape shifters. You name it, I've heard it. I always thought it was just stories, you know? Tired people seeing things that aren't there." He pulls Zorah's gown down and wraps her back in the sheets. "And now I have my own story that no one will believe." He rests a hand on the shape of her leg. "I'm going to give her a blood transfusion. That should buy us some time."

I ask the only important question. "Will she live?"

Chavez runs a hand through his hair, dislodging his green cotton hat and making his short hair stand up. "If it was anyone else I would say that the prognosis isn't good. With her? I don't know."

A nurse brings in bags of blood I smell even through the plastic. Chavez hooks the bag up and slips a new needle into Zorah's arm.

The effect is instantaneous. Zorah's eyes fly open and she sits up in bed so quickly that the startled nurse steps back and trips over a chair.

"Shit," Chavez says and darts forward, but I am faster. I reach Zorah in a heartbeat, my hands on her shoulders, ready to restrain. She looks at me and her eyes focus on mine. The blood-filled right eye is much clearer.

"Leave," I growl at the nurse.

Her lips part in response, but Chavez touches her on the shoulder. "He's right." The doctor nods toward the door. "We'll call if we need you."

She goes, glancing back over her shoulder. But she follows orders. The door closes, and it's just the four of us.

Zorah reaches for the needle in her arm but pauses, her fingers exploring the place where the metal pierces her skin. She looks at me doubtfully.

"Zorah, can you hear me?"

"Of course I can hear you," she says tartly. "My ribs are broken, I'm not deaf."

I tilt her chin up with one finger. "Zorah, who did this to you?"

She glances away, her brow furrowing. "Where am I?"

"San Francisco General."

Her eyes rest on Nicholas. "I didn't call you."

He steps forward. "The hospital called me."

"Oh." She glances at the needle in her arm again, and suddenly holds her hands up before her face. "Where are my rings?"

For the first time I notice that all of her jewelry is missing.

"I have them." Nicholas steps forward and pulls a handful of silver from his pocket. "The nurse gave them to me." He places them in her outstretched palm.

She closes her fingers over the rings but does not look at them or put them on. Instead, her attention focuses on Chavez. "Who are you?"

"I'm Doctor Guillermo Chavez. I've been caring for you."

"What's wrong with me?"

He glances swiftly at me, a move Zorah doesn't miss. "You've been badly beaten. You have a concussion, broken ribs, internal bleeding."

"So that's why I feel as though I've been hit by a Mack truck." She scratches absently at the needle. "I want to leave."

I run my hands down her arms, feeling the coolness of her skin. A bloom of color brightens her cheeks, but the rest of her is still pale, almost greenish. Dark circles have formed beneath her eyes, and I see blue veins clearly through her skin. "Leaving is not a possibility right now, pet."

Her navy eyes swing back to me, her jaw tightening. The intensity of her gaze alarms me. I don't like the way her eyes narrow. Her movements are too abrupt, nervous, almost spastic. Her skin jumps under my palms. She feels like a bomb.

"What are you going to do? Stop me?" Her blue lips curve up.

"Zorah, it's best if we stay awhile longer. You're not stable."

"Is that a comment on my physical health or my mental state?"

Nicholas shifts, making a small sound, and her face turns back toward him. She blinks rapidly, tilting her face, birdlike.

"Zorah," Nicholas speaks her name softly, and I feel her relax in response. "We're so worried about you. Doctor Chavez has been amazing."

She digests this, eerily motionless, her face still tilted to one side. "Her name is Kelli," she says. "She is nineteen years old and failing Biology. She gives blood in a room the color of ashes."

I consider this new information and realize that Zorah is picking up on the owner of the blood that pours into her veins. Vampires get this sort of reading when we feed, and I am the first to catch on. "You're talking about the blood."

Chavez and Nicholas look at me surprised, but Zorah smiles as though I have solved a difficult problem. "Of course," she says.

"That's amazing," Chavez whispers.

"I want to leave," Zorah states again. I feel her tense beneath my arms.

"That's not a good idea, dear," Nicholas reminds her.

Her disconcerting eyes jerk back to him. "But I don't care," she informs him in a tone that sounds disbelieving and a bit petulant.

Before I can move to prevent it, she swings her legs out of the bed and stands up. I can't believe how quickly she accomplishes the maneuver – she is out of my grasp and away from me before I can anticipate it, much less restrain her. I leap after her, but she looks at me with her navy eyes, and I run headlong into the barrier only she can erect against me.

"Damn it, Zorah." I push but to no avail. I am dimly aware of Chavez and Nicholas watching, identical expressions of amazement on their faces. Under other circumstances it would be funny.

Holding me easily at bay she pulls the needles and wires from her skin, making the machines bleat with dismay. She unhooks the half full bag of blood and rips off the top. Lifting it to her mouth she drains the bag. Not a drop spilled.

"Kelli is in love with a boy names Travis, but he doesn't love her back," she informs us. "He gave her an STD and now her pussy smells like rot."

"Oh, my god," Chavez whispers. His eyes are huge in his white face. He overcomes his shocked paralysis and reaches for her. With a glance she sends him crashing back into the wall and holds him there, splayed like a bug on a windshield.

"What does your blood taste like?" she asks him, and her lips bow up sweetly. Her hands open, and the rings fall glittering to scatter on the floor with a sound like bones against stone. I see her wedding ring spin like a top. She's dropped it without a thought.

Her attention, diverted from me, slips a little. I push against the invisible barricade and break through, feeling an odd sensation like air displacing as I do. I wrap my arms around her from behind, pinning her, lifting her off the ground. Chavez, released, slides down the wall.

Fury pours off her like acid. I feel it eat into my skin, but I do not let go, only squeeze her tighter, my flesh healing almost as quickly as she burns it away. My arms turn black, smoldering, and I still do not let go.

"A little help would be nice," I say, and Nicholas hauls Chavez to his feet.

Zorah screams, louder than should be possible for a set of human vocal cords, and my ears begin to ring. The sound is like an air siren, impossibly loud, and I feel something rupture inside my ear canal. Nicholas claps his hands to his head with a shocked expression, his eyes wide and white.

I feel her power gather, and then I am swatted away as though I am of no consequence at all. Chavez slams back into the wall he had just slid down, and the furniture slides across the floor to pile against the door. Nicholas smartly sidesteps a careening IV pole. Outside, fists hammer against the door, but it does not budge.

Zorah rises into midair, and my memory of *The Exorcist* returns in force. She hangs, her head thrown back, her long hair waving. I'd seen that film in the theatre along with half the world, mesmerized by the blasphemy and amused at the public outrage.

I hear a musical note, and realize that she sings up at the ceiling, her sweet tenor voice whispering eerily. "As I went walking up the stair...I met a man who wasn't there..." It is a ghostly singsong that raises shivers along my skin.

There is a loud *crack* and the whole wall peels away, the glass in the window shattering, as though stripped back by the hand of some monstrous god. The night rushes in, cold and metallic and salty from the sea. I hear screams from the street below as the bricks and concrete hit the pavements, sending up clouds of dust. An alarm begins to blare.

Zorah drifts to the floor and I rush her. She looks at me, and I see that her pupils are huge, eating the color of her eyes. To my horror, I see blood dripping in thin rivulets from each nostril and from her tear ducts. Her glance sends me back into the wall so hard I feel the plaster crack.

She walks to the gaping hole in the wall as I slide to the floor. And then she steps out into the night sky and falls from sight.

A glimmer catches my eye and I scoop up her rings, lying discarded on the floor. I slip them over my little finger one by one, feeling her wedding ring burn into my skin with a small residue of her power. She'd left it with no thought, and that scares me as much as anything.

I run to the edge. Six stories down I see Zorah stop her fall five feet above the ground and drift down to the pavement. She looks quickly around and then decisively turns left walks away.

"Zorah!" I yell.

She begins to run.

"Fuck, this is going to hurt," I say, and leap into the void.

# CHAPTER 15

# AMEN TO NOTHING

I CRASH TO THE ground and my ankle shatters, but I am able to catch myself on hands and knees. "Need to work on my superhero landing," I mutter and push myself to my feet, brushing sand and glass from the blue scrubs, now torn and dirty. I long for my own clothes and my boots, leather and thick and strong. My toes, broken by the fall, heal and I take a careful step forward as the bones mend. I am finding it difficult to focus. If I do not eat soon, my strength will begin to fail.

Zorah is a block down. She doesn't even pause, stepping into the street. Her hands rise. At this late hour there aren't many people. But a Volvo stops as though it has run into a wall, the hood crumpling. A Civic slams into its rear bumper. Zorah walks through the carnage without a glance.

"Oh my god! Oh my god!" A woman screams it over and over, and I look up to find her pointing at me, her face one long expression of horror.

"Oh, shut up," I tell her and to my surprise she does, her mouth closing with an audible click of teeth. "Thank you," I say, and head after Zorah. The people in the street are sorting out the fender bender. They don't notice me.

I cannot see her now, and so I lift my nose and scent her like a dog. I find her sweaty musk, still coated with the cloying jasmine. She's turned off the pavement. I push into a low stand of juniper bushes, smelling her on the spicy boughs. Cast off bottles of cheap wine clatter underfoot as I push through the dense thicket.

I emerge into an alley, the backs of narrow row houses looming over me. Zorah's scent mixes with rotting food and stale alcohol. I trot swiftly down the street, ignoring a man carrying a grocery bag who steps out of my way, eying me cautiously. Sirens from the hospital fade behind me.

I turn onto the street in front of the houses. There are a few shuttered shops. Zorah stands halfway down the block with her back to me, another smaller figure in front of her, blocked from my vision. I break into a run as her pale hands come up, and I hear a thin cry, blown away on the night breeze. I'm grateful it's late, and no one is out.

Zorah's white hands close on the figure before her and I hear the echo of her voice in my head, her smile as she asks Chavez, *What does your blood taste like?* Red washes down over her arms and the aroma of hot blood washes over me, dazing me with desire.

She has ripped the girl's head entirely free from her body, and I catch a glimpse of staring and horrified eyes that are already glazing over. Zorah discards the head and it rolls away with a flip of brown hair.

The blood fountains up and Zorah places her face into the gush, greedy and gluttonous. The gore coats her, matting her silver hair, running in menstrual rivers down the stained hospital gown. I draw even with her and she looks up, giving me a ghoulish grin, her lips curving open over stained teeth.

"Good," she informs me and then her eyes roll up and she collapses onto the sidewalk.

The body of the girl sinks to its knees, the pink dress soaked with scarlet. She's young enough that I wonder what she'd been doing out.

I look at Zorah lying still on the pavement. I see the gentle rise and fall of her breath. The scent of the gushing blood is intoxicating. "Waste not," I murmur and let the hunger take me.

I cannot drain the body completely once the heart has stopped. I'll have to leave the shattered and bloody mess on the sidewalk. I feel new energy, but I also know that I'll need more. I can't stay here long. The body will be found, opening a whole new slew of trouble to avoid.

I go to Zorah and find her deeply asleep. She snores lightly. I lay my head against her chest and hear her heartbeat, slow and regular.

"Zorah!" I slap her cheeks gently, but she doesn't move. I don't know what this means. But I can't stay here.

I pick Zorah up and put my nose into the wind, scenting out the dank smell I know will lead me into the maze of sewers and train tunnels that underlay San Francisco. I am in luck: I find an opening less than a block down, an old storm drain that I slide into easily, pulling Zorah's limp body after me.

I sit for a moment in the dark and blessedly dry tunnel, hugging Zorah's body to me, listening to her heartbeat, thinking. Taking her back to the hospital seems like a bad idea. Especially after the stunt she had just pulled. *Restrain her and keep her still*, Chavez had said. *Give her another transfusion.* Well, she had gotten the blood for herself, and I stood a better chance of restraining her than any psychiatric ward, especially since she had just proven that she could literally walk through walls.

Decided, I walk in the direction of the place I call home, led by my internal radar, vampire and alien and never wrong.

I have just maneuvered Zorah through the portal into my apartment when she seizes for a second time. Her head twists back, her fingers clutching at the air, her jaw grinding her teeth together. Her nose begins to bleed again and her eyes pop open, vacant, her pupils huge and black, eating the whites of her eyes.

She begins to thrash, more violently than before, and I launch myself across her, cushioning her as she batters herself against the floor. A low growling hum emanates from her, and I brace myself against the unearthly screams, but they do not come.

At last, she quiets, the shudders stopping and the tension draining from her body. I release her and sit up, shoving the cover over the gaping hole of the sewers. She lies twisted on her side and I hear a strange liquid gurgle in her breath. Her skin is pallid and gruesome though the bruises have faded and the cuts have sealed into angry pink lines. She stares vacantly at the opposite wall. The heat pours off her in fever waves.

I pick her up and carry her to the bathroom where I lay her carefully in my large tub. Retrieving a pocket knife from the nightstand I begin to cut the hospital gown off her. The surface damage is definitely healing, but her abdomen blooms with livid brands. When I touch her flesh my fingers sink as though into dough, leaving fingerprints. Her flesh is bloated and so dark she looks painted.

I run cool water into the tub and begin to gently wash the filth from her skin. She lies limp and hot. It seems as though her skin cools some in the water but now her breathing is frightening, liquid and shallow.

I hear when her heart stops.

I do the only thing I know how. Hauling her out of the water, I pull her across my lap. Tilting her head back I sink my teeth into her jugular and pull her blood into me, my arms across her chest constricting, willing her heart to beat again. My eyes are closed, but the colors bloom on the darkness of my lids as her witch's blood pours into me. She tastes of Calcutta altars, fetid and filled with ash.

I bring my wrist to my mouth and bite deep. Bringing my arm to Zorah's mouth I force it between her teeth, massaging my arm to make the blood flow freely.

At first it only pools in her mouth and I shove her face back, opening her throat. After a moment she swallows convulsively and I laugh with relief. "Yes, that's it, love. Take it in."

She swallows and takes a deep breath, then screams up at the ceiling, her back arching away from me, her fingers drawn into claws, nails tearing through the thin skin over her ribs. Small droplets of blood well in the red welts.

I catch her hands and pull them tight against her body, feeling the fragile bones in her wrists grind against one another in the restraint of my grasp. "I see them!" she cries.

I look up and see nothing but the cracked plaster on the ceiling. "See who? Who do you see, pretty Zorah?"

She wrenches away from me and I almost lose hold. My grip on her wrists pulls her arms painfully backward. I watch her shoulder blades push up through her skin, her ribs standing out in a ladder up her back.

"They're falling!" She is so loud that my ears begin to ring. I haul her back against me, listening to the rapid, sporadic beat of her heart. That heartbeat had ceased when I had taken her blood into me, and now it seems to pulse without rhyme or reason, speeding along and then falling silent.

She stops resisting and twists, tucking her head beneath my chin, her arms thin around my shoulders. I cradle her gently, feeling the shallow rise and fall of her breathing.

I do not know what any of this means, I do not know what is happening to her. The ones I had tried to turn before had burned away within hours. Zorah has been in this state for days, maybe weeks, but she does not die and she does not turn, trapped in a limbo state between life and death, between human and monster. And I fear that her mind has gone, slipping through the cracks of reality, never to be heard from again.

I gather her into my arms and pull myself up. Her naked skin cools against me. I wonder if this sudden drop in temperature is a good sign. It seems her fever has broken.

I carry her to the bed and lay her on the cool sheets, pulling the comforter up over her, my fingers grazing the livid bruising that covers her abdomen like an inkblot. Unwilling to release her for long, I lay down next to her, pulling her against me, my arms around her shoulders. I pick up my cell phone and open a search for San Francisco numbers. Nicholas comes right up and I hit *call.*

His voice is simultaneously weary and alarmed; the predator in me hears the tension of fear in his one-word answer.

"Nicholas. It's Zeke."

I register the sharp inhalation and then he says cautiously, "Is Zorah with you?"

I run my fingertip lightly over the blonde lashes resting against Zorah's pale cheek. She makes a small, hurt sound and presses closer to me. I hear her heartbeat quicken and then even out.

"Yes, I have her."

"The police found a girl." Nicholas's voice falters. "Decapitated. A few blocks from the hospital. Do you know anything about that?"

Zorah's eyes suddenly pop open and I tighten my arms around her as she glares up at me. "July twenty-seventh," she says.

I place the phone against my shoulder, blocking the microphone. "What happens July twenty-seventh?"

She tilts her face like a bird, looking past me into visions only she can see. "Nicholas Weal dies."

I am glad that I have the microphone covered. "July twenty-seventh of what year?"

She blinks rapidly three times as though trying to clear her vision. "There are red tulips." She looks back at me, a tiny line appearing between her brows. "Tulips don't bloom in July."

"Not usually," I agree.

In slow motion, her mismatched eyes roll up into her head, and she sinks back against me. Her breath comes harder, but her heartbeat has evened out. I pull her against me and put the phone back to my ear.

"Are you there, Zeke?" Nicholas is asking, a note of worry in his voice.

"Nicholas, I am taking Zorah away," I say. "I wanted to let you know because I know you care about her."

There is a moment of silence. "Zeke, what's happening to her?"

"I don't know."

"Will she live?"

I listen to the rapid beat of her heart, the soft sound of blood moving through her veins. "I don't know. I think so."

"Thank god."

"Amen," I say.

Beneath my chin Zorah whispers, *Amen to nothing.*

"Nicholas, I need your help."

I hear all of the hesitation contained in his being in the length of time it takes him to ask, "What do you need?"

"I need restraints." When he says nothing, I continue. "Strong ones. Steel."

"Where the hell am I supposed to get steel restraints at six o'clock in the morning?"

"You're a college professor, Nicholas. With the internet at your fingertips. Figure it out. Call me at this number if you get what I need." I hit the *end* button.

I feel Zorah's lips against my throat, her breath cool against my skin. I have never been so wrapped up in anyone not even, if I remember correctly through the long years of my life, Yrsa. Zorah is a completely new thing, unimaginable in a world filled with marvelous horrors.

The vampire world underlies the human one, a realm of shadow mirroring the bright light of day. Monsters move beneath the surface of waking reality, unseen behind the veil of human ignorance. My kind are not the only creatures inhabiting the depths that lie beyond mortal perception; I have met all manner of beasts in the far reaches of the earth. But I've never met anyone like her.

Zorah suddenly pulls away from me and sits up. Her eyes remain closed, but she tilts her head up toward the ceiling. "I killed a little girl," she states matter-of-factly.

"Yes, you did."

Her eyes open, the dilated pupil making her gaze mismatched and deranged. "I can hear her mother screaming." She raises her hands to shoulder height, her palms open toward the sky. "A sound to shatter heaven." She twists toward me. I see only madness in her beautiful face. "Watch and whisper as those above fall."

"Zorah, what does that mean?"

"That angels are falling, smoking, from heaven." She slides off the bed and stands up. The bruises across her stomach are faded, greenish.

I stand up but she moves quickly away from me, and I realize too late. She opens the door and steps into the morning light falling through the window at the end of the hall.

For one terrified second, I see her skin smoke, but then I realize that it is only the dust dancing in the breeze of the opened door. But now she is beyond my reach in the deadly light.

"Zorah, come back to me." I hold out my hands toward her.

She tilts her head, birdlike. She glows in the light, her drying hair stirred by the breeze. The sunlight, even diluted and amorphous, brings tears to my eyes and flushes my exposed skin.

"Zorah, please don't leave me." I cannot imagine her loosed on the world in her current condition. I am the only one with any chance of stopping her, and I cannot follow her into the daylight.

"I have to go to her," she says and spins, running into the light and away into a world where I cannot follow.

"Zorah!" But she does not even falter.

# CHAPTER 16

# RUPTURE HEAVEN

C OLOR SURROUNDS ME. IT pours off everything, so bright that I can't see. My eyes leak tears and I block the sky with my hand.

I hear her in my head, screaming. A sound to rupture heaven. I remember how the blood tasted, how sweet. How nourishing. I remember her heart stopping.

But now her mother screams, and I can't hear anything else. I have to stop that sound.

A woman runs toward me, her face opening but I don't want her and I close her eyes to me, make it so that she can't see. She falls to the ground and I forget her.

It is easy to be invisible. I slip through the cracks, unseen. I have to get to her, have to stop the screams. Better she is dead than making that noise. I know what it feels like to make sounds like that. I feel her pain in my bones and in my breath. How can the world allow such grief? I can bring her sweet silence.

My mouth waters.

# CHAPTER 17

# ALTERED FLESH

I PACE, TRAPPED IN a cage of sunlight. I would take to the sewers, but I do not know where to go, and so I stalk back and forth, raging. At some point, Nicholas calls and I recite my address.

This is how he finds me, captive before the television, flipping channels. I don't watch network television, so I don't understand what I'm seeing: reality competitions, a cooking show, drama on overpainted faces. I'm hunting for news.

He knocks on the open door, the door I have been unable to close due to the light flooding the hall. He has a black plastic bag in his hands.

"Come in," I say and flip to the next channel. A news anchor appears, and I pause. But she's talking about a local sports competition, not a decapitated girl.

He enters hesitantly, glancing quickly around the sparsely furnished room. "Where's Zorah?"

I flip to the next station. "She's not here."

He sets the bag gently on the bed and I hear the soft clink of metal whispering to itself. "Where is she?"

I flip again. "Now, that is an interesting question." I watch five seconds of a local news anchor telling of a dog rescued from a storm drain and flip again. Crime scene tape fills the screen and I see the street, the body covered by a sheet, all drenched in daylight.

"You lost her."

"Not for long, I'm sure." A thought suddenly occurs. "Nicholas, do you know where the police would take the mother of a murder victim?"

He glances from the television to me, all the weariness of the world in his eyes. "The police station?"

I hit the power button, and the television clicks off. "I'll drive. You bring the bag."

He glances around. "You have a car?"

I sweep aside a tapestry to reveal a door opposite the front door. It opens into my private garage, revealed in stark fluorescents when I flip the switch on the wall, gleaming off the black paint of the Mercedes CL 550 coupe parked in the middle of the open floor. Behind me Nicholas whistles appreciatively.

"That's a hundred-thousand-dollar car," he says, running a fingertip over the shining fender.

"Not with my options," I say, opening the door. I take the bag from his hand and sling it into the backseat with a clatter. "Come on."

Nicholas walks slowly around to the passenger door, eying the Indian Scout parked next to the Mercedes. "Nice bike."

"Yeah, it's great for picking up chicks," I say, pulling on the leather gloves waiting for me on the seat. I make sure that the cuffs of my shirt cover the flesh on my wrists and slide into the luxurious seat of the car. "You coming?"

He gets in and glances quickly at my gloved hands. But he doesn't say anything.

I start the car and hit the button that opens the garage door leading up to the street. I pull up the ramp into what is becoming a damp and foggy day, the sun flickering between mist and clouds.

"Why do you want to help her?" he asks finally. I notice that his hand rests on the door handle.

The question surprises me almost as much as the effort it takes to answer. "Because..." Now I hesitate. I have not said the words, hardly even thought them. "Because I am falling." I can't speak the word *love*.

"Oh." His brow furrows as he contemplates my answer. "Do you know what you're getting yourself into?"

His question is so unexpected that I laugh. "No. But no one ever does do they?"

He smiles slightly. "I guess not."

I guide the car through the midmorning traffic, flipping the radio on to a local news station. I keep thinking that I will hear something, some mention of a naked and crazed woman wandering the streets.

"What's the plan, then?" Nicholas asks as I cross traffic and pull the car to a halt facing the wrong way in front of the police station. The hospital is only five blocks away, the place where Zorah had decapitated a young girl fewer than two.

"Well, we have to find her first. Then I want to get her into those chains. Slow her down a bit."

"Will they?"

I glance at him, puzzled.

"Slow her, I mean. She walked through a wall."

"She's weaker, now." I shoot him a wry grin. "I hope."

"But we have to find her first."

I look past him down the street. "I'm thinking that won't be a problem."

He follows my gaze. "Oh, my god."

She stands in the middle of the block looking up at the building behind us. She has a dirty blanket wrapped around her middle and thrown over her shoulder toga style. It is oddly elegant, almost regal, combined with the arrogant tilt of her head and the silvery hair streaming over her shoulders. Her skin is white and flawless in the muted light. No mark remains to mar her skin. And yet she stands in the bright light of day unscathed and shining.

I kick the car into reverse and back up even with her, rolling down the window. "Zorah."

She turns toward me, and I see that her pupil is still dilated and concussed. "I am the princess and you are the dark prince," she says. "Just like in a fairy tale."

"Just like in a fairy tale," I agree. "Come to me, Zorah."

She takes a hesitant step but suddenly stops, her head tilting back toward the police station. "She's screaming."

"Zorah." She looks back toward me. "We live in a world of screams. What are these?"

"I caused these."

"But I thought we agreed that the world is a cruel place. Death happens. It's a part of the nature of things."

She tilts her head, and I am again reminded of a bird, fragile and inquisitive. "Did we agree?"

"Zorah, please." I extend my hand toward her through the window. My sleeve rides up slightly. I feel the burn start on my wrist. "Please."

Still, she hesitates, blinking rapidly three times as though listening to sounds I cannot hear. Something inside her head and out of my range, in a reality only she can see. Behind me, I hear the door open and Nicholas slide out.

"I am the dark prince," I say, and her navy eyes fixate on mine again.

"Our kiss will be for all time." She is so close and yet so far away as the smoke begins to rise from my searing flesh.

Nicholas enters her vision and she turns toward him, the hem of the blanket fluttering in the breeze. Behind her a man and a woman stop to stare.

"There are red tulips when you die," she says conversationally.

I have to give him credit—he does not flinch. "I like tulips," he says, and extends a hand toward her.

I hear the rumble before I see it, and then a huge crack splits down the sidewalk, the concrete heaving up as though pushed by some unimaginable force. The man and woman leap aside, their arms up against the shower of earth that bursts up and falls. Nicholas stumbles back against the fender of the car, and I act.

I throw the door open and leap into the deadly light, feeling it against my skin, muted by the mist but beginning to burn. "Zorah," I call, and then she is in my arms, her skin soft against me as the blanket falls away. I lift her easily and feel her arms go up and around my neck, the warm smell of her hair in my nose.

Despite the smoldering on my exposed face, I lay her gently in the back seat before crawling in after her, feeling the heat in my skin dissipate as I heal. With the blanket gone, I see every exposed inch. There is no bruising on her stomach, no scars, and her skin is cool to my touch. I can smell the blood moving in her veins, the rich, caramel scent of it.

I tear open the bag and pull out the cuffs. Nicholas had done well—they are thick and steel, restraints for wrists and ankles connected by heavy gauge chain. I fasten them quickly, bending the steel closed with my bare hands, twisting and knotting the metal back on itself.

Beneath me the car shutters. I look up and find her eyes on me, mismatched and vacant. Outside something immense falls, and I throw myself across her as a huge object shatters on the sidewalk. Dimly, I hear Nicholas cry out.

I take Zorah firmly by the shoulders and give her a sharp shake. "Zorah, stop it. You'll hurt Nicholas."

She stares up at me, a small, puzzled line appearing between her eyebrows. "I can hear her scream."

I shake her again. "Then shut it out."

"Do you think her blood will taste as rich?" She shoves against me, hard, and I struggle to hold her. In front of my eyes, I see the metal I had twisted together with all of my inhuman strength begin to smoke and melt.

"Shit," I say.

A shadow falls across the window, and I look up to see the young man who had just been cowering on the sidewalk beneath the shower of earth looking in the open door at me.

"Do you need help?" he asks.

I laugh before I can stop myself. "Look, pal. You need to get out of here."

His gaze shifts from my face to the smoking metal encasing Zorah's wrists. Inexplicably, I do not see surprise or shock on his face. Instead, his dark brown eyes shift back to me.

"She's going to get out," he observes.

"No shit? You think?" I shift my grip to Zorah's arms, ready to hold her the instant the restraints give way. "You think you can stop her?"

"Yes." He looks back at her and reaches in the door to rest a hand on her leg.

The sight of this strange hand against Zorah's bare flesh drives me mad, and I piston a leg out, intending to catch him in the stomach to shove him back. Zorah tenses under me, and I know that it is only a matter of seconds.

Moving almost faster than even my preternatural eyes can follow, the stranger catches my foot. And he stops me.

His odd brown eyes bore into mine, hypnotizing. I feel the mist in the air enter my mind. My hold on Zorah relaxes. I shake my head to clear it. His eyes are like pinwheels, riveting.

"You're a vampire," he says.

I pull my foot free of his grasp and twist, feeling suddenly vulnerable lying prone across Zorah. All this weird man would have to do is pull me backward into the deadly light. "What the fuck are *you*?"

He looks back at her again, and his lips curl softly up. He is young, no more than twenty. "I'm like her."

Zorah's eyes open and she glares at him, her lips lifting over her teeth. "You fell," she says.

"Yes, I did," he agrees, and Zorah blinks rapidly at him, her brow furrowing. "As did you."

She looks up at me, and I smell her breath, warm and rich as her blood. "I fell," she tells me.

"Yeah? Why did you fall, pretty Zorah?"

She freezes, her eyes unfocusing, turning inward. "I wanted to." She shakes her head slightly. "I think."

"I can help you," he says.

"I don't want you laying a hand on her."

He lifts his hands to shoulder height in surrender. "Then it's going to be kind of difficult."

I flip off Zorah and onto the floorboards, rolling her over into my lap, her body heavy and warm against me. It's not a lot better but at least now I am sitting up and facing him instead of lying down and peering back at him over my shoulder.

"What can you do?"

"Do?" Zorah whispers, shifting in my arms but thankfully distracted enough to not struggle. The metal restraints have stopped smoking. Outside I hear voices and realize that the cracking sidewalk and fallen façade have drawn attention. I need to get out of here, I need to have her safe. I need to be out of the goddamn daylight.

"Well, I can see that she doesn't get out of those restraints. And I can make her sleep long enough that you can get her to a safe place."

*Sleep.* Zorah's head falls back against me as though at the power of his suggestion. She laughs softly.

I desperately need both of the things offered by this strange man. I size him up, taking in his unassuming khaki pants, the black button down and the fleece unzipped in the cool morning air. I cannot know, there is no time.

"Okay," I say. "But one wrong move..."

He grins at me. "And you'll eat me for breakfast?"

"Yeah. After I break all your fingers."

That wipes the grin off his face, and he nods seriously. "Fair enough." He extends his hands. "I'll need to touch the restraints."

I lean forward, sliding my hands down to take Zorah's forearms, lifting both her hands toward him. He lays his fingertips against the metal where I had twisted it together. His eyes close.

It only takes him seconds, and then his eyes open and he moves his hands away. I pull Zorah back against me. I cannot see her face, but I know that she is awake and watching, blessedly silent for the time being.

"What did you do?"

He shoots me a crooked smile. "I made it impossible for her to use her magic on the restraints. You'll be able to sever the metal when you're ready, but she can't use her mental powers on it."

Under my chin Zorah snarls, and the car begins to shudder.

"You said something about making her sleep?" I tighten my arms around her, hearing a growl build in her throat.

He reaches in and places one palm on either side of her head. Almost instantly her head slumps forward. The shuddering ceases.

She is heavy in my arms now, relaxed, her breathing even and deep. I hear her heartbeat slow and even out.

I look up at this impossible person standing silhouetted against a daytime sky that has begin to lighten as the fog breaks up. I realize how tired I am and how hungry. I can smell his blood now, sweet and delicious and human.

"Help me get her back onto the seat," I say, lifting her upper body into my arms. I am past distrusting him now – I am hungry enough to eat him in an instant if his intentions turn.

He grabs her by the ankles, his eyes fixed modestly on his hands. I like him for that little gesture. Together we lift her back onto the seat. She curls into a ball, her knees drawn up, one hand pillowing her cheek, deeply and perfectly asleep.

"She had a blanket," I say. "Can you find it?"

He disappears, and I crawl between the seats into the driver's chair, risking my vulnerable skin long enough to pull the back door closed. I roll my window partially down.

The man reappears, Zorah's filthy blanket in hand. He passes it through the window to me. I turn and cover her. One of her hands snakes out and pulls the fabric tight around her and over her head, hiding her completely. I hear her sigh softly and quiet.

"Your friend is injured."

It takes me a moment to remember. "Nicholas!"

"He was hit. It appears your witch girl pulled a piece of concrete siding off the building." He points up, beyond my sight.

"Shit." The sunlight breaks suddenly through the clouds and I pull my Ray-Bans off the visor. "I hear sirens." There are several people gathered on the sidewalk, and I watch one man pull Nicholas gently away from the front fender of my car and into sight. There is blood on his face. I smell it. But he's breathing.

"Seeing as you'd probably respond to the demand to 'step out of the car, sir' by bursting into flame, it's probably best to go."

"I shouldn't leave Nicholas."

"Is there anything you can do to help him?"

I consider this. "Probably not."

"Then you can drop me down the street a ways."

I glance at him over the tops of my sunglasses, risking burned corneas. "What's your name?"

He grins and sticks his hand through the open window. "Sorin. What's yours?"

He has placed his open palm courteously out of the light. I shake with a rueful smile of my own. "Zeke."

"Zeke, I'm sure the pleasure is all mine. You're my first vampire." He jogs around the car and gets in just as the first police arrives and begin shouting instructions.

I pull smoothly away, rolling up my window against the blistering light. "Sorin, you should start talking. Just tell me everything you think I need to know." I navigate too fast through the traffic, the car purring beneath us. I shouldn't risk attracting attention, but I just want to get far away. I want to be alone with Zorah, out of the city, out of danger, where I can really look at what she's becoming.

Sorin sits biting his lip contemplatively.

"I said start talking." I cut into the left lane and blast through a yellow light.

"I'm gathering my thoughts." He seems perfectly at ease, both with what I am and the reckless pace I set through the narrow streets.

"You said you're like her," I prompt to get him started.

He laughs. "Well, not exactly. I can't break concrete and pull buildings down. My main talent is that I can make it impossible for others to work magic." He glances into the backseat but there's nothing to see – Zorah is completely hidden except for the tips of her silver hair. "I've never seen anything like her."

"Neither have I."

This turns his attention back to me. "And I bet you've been around awhile, haven't you?"

"I have."

His brown eyes fix on me. "You've been around, and you have never met one of us?"

"Not to my knowledge."

"Well," he turns his gaze back out the windshield. "We're kinda few and far between. And we keep to ourselves."

"What are you?" I make a left turn and pull to a stop at the curb. We are far enough away, and I want to focus on Sorin.

He twists toward me in the seat. "Okay. I don't know everything, and half of this is just speculation, but I'll tell you what I can."

I gesture expansively. "Please."

"I come from a family in Romania. We have been there for generations, hundreds of years. And we can all do things. Our abilities are different, but we can all do something. Make it rain, foretell the future. My aunt Anamarie can make anyone fall in love with anyone else."

"That's kind of a scary gift."

He grins. "Yeah, tell that to my uncle Saadhik."

"Go on."

"Well, like I said, we've been there for generations. Our whole history is chronicled in the family library. We have records that go back almost twenty-five hundred years. The earliest ones are written in Greek."

"That's impressive."

"Yes, it's rather unusual. My point is, we have some pretty solid evidence of these gifts of ours. And we have legends."

"Legends."

He pauses, regarding me speculatively. "Stick with me here. How familiar are you with the Bible?"

I blink, surprised. "It's been a few years, but I've read it."

"Okay so the Book of Isaiah and the Book of Revelation both mention what they call angels falling from heaven."

"Sure, Lucifer, the Morning Star. He's a Roman god written into the Judeo-Christian chronicles."

"Exactly. But my family has a different version of the stories. The way we tell it is that there was a war, but it wasn't in heaven. It was in a different dimension, a war between species or maybe races. The winners thrust the losers not just out of their country but out of their reality."

I pull my sunglasses off to glare at him. "Are you telling me that you're descended from some inter-dimensional alien species?"

He spreads his hands out, palms up, mollifying. "More or less."

"I find that pretty fucking unbelievable."

His eyebrows lift. "And I find that pretty fucking funny coming from a *vampire*."

He's got me there. "Well...okay. So you're telling me that your family can do magic because they're not human."

He nods. "Precisely." He shakes his head. "Or...almost."

"Almost?"

"We are human." He tilts his head toward me. "Just not completely of this world."

I turn away and stare sightlessly down the street. "Do you have proof of any of this?"

"You mean besides the ability to levitate things?"

"I can bite you," I remind him, but he only grins.

"I have a sister who can open portals to other worlds. Twelve other worlds, to be precise. And she can take people with her."

That silences me. I gape at him in astonishment.

"I've been." His grin widens.

"Have you been to your home world? The one your species came from?"

He shakes his head but not in denial. "It's difficult to say. There are humans in all the worlds, or something close. Minor genetic differences."

"Like the minor genetic difference that allows Zorah to cause earthquakes."

"Yeah, like that. Some differences in appearance, height, skin color, small stuff. There's one world that has no sun. Everyone is white there and blind."

"A world with no sun." I can hardly imagine it. A place where I could not burn.

"And you have two eyes," he says with a smirk.

"What?" It takes me a minute. "Oh, what a king I would make." Another thought occurs. "Are there vampires?"

His smile fades. "On every world. In every humanoid species. Especially on the world with no sun."

"Really."

"Yes, my sister got bitten but she got away. Personally, I think that's where your kind originated."

It makes an odd kind of sense. "That's why we can't be in sunlight."

He shrugs again. "Maybe. Like I said, it's a lot of speculation."

"But you've been to these other worlds."

"Yes."

"And you think that Zorah is like you."

His gaze is steady and serious. "Not for long."

"What do you mean?"

His smile is gentle and sad. "Soon she'll be like you."

"She's turning? How do you know?"

He brings one finger to his temple and taps three times. "I can feel it. To my knowledge, none of my kind have ever been turned by a vampire. Not on this world, at least. That's why it took so long, I think. That's why she's responding so oddly. Vampirism is like a genetic mutation, but she already has a genetic mutation."

It makes as much sense as any of this. "What will happen to her?"

He shakes his head. "I don't know."

# Chapter 18

# As Those Above Fall

IT ALL BEGINS WITH fire. As those above fall. Searing flesh from bone, plummeting through a darkened sky filled with strange stars, unable to focus as my body tumbles.

She recedes, surrounded by red flames that pour from her skin like sweat until she is but another point of light in the sky. There is glee and horrible fury in her orange gaze.

My family falls as well. Their screams surround me, but I am silent, my throat parched beyond use. I close my eyes against the wind, thinking that this must be a dream. It's one of those falling dreams where you wake before impact, jerking out of sleep with a cry and a sheepish chuckle.

This new world is dusty and verdant and alive. I smell its creatures, the sweet scents of skin, the rich smell of the blood pumping in their hearts and animating their fragile bodies. I open my eyes into the wind and see the ground rushing up to meet me.

I cry out and jerk awake to blood scented breeze and vibration beneath me. Outside the trees race past the stars. Each frond of green life is surrounded by a glow so bright that I squint against it. The energies of animals flash like multicolored fire in the forest and I gasp in wonder at the beauty of this world.

"Zorah?"

I turn toward the voice and mistake his face for mine, the sharp cheekbones, the narrow chin. But the lush mouth is not familiar, nor the silvery eyes. He is the most beautiful thing I have ever seen, his white skin shining through an aura red and dark like Shiva in his cave of fire.

It feels like recognition.

"Who are you?"

He blinks at me. "I am the one who cannot die."

Do I know him? Did he fall beside me?

He turns away and guides the car onto the shoulder of the road. I know these things (*car, road*) but this reality has been supplanted by other worlds older than time, and I cannot decipher between the present and the memory of falling though space with my skin on fire. I have cryptomnesia and reality melts into memory.

It began with fire pouring from the mouth of a woman not human, her eyes orange as flame, her aura like a burning star, white and blistering and merciless. She ripped though the fabric of reality, and we had been sucked backward into a black void filled with the light of dying worlds. And we had fallen like comets with our wings blazing, Icarus broken, fading from blue to black. We had died, smashed against the stones of a foreign planet, our bodies bursting on the hard earth like ripe fruit.

But my kind is hard to kill. We are resurrected, our bodies healing, the indigenous people of this world approaching with wonder, stroking our shining skin, peering into our luminous eyes. They had mistaken us for gods.

"Zorah." He opens the door and gets out, the moonlight pouring over his skin. I sit up in the seat and open the door, sliding naked out into the bright night.

The green world whispers to its secret self in dulcet dark tones. Night is the time of predators and their red flashes in the dark, bright bursts of white as they kill. The magic of predators is magic of flesh and bones and blood and it calls to me as nothing ever has.

I look up into his face, tracing his high cheekbones and hard jaw narrowing to a sharp chin below a luxuriant mouth. "There is magic older than words," I whisper and his face tilts down to mine, shadows swarming across his features. "And it lives in your blood."

This is death incarnate, the moment before dying. He is the face of eternity, and the predator in him lurks just under his beautiful surface. It is red.

I take a step back. I see now, know what he is, it pours off him in turgid scarlet waves and yet his silver skin and shining eyes glow through, his scent like desert rain.

"You are flesh magic." I take another step back.

"Zorah." He holds out his hand. His entire being cries out with hunger and all of life is sucked into the void of his need. A vortex surrounds him. He is a nexus of death, and all mortality shudders before him.

"You cannot die because you are death. And death is eternal."

His hand out, beseeching and seductive. "But you're eternal too."

"You were the first thing. It was not desire or dreams. You came first."

"But you called me." His face tilts sideways and the silver light of the moon coats his features in molten light. "So what does that make you?"

Searing flesh in falling flight. Bones and wings melting only to be formed anew in this strange world. "I fell."

"From where?"

I catch glimpses, a vast ocean under two moons, twisting spires of rock rising from the floor of an immense desert but I cannot see, I cannot remember. It is all devoured in flaming eyes. "I don't remember."

"Do you remember Alex?"

Agony twists through my belly though I cannot at first understand why. The power of the name breaks over me, but I cannot remember. I only see blood seeping into pavement under a luxuriant fall of dark, curling hair.

Then I see him against the darkness of the forest. His back is to me but I'd know him anywhere, those curls, his broad shoulders and tapered waist.

"Alex!" I scream his name but his form fades. He is not really there. He died on the highway at night.

I throw my head back and howl up at the moon. He is there, this other one, so unlike Alex in form, his arms around me, his aura enveloping me, and I shove against him, discovering that my hands are manacled and immobile.

That's when I see it. My aura is as red as his and they blend together, oily and thick and viscous.

"I'm like you." I look up into his face, smelling the sweet scent of his breath. My eyes are drawn to his full mouth.

His eyes darken from silver to gray in an instant. "Are you hungry?" he asks.

Taking a step back I stumble, but he is there to catch me and I realize that my feet are shackled as well. I reach for the metal with my mind, but it does not give. "I have forgotten how to do magic," I say.

To my surprise he laughs, his luscious mouth curving up. "I doubt that," he says. "It's just that I can do some magic, too."

There is a new scent, the sharp lightening scent of glass and a sweet, acrid smell. "I want the wine in the trunk," I tell him, and he laughs again, a wild sound that echoes through the trees, making the animals still.

"You got it, love." He steps away and pops the trunk. I look up at the sky, framed between tall mountain peaks. This place is desolate, only the curving pavement of the highway cutting through the wilderness. The moon hangs above, heavily round, lighting flickers from mica and quartz in the boulders tumbled along the highway, lining the wide place he'd pulled over.

The wine slides down my throat, and I swallow convulsively, draining the bottle in seconds. The sound it makes as it breaks against the gravel releases a tiny flash of green light, lost against a cacophony of color from the gravel itself, each microscopic piece shimmering with its own soft pink light.

Zeke hands me another bottle, amusement curling the corners of his mouth. "I think we're going to have to stop at a liquor store."

"Your name is Zeke." I push the cork down into the bottle.

He stands with his hands shoved into the pockets of his black jeans, disarmingly relaxed, though I can see the tense muscles in his shoulders. "And your name is Zorah."

I look up at the stars and take a pull on the bottle. "What's in a name?" I ask the stars. Each one is a pinpoint of light surrounded by a starburst of color. "The Greeks believed that to name something was to gain power over it, to control its destiny. And the Mormons believe that everyone has a secret name known only by God. To know someone's secret name is to possess their soul." I look back at him and swallow more wine. I can feel it alive and scarlet in my stomach. "Your name is not really Zeke."

The monster is in him now, a mad and capering thing, the monster that lives in him. "Zeke is not the name my mother gave me."

"What name did your mother give you?"

"I forgot." His silver eyes glow through the gloom. And the shine of his teeth exposed by his mouth curving up in a grin.

"You forgot the name your mother gave you?" I wag my finger reprovingly, forgetting the shackles and almost spilling the wine in the process. He laughs and I laugh back at him. "Then how will you get into heaven?"

He says nothing, only watches.

I take another sip of wine and look around at the forest. It is evergreen with splashes of white in the trucks of aspen groves. "Where are we?"

"Colorado."

I concentrate on my last memory, Zeke pulling away from my curb. "What day is it?"

"The third."

I glare at him doubtfully. "That can't be right. Isn't it the fifth?"

I see his tongue move over his lower lip. "It's the third of April."

This startles me so badly I almost drop the wine bottle. "What? How can that be?"

He takes a step toward me. "What's the last thing you remember?"

"I..." I pause. "I remember you leaving. I remember you refusing..." I trail off uncertainly.

"Refusing what?"

His red aura fills my vision. "You're a vampire."

"Yes. And?"

"And..." I swallow. "And you refused to make me one."

He claps his hands together, the sound loud in the still forest, making me jump. "Now we're getting somewhere! So tell me, pretty Zorah." He takes another step toward me, his chin dropping, menacing. I take a small step back, hampered by the shackles around my ankles. "Tell me how, if I refused you, tell me how you became a vampire."

It all comes back. Malachi with his knives and teeth and jasmine skin. I remember it all in a flash. The girl in the pink dress and Nicholas stepping back in horror, his eyes wide and terrified.

*Nicholas.* "What happened to Nicholas?"

"You almost killed him."

The memories are immense and immediate, and I throw the wine bottle at Zeke with all of my strength to make them stop. "You left me on the sidewalk to die!"

He catches the bottle easily and wine slops over his hand. "And you went and found another goddamn vampire!" He yells back at me, matching my volume, his red brows coming down sharply over darkened eyes.

"You left me no choice."

He does not come closer but his finger, sharp and accusatory, jabs at me. "Don't you fucking put this on me. Don't you dare hold me responsible."

"But I chose you!"

"And I asked you to wait."

"I explained why I couldn't."

He makes an exasperated gesture. "And that makes it your choice."

I tug irritably at the chains, but I cannot even make them flex. "I wanted you." It comes out petulant and he snorts.

"So who did you find?"

I can still taste Malachi in the back of my throat, sweet as syrup and poisonous as nightshade. "What does it matter?"

His eyes narrow dangerously. "Call it my need to know."

It gives me perverse pleasure to deny him. "But I really don't see why you need to know. What's done is done."

He forces himself to relax and leans back against the gleaming flank of the car. "You could have died."

I smile smugly. "But I didn't."

He exhales irritably and shoots me that grin, full of danger and suggestion. "I suppose you're right. You are not dead."

"What happened to Nicholas?" I ask again.

Zeke runs a hand through his hair. "I think he's okay. Just banged up a bit."

"You left him?"

"We left him. In a big pool of sunlight."

"I feel bad for that."

Zeke shrugs. "He had people taking care of him. He'll be alright."

I feel the vibrations as a tiny ripple through the blazing auras before I hear it. Then the rumble rises and I realize that a car approaches.

Zeke is by my side before I can blink, and I wonder if I will be able to move that fast, freed of my chains. "Let's get you back in the car," he says.

"Why?"

"Because you're naked except for shackles and that's going to attract some attention." He guides me toward the open door, and I let him tuck me inside. He pulls the blanket up around me. I get lost in the glowing fibers of the wool. Though only dead hair it gleams with life, tiny creatures twisting through the weave, each glowing with their own distinct shade. And there are scents as well, the putrid smell of rotting blood, dark earth, and sweat. I put my tongue to the taste and breathe it in, catching glimpses, flashes. So much life everywhere, it overwhelms me. I had thought only of death recently. The whole world is a cemetery, and my focus had gotten lost in that, but now I become aware of the life surrounding me, and I can't see anything else. Everything pulses, and I lie still against the seat, listening. A great heartbeat, a vast inhale. I reach out with my mind and feel the decay all around me, but now I see that it shifts and transforms. Nothing is ever lost; it only becomes something new.

I tremble with this awareness. *Nothing ever dies.* The body stops, it decays, it transforms. I do not know what this means, but I feel on the edge of a vast discovery. Did death not exist except in limited human perception?

I hear the engine of a car pull in behind ours, but it is unimportant and far away. I push the blanket down and look up at the vast sky of stars. To my eyes it is light, bright even, and I am aware of a new way of seeing. I look and really see maybe for the first time in my life. Everything has its own unique pulse, but everything follows a larger rhythm as well, a deep inhale as though the entire planet breathes.

I look out at Zeke. I have to squint against headlights, and I see the light bar across the top, mercifully dark. A uniformed woman approaches, and I watch her aura with fascination. It is a strong pale purple. It wafts toward Zeke. I smile to see her pupils dilate. Zeke has that effect on people.

"Are you okay, sir?" I hear her ask.

"Just stopped to enjoy the night sky for a minute," he says, not a hint of nervousness in his voice. "No light pollution out here." He gestures up.

She follows his gaze. "It is beautiful, isn't it?"

I watch her aura with fascination. It is like the sunrise, lavender and lovely. She shines the light over toward the car and I duck, turning my eyes toward Zeke, who I can see through the side window.

His hair is longer, the red grown out, tipped with bright blond. I can't believe that a month has passed, but the length of his hair makes it true. I think of the modern vampire as the character has evolved over the past century. Zeke is that vampire, with his bleached hair, silver rings, and punk clothes. It is difficult to believe that he is hundreds of years old. The trace of the accent is all that remains.

The woman is close enough to smell and a rich, delicious scent washes over me. Incredibly my stomach growls, such a human sound that I laugh to myself. The pull is irresistible.

The gravel bites into my bare feet. I am dimly aware of a gun in Zeke's face as the cop reacts to the sight of my shackles. I reach for her with both hands and my mind, and she drops the gun without another thought. *How beautiful*, I hear her think, and then she is in my arms, that fragrance. I hear her heartbeat and feel her pulse against my lips, and I bite down firmly, my teeth passing through the thin skin of her throat, and then the scent fills my mouth and I pull deep, entering her with teeth and mind. *This must be heaven*, she thinks. The thought of her lover, slim and lovely and dark is before me, and I feel a tiny sliver of guilt in her heart. *You're dying* I say into her mind and feel a gentle swell of sadness. Then she blows to dust and my teeth snap painfully together. *Remember to let go* I tell myself and look up into Zeke's face.

A brow lifts. "Better?" he asks.

"Much," I reply.

"Good." He shoots me that curving, deadly smile. "Now let me explain why you shouldn't have done that."

I feel a slight niggle of worry. It had felt so *right*. "I was hungry."

"No doubt. But vampires who give into their hunger like humans give into their addictions live about as long."

It occurs to me that maybe being a vampire is not as freeing as I anticipated.

"Which is to say, not very." He gestures toward the police car. "Those things are equipped with cameras. Sometimes the feed is sent wirelessly straight through a satellite upload."

He materializes beside me and I realize that I had seen him move. My eyes are developing.

"Rule one, pretty, Zorah." His eyes drop to my mouth, and I take a shallow breath. "Rule one. Never let on what you are. The humans must not know."

"Why not?"

"There are more of them than there are of us. Strength in numbers. Besides, can you imagine what the U.S. military would do if they caught one of us? If they knew of our existence?"

I consider this. Modern surveillance is a truly frightening thing. "How can the military not know of vampires? I mean, you make mistakes, right? Get seen? Get caught?"

"That's the reason for rule number one." He moves toward the police car, and I can almost hear his mind work. "We're in the mountains so we may be lucky."

I roll that around and finally ask. "Why is that?"

"They probably don't have a wireless feed." He opens the door and leans into the vehicle. His voice when he speaks again is muffled, but I have no trouble hearing him. "Service is too spotty."

I watch him bend into the car, his eyes moving quickly over the interior. I look up at the sky and become immediately captivated by the stars. I realize that I can feel the earth move beneath me and sense the slow revolution of the heavens. *Heaven*, she had thought before dying. She had thought that I was taking her to heaven.

I jump when Zeke speaks.

"Can you bring the clothes, please?"

The clothing lies in a sad bundle next to the rear tire, and I gather everything up, catching a whiff of her scent again. My mouth waters.

I had not thought to watch when she died, forgot to see where that bright flash of energy went. I think I will be able to see now, watch in a new way.

I take the clothing and hand them in to Zeke. I smell a sharp new scent. It takes me a minute to place, and then I realize that it's gasoline. The odor is more complex than I can believe; it is as though I can smell each of the separate chemical components that comprise it.

Zeke dumps the liquid liberally over the seats and dash. I see that he has removed a laptop, radio, and a camera. I feel unease again, and I wonder if I have placed us in danger. The scent of the women had overwhelmed me, and I had given into the compunction as I have given into mostly everything in my life: without thought. I will have to learn a new self-preservation now, a new set of rules.

When the flame leaps, I gasp out loud. I have never seen fire before now, not like this, with vampire eyes. It has more colors than I suspected, blues and indigoes twisting through the reds and oranges. I see an aura, a deep violet glow, and I wonder if fire is alive. Life gives off aura, dead things glow only with the life that coats them. This flame lives.

Zeke breaks the electronic components into small pieces and begins to toss them into the growing conflagration. The flames flare as each brings a rush of air into the cab of the burning car. Finished, he takes my hand to lead me back to his car. I resist for a moment, watching the fire leap inside the violet glow only I can see.

Zeke tugs gently. "Pretty," I tell him, and his mouth curves up.

"It is pretty. But it's time to go."

I allow myself to be led. He tucks me into the front seat, and I twist around to sit on my knees, watching the fire through the back window. Zeke retraces our steps, pulling his feet across our footprints and the indentations the tires made as they pulled in. I understand that he is covering our tracks and wonder if his precautions are enough. It occurs to me that learning a bit more about police technology and procedure is probably a good idea. I wonder what else I need to lean about how to be a vampire in a world run by humans.

Zeke gets in the driver's side and looks across at me. "Ready?" he asks, and his eyes darken toward black.

I smile at him. "For anything."

# CHAPTER 19

# BLOOD SONGS

T HE MOONLIGHT GLINTS OFF the rocks in shatters of light, and I press my head against the cool glass, mesmerized. I see everything; situated in this high place, I see as God must see, every whisper of wind, the movements of small things.

"What's happening to me?"

He moves in absolute silence but his aura creeps in around me, red against the dim. His outline is a cool blue underneath.

"You're becoming," he answers.

"I can't..." I hesitate, unsure as to how to describe the change. "I can't see."

"What do you mean?"

"Everything is in shades of red and blue."

He laughs softly. "The virus is working in you. I call it predator vision."

"Predator vision?"

"You're seeing heat signatures."

"Really." I look again. "Heat signatures." I bring the block down, quash the auras, a flex in my mind. The slivery world beyond the window shifts and becomes a dreamscape of blue. Small life glows hot and orange against the cool of the background. I laugh in delight.

I hear him exhale and turn toward him. He is a statue of ice against the dark room, sculpted and glistening. He has showered, and his wet hair sticks up in tangles, the moisture shining on his bare skin. He wears only jeans, and I study his toes, long and supple, against the wood floor. Cold radiates off him.

"You're hungry."

He does not take his eyes off the moonscape beyond. "I am."

I hold out my arm with a clink of chains, making him glance down as my fingers brush across his chest.

"You're sure?" His mouth softens, and I see the tenderness in him, in constant tension with the monster.

"Of course."

His bite is sharp and sure. I feel the way his teeth pierce my hardening flesh, and there is no pain, only pressure. I become aware of my heartbeat, and realize that I hear his pulse as well, the rhythm matching mine as my blood pours into him. I watch his aura darken as his heat signature brightens.

"A vampire can drink another vampire to death?" I think of blowing away, dust in the wind, like all his victims.

He lifts his mouth from my arm, my blood on his lips before he runs his tongue over them in a quick flick, a fleeting, sensual gesture.

"Yes, it's possible." He straightens. "Of course, another vampire is very strong and makes for difficult prey. But vampire blood is..." He hesitates, his mouth curving up. "Good."

I hear the accent again, clipping his words, elongating the vowels. "What's your accent?"

His red brows lift at the change in topic and he smiles, breathtaking, very human. "All over, I expect. Here I try to sound American."

"You don't." I study him, feeling as though I am seeing him for the first time. The sense of recognition is stronger than it has ever been, like déjà vu, and I shake my head, trying to remember. It is a dream, coming in flashes and glimmers.

He looks away again, out into the darkness. "Come outside with me."

"Can you take the shackles off?"

He glances at me, his lower lip caught between his teeth, mouth curling up at the corners. "Promise not to run away?"

I cock my head and catch my lip in imitation. He grins at me and sinks to his knees, hands running lightly down my bare legs. A coil of warmth blooms in my belly.

He twists the metal apart, and the chains fall to the floor with a metallic jangle. I hold my hands out and rub my wrists in freedom. He grabs a shirt from where it is draped across the back of a small couch and holds it out. I pull it over my head. It smells musty.

He leads me out onto a small deck overlooking a vista of windswept shrubs and scattered boulders. The car gleams in the moonlight, pulled up to the four steps leading down. The cabin is set atop a rise, backed against a bank of pine trees, stunted and twisted by altitude and the wind that sweeps down from the high expanses above. We are only a few hundred feet below the tree line, and the Rocky Mountains, snow topped and desolate, rise into the moonlight beyond. It is cold but I do not feel it, though I wear only a shirt that barely covers me.

He picks up an old fashioned glass milk jug that sits on the railing and looks back at me over his shoulder. "Stay here."

Graceful as a gazelle, he vaults over the railing and lopes off into the moonlight. I rest my hands on the railing, running my fingertips over the rough wood. I let the auras flood back in, and I can make out Zeke against the cold blue of the frozen fields. I begin to be able to distinguish the heat signatures from the auras, and I see that Zeke is almost the same temperature as the earth. Heat spots shine from his shoulders, pelvis, and knees, and I recognize that I am seeing the friction from his movement.

He disappears into the woods, and I walk down the short set of steps. The ground is very hard beneath my feet. I walk to the car. Resting my hand on the hood, I feel the warmth I can see. Looking out over the moonlit vista, I concentrate and push both the auras and the heat signatures away. It feels like looking at an optical illusion, shifting the way I perceive in order to filter out what I do not want. The night springs into focus, fading into a palette of black and silver. It is comforting to know that I can still control my perceptions, and I smile at the familiar world.

Even though my sight has returned to normal, my vision is much sharper than it has ever been. I see minute details in the waving grasses, each strand of moss on the distant tree bark distinct.

I look up at the moon and gape in wonder. It looks huge and I make out craters and pits that I have never seen even through a telescope. The Old Woman in the Moon is entirely erased from my sight, and a maze of hidden things shine forth. The light has an aura as well, silvery blue, coating my shin in molten light.

The periwinkle of my human aura still coats my skin under the vampire glimmering off my body. All of the tiny mites and parasites on my flesh are gone. I run my fingertips across my cheek. My skin feels like silk, perfectly smooth and firm.

I draw a deep breath of the cold, pine scented air and realize that I am happy. For the first time in a long time. I laugh softly. It had worked; I'd gotten what I wanted. I'd defied death, and I feel the power rising in me.

I hear him and turn to watch him jog back up the hill toward me. He carries the jug, and I catch the scent of some delicious thing. I restrain myself from running to meet him.

He is not breathing hard as he stops in front of me and holds out the jug, now filled with blood. My mouth waters.

I drink it all, upending the jug for the last drops, feeling power surge through me  in a palpable wave. It is still very warm and my parched cells expand.

"What is that?"

"Elk." He grins at me.

I feel a stab of remorse. "But I don't eat animals!"

He throws his head back and laughs.

I frown at him sternly. "Why are you laughing?"

He howls, his hands crossing over his sides.

"What?" I demand, beginning to smile myself.

He shakes his head, transfixed with silent laughter.

"Zeke? What's so funny?" I glare at him reprovingly, fighting to control the twitching of my lips. He is unable to meet my eyes, going off into chuckles every time he glances my way.

He wipes his eyes with the back of his hand. "You are the first vegetarian vampire I have ever met."

I consider this, beginning to understand his hilarity. "I *like* animals."

He grins at me. "So do I."

I narrow my eyes at him. "Not what I meant."

"What did you mean?"

"I mean that I like animals and don't eat them. I find it..." I try to find the correct word. "Arrogant."

"And what is eating humans?"

I reflect on this. "Humans are a pestilence," I finally say. "As far as I can tell, the vast majority of them are stupid, irritating, and basically incompetent. They deserve to be eaten."

Zeke's left brow arches, silvery eyes boring into me. "Not pulling any punches, are you?"

I spin in a circle, looking up at the moon. "I've always felt this way. But I've followed the rules because that's what everyone does. I don't have to be everyone anymore."

He reaches out to me and pulls me into him. "You aren't anyone anymore."

A feeling of liberation flows through me. "I'm not, am I?"

His mouth comes down on mine, and I taste him for the first time as a vampire. He is rain in the desert, musky and sweet. Images flash before my eyes, Zeke in sunlight, Zeke in the rain, Zeke in my bed his white skin against my black sheets, Zeke that first night, his chin tipping down as his silver eyes met mine. I knew him, I *knew* I knew him.

"Who are you?" I ask against his mouth and feel his sharp teeth through his lips.

"Who are *you*?" he responds. "What name did you mother give *you*?"

He pulls away from me, and I look up into his eyes. My whole body shivers. The weight of what I have become presses down and my breath catches. This cannot be real; this is some dream. I have died with Alex on the highway and my brain, oxygen deprived and losing blood, creates phantasms in flesh magic and blood songs.

Zeke's arms tighten around me. I look into his face, seeing him in three dimensions: aura, heat, and flesh. This is the really real, more than I could have imagined. I am fearless, this is a dream and immortal I have become. I face the mouth of madness and succumb.

I fall back against the steps, his weight on top of me, and look into my mind, feel, see. "I see us falling." There he is, that face, falling beside me. Everything is fire, flame. And my family falls, all as one, all the same.

He is in me, skin melting, heat rising from our flesh like flame in the silver light of the moonlit night. I taste his blood in my mouth, his tongue on my teeth, and I draw him in deep. The shirt is gone, and I am naked again, in his embrace. His skin in me, his scent permeating. Take me, fuck me, breathe me in. Reality slips and I realize that I am falling over the edge for real this time, beyond the pale, into the red, pilot error, fetal distress. Dark curls blowing in the breeze of passing traffic, and I see it again, death on the highway, pleasure and pain, Alex dies and I come again. I throw my head back and scream. And scream. And scream.

I stand at the windows and look out at the frost glistening in the scrub, coating the stones with ice. Something immense looms on the horizon just out of sight. I can feel it burn in my retinas and tug at my mind.

"It's coming."

Zeke appears beside me. He is dressed again, jeans, soft black shirt, but his feet remain bare, clever toes against the wood.

"Yes," he agrees.

"What is it?" I glance sidewise at his sharp profile, the clean lines of his face. His features shine softly in the gloom, shadows in his eye sockets and in the caverns beneath his cheekbones.

"You don't know?"

I look back out into the night. I can feel it in my blood and in my brain, growing, coming closer. I resist the urge to flee, to draw back, hide behind Zeke's body. His lack of fear reassures me.

"It's the dawn."

When he says it, I see it, the subtle lightening of the sky, the softening of the silver light. The moon is behind the cabin now, and the shadows have grown long, but they are no longer as deep.

"Sunlight."

His lips curve up as he turns to face me. "Death," he says.

I perceive the first light of day in the tips of his hair. That bleached mop looked pure silver at night, but now I see the first hints of gold. "Sunlight kills vampires."

He looks toward the lightening sky. "It's one of the only things."

"What else?"

"Beheading. Burning. That's about it."

"What about starvation?"

He shakes his head slightly. "Nope. It gets pretty rough. Brain stops functioning, you look like shit, but you won't die."

"Stake through the heart?"

"Nope, that's a myth. It will prevent the heart from beating which deprives the body of blood. But as soon as the stake is removed, we heal."

"Garlic?"

He laughs, his sharp teeth flashing. "No. But strong scents can be quite unpleasant to us."

"Holy water?"

He turns toward me, his chin dipping. "Well, that can sting. It has to do with that whole magic of faith thing."

"Like my charms burning you."

"Exactly. But the one throwing it has to have faith."

I see the warmth of his skin tone now, pale rose on the tops of his cheekbones, and I squint. It feels like my eyes are close to a furnace. Zeke grasps the pull rod and draws heavy velvet drapes across the window, shutting out the light as though flipping a switch. My eyes water and cease burning.

He moves from window to window, muffling each one in dark blue fabric. The curtains are made from double panes, white linen on the outside, heavy velvet facing inward. Closed, only a dim glow comes in against the walls to either side.

Finished, he comes to me through the gloom, shining pale in the darkness. His arms slide around me, and I feel heat burn in me again as he pulls my body against his, hands sliding down my back to press me closer. I lean into him, head on his shoulder, and then, for just an instant, I forget that Alex had ever been. Everything melts away, my mind stills, his breath in my ear, lips cool against my throat. I am me again, the me who loves life, the me from before.

Then I see him in the dark, a shade against the black. His dark eyes bore into mine, a curl falling across his forehead. I stiffen in Zeke's arms.

"What?" he whispers, his breath in my hair.

I pull away, shaking my head. "Ghosts." Alex melts away, his smile a burn in my mind.

Zeke pulls me gently toward the ladder leading to the loft. A king size bed takes up almost the entire space, and Zeke picks me up and sets me in the center. Moving quickly, he sheds his clothes and then climbs in, pulling a soft down comforter up around the two of us. He pulls me close, and I relax into his body, his skin cool and smooth against mine. I feel his lips move against my ear. "Σ'αγαπώ," he whispers.

"What does that mean?"

He pulls me closer. "It means I'm happy you didn't die."

Outside, the sunlight comes in deadly rays. I tuck my head beneath his chin and close my eyes. Alex dies on the highway, Malachi slinks into the dark. Zeke's chin tips toward me across a crowded room. It feels like recognition.

# CHAPTER 20

# NIGHT AWAITS

LIGHTNING ARCS ACROSS THE sky, and I hold my arms out. All of the small hairs in my flesh stand up, and I pull the electricity out of the air, drinking it in. The light races down toward me. I catch it in my hand, the bones glowing blue through my skin as it strikes.

"Holy shit," Zeke says behind me, and I laugh.

It moves through me in a wave of warmth like blood. The thunder booms close enough that I feel it in my chest. Rain falls in a sudden deluge. I tilt my face toward the sky, the freezing drops penetrating the thin shirt I wear, soaking me instantly. I reach out with my mind and pull the storm toward me, drinking in its power. It has never been this easy. I think about flash floods and mud slides. Lightning smashes down all around. Zeke flinches and ducks, his arms coming up defensively. I laugh.

"Don't set the house on fire, pet," he says. "We kind of need it to keep from dying when the sun comes."

I breathe deep, drawing the charge into my body, and release the storm. The clouds swirl uncertainly, and the wind shifts. "See? No fire."

Zeke stands up and grins. "That was something else." His skin gleams with water, shining in the flickering storm light.

I turn my face up into the rain and release the energy I had pulled in from the wind, palms out toward the trees. They whip and blow, and I throw my head back. This gets better every night. I'd been powerful before but now...but now.

"I'm hungry," I say.

"Want me to catch you an elk?"

"No." I turn to him. "I want to go to town."

He gazes at me, eyes narrowed. "Promise not to walk through walls and decapitate people?"

I wrinkle my nose at him. "I'll make sure there are no surveillance cameras around."

He looks at me a moment longer, the storm light playing along his cheekbones, his expression inscrutable. "Fair enough. Let's go."

I clap my hands together and laugh like a child. "I want to go shopping."

He grins at that.

"I'm tired of wearing your clothes."

"I like you in my clothes." He comes to me and pulls me into him. "And I like you better naked."

I let him caress me and then step away. "Shopping!"

"Fine." He shakes his head and sighs, his eyes wandering down my body regretfully. "Let me get my keys."

Aspen, Colorado runs along highway 82. We enter from the south and Zeke drives slowly down Main Street until I spot what I want and point. He pulls the car into a parking space and kills the engine.

It is late, after eleven, and cold. Though the restaurants and bars spill light and laughter onto the street, there is almost no one out, no one to see as I step barefoot onto the pavement. I wear a pair of Zeke's pants cinched around me and one of his white shirts but no shoes, no coat, no hat. My hair blows in the wind, and I tilt my face up to the sky.

It keeps overcoming me, this world through vampire senses. Motes of life, glowing soft blue, blow by in the breeze, landing on my skin and then whirling away. I smell each one, their wild sweet scent.

"Zorah?" Zeke appears beside me, taking my elbow gently. I see worry in the crease between his brows, and I smile at him.

"Just smelling the night," I say, and he relaxes.

I move quickly to the shop I had spotted from the car. It is closed, of course, a dim security light burning in the depths between racks of clothing.

"Western Wear," Zeke reads the sign and looks at me doubtfully. "I never pictured you as a cowgirl."

"I just want a pair of those sexy boots," I say and lay my hand against the door. I see the wires running along the lintel and spot the small sticker for the security company in the corner of the window. I reach out with my mind, tracing those wires, my eyes sliding closed as I look with another vision. Security system, cameras, silent alarm, I trace it all to the breaker box. I can see it clearly, square, metal, gray. I am vaguely aware of Zeke speaking, but I lift my hand to silence him, concentrating on all those wires, all that electricity. I feel it as an uncomfortable buzz between my ears, and I reach out with my will and flip one of the breakers to off. The particular buzz I concentrate on silences, but I look again at the security monitor to be sure. It has a battery backup, of course. I see it in my mind, the dark screen, the small glass light bulbs. I flex, and the back explodes, the batteries falling smoking to the floor. All dark. Opening my eyes, I shift my focus to the door lock, a simple deadbolt and key. The pins in the lock disengage, the bolt slides, and I push the door open. The bell tinkles.

"Security?" Zeke looks at me doubtfully.

"Disengaged." I grin and pull him inside, closing and locking the door behind me.

He gazes at me appraisingly, a small smile playing at the corners of his mouth. "You are very useful," he says, the muted light playing along his sharp teeth.

"Aren't I, though? Don't you wish you'd had a witch all this time?" There are blinds on the windows, but they are open all the way. I begin to let them down one by one, keeping one piece of my mind on the street, alert to passers by.

"Yes, you definitely would have come in handy when I had to escape Paris in 1181." He moves to the other side of the window and lowers the blinds on that side.

"What happened in 1181?"

"The Inquisition."

I remember him mentioning this before, but I had been too distracted by other things to take note. "They came after you?"

"Oh, yeah." This time his teeth positively glint through his grin.

"You obviously survived."

"And they didn't." He pulls a shirt off the rack nearest him. It is bright white cotton, unadorned except for pearl snaps and the triangular Western cut pockets. "I actually kind of like this."

I spread my hands in a wide gesture that takes in the whole store. "The candy is yours."

"Why, thank you." He laughs softly and moves away from me into the dim light.

I select several pairs of jeans, both black and denim, tank tops, boots. I make a large pile on the counter and then go through the glass display next to the register, selecting leather wrist bands, silver tips for one pair of the boots I had selected, a thong to pull back my long hair. Zeke takes only a few shirts and a pair of black boots. He fits the silver tips on the toes of my boots while I put everything into bags.

"I need underclothes," I say.

"Why?" Zeke looks up from my boots with a wicked grin.

I shake my head. "Boys will never truly understand why girls need bras." I pull open a door in the wall behind the register. "Oh, ask and you will receive."

Zeke sets the boots on the counter and comes to stand beside me. "Look at that," he says.

The door opens into the shop next door, a funky boutique filled with lingerie, jewelry, handbags, and some long winter coats that hang on display toward the front of the shop.

"No blinds," I note, looking out into the street.

"But there's also no security light. Just stay low." Zeke takes his own advice and vanishes into the gloom.

Heightened vampire sight comes in handy. I select matching panties and bras, several pairs of socks, and some earrings before heading to the back of the store to find Zeke. He kneels behind the display counter, and I see that he has found hair dye and makeup.

"Look!" He holds up a canister. "Blue!" He sets the container on the counter next to a hair bleaching kit and three bottles of nail polish.

I have to laugh. "You are so vain!"

He glances up at me, his face elfin and mischievous in the dark. "I do not understand why, in this century, men do not adorn themselves more often. Even with the changing gender roles it's still considered a bit risqué for men to decorate themselves. The sixteenth century was so much more fun."

His age strikes me again – it is so easy to forget how old he is, how ancient, how much he has seen. For the majority of his long life, upper-class men had bedecked themselves as much as the women. How conservative modern America must seem with its dark suits and restrictive ties. No wonder he went punk.

He sweeps his selections off into a bandana he has also swiped, and I lean in to pick out lipstick and eyeliner, a tricky task in the dark even with my sharp sight.

Back in the Western store Zeke packs our selections into shopping bags, and I go find the dressing room behind a curtain at the back of the store. I flip on the light and strip to the skin, redressing in matching red bra and panties and black knee socks. Over this I add black jeans, a black leather belt and a black tank top with a red tribal style design. Matching red lipstick, the black boots with their silver embellishments, and lots of black mascara completes the look.

I look into the mirror and stare back at myself. Mirrors fascinate me. I cannot see the auras in them, I have to be looking at the object itself. Now I let the heat signatures creep in and notice that I cannot see them in the mirror either. I wonder if this is the reason some cultures believe that the mirror reflects the soul and not the person.

I decide that the traditions have it backward. Mirrors reflect only one kind of reality, the purely physical. They cannot see auras or temperature, and thus they fail to reflect the whole person. Vampires are physical beings, in addition to whatever else they are, and so mirrors reflect them. Me. Us.

I still look more or less the same. But the differences are obvious. The shadows have disappeared from beneath my eyes, and the fine lines around my mouth are gone. My skin is even paler and gleams softly. I can clearly see the blue veins beneath the skin at my temples and across the backs of my hands.

Zeke appears in the mirror behind me. He places his chin on my shoulder, his hands on my arms, pulling me back against him, his chin dropping, eyes shining silver. His bleached hair matches mine almost perfectly, and our skin is identical. Even our features are similar, oval faces, narrow chins, full lips. Only his cheekbones are much higher and his eyes lighter.

"We match," I say.

"You belong in the darkness," he whispers, his hands tightening on my arms. "With me." His hands slide down my arms and I feel his breath in my ear.

"You're not angry with me anymore?"

His eyes flash silver at me. "Oh, yes. You could have died."

"But I didn't."

He inhales, stirring my hair. "No, you most certainly did not."

"Then you should forgive me."

He bites gently, not enough to break the skin, just letting me feel his teeth at my throat. "I have centuries to forgive you."

It stretches before me. Life. I had felt so rushed since Alex died, like I didn't have enough time. I had wanted to die to be with him, and yet I had wanted desperately to live, to figure out how to bring him back, to continue our interrupted life. Nothing in my experience led me to believe that an afterlife is possible, much less probable, and so I had clung to life, afraid that by dying I would lose him again.

Alex had been my destiny and I had been his and then it had all been stolen in one instant when his car swerved. Now I have forever, millennia, to solve his death, to find him again, to bring him back. But the price is Zeke, this impossible creature at my side, the one I knew I knew, a new mystery.

I laugh, making Zeke lift his face from my neck. "I'm hungry," I say.

He steps back, taking my hand. "The night awaits."

# CHAPTER 21

# THE INSTANT BEFORE DYING

S HE WALKS INTO THE room, and every head turns. "Did you do that on purpose?" I ask. She laughs.

She moves into the pulsing light and I follow, watching them watch her. The music throbs, the lights flash on her glimmering skin, and everyone looks.

"I'll have whiskey. Neat," she says to the dark-haired bartender. He nods, his eyes skating down her slim form. I slide up beside her, and he gives me the same appraising once-over.

"I'll have the same. Make it a double." I feel the hunger in me, more than just the need for nourishment. The hunt, the kill, the seduction of finding and taking a victim, it all sustains the predator in me. It has been too long.

I glance around, looking for who is watching me. Everyone, of course, their eyes glancing away as I see them. I observe the way the blood rushes into their cheeks, their heartbeats speeding up.

Zorah knocks back the whiskey without a grimace. A flush rises into her skin as the alcohol warms her. She looks too, and her eyes land on a girl at the end of the bar.

"Underage," she murmurs.

"How do you know?"

"I can see it in her thoughts. It's all she's thinking about." I watch Zorah's tongue wet her lower lip, tasting the air. "Her fake ID worked at the door, but now she's afraid the bartender will card her again. And the light's better here." Zorah glances toward the bartender. "He won't card her." She looks up at me, navy eyes dark in the dim light. "He's too busy thinking about me." Her mouth curves sweetly up, her sharpening teeth flashing.

I take my whiskey and swallow it. "Happy hunting."

Her brows crease slightly. "I'm on my own?"

"Why?" I lean in close enough to feel her breath, and watch her pupils dilate. "You need help?"

She pulls back from me and shakes her head so her hair slithers over her shoulders and down her back. "No."

I place one fingertip beneath her chin and draw her mouth to mine. "Remember rule number one." I whisper the words against her lips.

Her lips lock softly on mine, her mouth cool.

I watch her walk away from me, resting one elbow on the bar so I can keep her in sight. The girl at the end of the bar turns as Zorah approaches, her face a confused mix of emotion. Zorah speaks, and the girl's eyes go starry. I wonder if this is magic or just Zorah.

I tap the bar. "I'll have another."

The bartender obligingly pours, and I slide two twenties onto the polished wood. "Keep the change."

He glances at me quickly. "Thanks, man."

His eyes shift over my shoulder. I feel the heat of a body behind me, and then a man slides onto the stool next to me. I roll my eyes in his direction without turning my head, a coy, seductive gesture.

I am pleasantly surprised. The bold ones, the ones who make the first move, are rarely the ones I desire. Their blood tastes of bitterness, cloying, bringing visions of loneliness and pain. I like the ones who want but don't approach. They're more fun to hunt, and their blood tastes of gratitude and guilt.

The man is in his fifties if I had to guess. He is dressed in simple but very expensive clothing, and I spot subtle eyeliner, the gleam of gloss on his lips. I also see the wedding ring, a discreet but flashy band glittering with small stones. He smells of money. Widowed, I'd guess. People like him don't cheat.

He looks over at me, direct but shy. My hands rest on the bar and I bring them up, resting my chin on a palm, my mouth hidden behind laced fingers. I have had a thousand years to perfect seduction. I know exactly how I look, and the precise effect each shift of my face has on prey.

"May I buy you a drink?' he asks.

"I'm drinking whiskey," I reply, and the bartender places another glass in front of me so fast I wonder if he had begun to pour before this man finished speaking.

I smell him now, the discreet herbal scent of shampoo overlying the soft musk of his natural odor. I lean toward him and inhale.

The myths claiming that vampires are dead things deny that we breathe. I know that I cannot die from oxygen deprivation; I can stop my lungs for as long as I want. But I scent the air, inhale cigarettes when I felt like it, and take breaths unless I intentionally stop.

His eyes turn toward mine, and I drop my fingers a fraction. Some vampires keep their human discernments and buy into the idea that feeding is sexual. I'm an opportunist, both in feeding and in bed. My prey takes many forms.

Humans love it too, the initial thrill of attraction. Both relationships always end the same: death. Falling in love is the same as dying. Meeting, joining lives, having babies, it all leads to death just as surely as meeting me. It is in the moment that we encounter our mortality that we are most alive and my victims, falling prey to my charm, are all the same, their blood rising in response to the only gift I offer.

His breath quickens as I breathe in, but he does not lose his poise. "I'm Evan."

"What a lovely name." I shift to face him, taking ringed fingers in my cool hand, bringing his hand to my mouth, brushing my lips across his knuckles, letting him feel my breath. I admire the perfectly buffed nails. "My name is Zeke."

"How unusual." The corners of his lips lift.

"Is it?"

"Short for Ezekiel of course?"

I smile, dropping my chin, holding his eyes with mine. They are hazel and very bright. "Of course."

"It's Biblical, right?"

"It is." I keep his hand, my fingers lightly encircling his, and reach for the whiskey with my other hand. "In Hebrew it literally means 'to fasten upon.' Or 'the one God strengthens.'" The whiskey pours down my throat, a river of warmth. "According to the Midrash, the prophet Ezekiel has the power of resurrection." I smile at the irony of this. I had resurrected no one and yet Zorah lives.

"Do you have the power of resurrection?" He drops his eyes as he asks, and I laugh, low in my throat. He darts a glance at my face.

"Is that the question you really want to ask?" I bring his hand back to my mouth, rubbing along his fingertips.

"No." He shifts self-consciously. "I'm sorry. I'm not very good at this."

I risk a look at Zorah while his eyes are down. My silver haired lover sits at the end of the bar, her head tilted toward her catch, her features in shadow. The girl says something, and Zorah looks quickly up, her dark eyes flashing, lips curling upward.

I turn back to Evan. "What do you really want to ask? Evan." His name is a solicitation.

His eyes come up, and the shyness dissipates. "I just want to talk to you." The wine glass he lifts to his lips tremors but only a little.

The hunger in me burns, building at the base of my spine, arousal and anticipation. "What would you like to talk about? Evan." Every time I say his name his pupils dilate, and he leans a bit closer. This is vampire magic, predator attraction, the death wish in the language of desire.

"I haven't seen you here before."

I drop my chin and grin at him, letting my teeth show. He does not flinch, and I know he is in thrall, under my spell, already numbered among the dead. "Well, I have not seen you here either, Evan."

He laughs a bit at that, a hand coming up to cover his mouth like a schoolgirl. The fine lines at the corners of his eyes wrinkle. I love this, the dance. I have always been a sucker for class.

"I come here a lot and I haven't seen you." He stutters, and I realize that he has had more than one glass of wine. "I mean, I don't come here a *lot* ... just ... sometimes." He flushes.

"So tell me." I take another shot of whiskey, draining the glass. Evan gestures, and the bartender appears like magic to pour the refill. "When you do come here. Do you always pick up men?"

He pulls his fingers from my grasp and knots both hands in his lap. "No!" He can't lift his eyes. "No," he repeats.

I reach out and lift his chin, forcing his face up to mine, running one finger along his jaw. The skin is very smooth, waxed or maybe electrolysis. "So what makes me different?"

His eyes stay firmly on my mouth. I watch the blush deepen. "I don't know. I'm sorry."

I trail my thumb down his jaw, loving the silky texture of skin. He risks a quick glance at my eyes. "Never say sorry. It is not befitting one of your class." He does look up at me now, and I see that his eyes are flecked with a darker brown. "If you never pick up men, why are you talking to me?"

He hesitates. I tilt my head toward him, parting my lips, breathing in, a sigh in reverse.

"You're so..." He trails off and chuckles softly.

"So what?" I whisper the words, stirring the fine hairs at his ear.

"So ... different. Different than ..." He stops.

"Other men?" I wonder what type of men come to Aspen, Colorado looking to be picked up. He probably thinks I'm the son of some millionaire, playing at rebellion.

"Yes." He looks back at me, swallowing. "You're different than any man I've ever ..."

I lift my brows, and he stutters to a stop. I pull away and take the glass of whiskey. Alcohol does not make vampires drunk in the same way as humans, though we do feel the effects if we drink enough of it. A heightened warmth, a calm buzz. I swallow, feeling my jaw tighten against the oak taste.

I turn back, flicking my tongue to the corner of my mouth to draw in a stray drop of the whiskey. I watch his fascinated eyes follow the movement.

This is what I love about classy people. They're so repressed. It's been true for the entirety of my long life. Upper class women have to hide their sexuality, learn modesty and the illusion of chastity at their mother's breast. Upper class men have more freedom but only if they fuck women. By the time they reach Evan's age they have lived through enough social danger that venturing out into a mixed space like this buttons them down. It makes them very fun prey. I can sit and press their buttons until they're ready to tear my clothes off. It sweetens their blood.

I bring the glass slowly to my mouth, wetting my lower lip, watching him watch me. I see Zorah in the mirror over Evan's shoulder, twining a long strand of hair around one finger.

"Well?" I ask. "I'm yours. What would you like to know?"

He takes a fortifying swallow of wine. "Okay ..." His eyes narrow daringly. "How do you get your hair that color?"

I laugh aloud and knock back the last of the whiskey. This time, the bartender hesitates before pouring, but I smile at him, eyes clear and steady. He pours with a slight shake of his head and walks away.

I run my fingers through my hair, making it stand up. It is naturally curly, but the bleach relaxes it, changing the texture, so that it stands up on its own in wild tufts and spikes. "Bleach," I say. "Lots and lots of bleach."

"It makes you look like that old singer. Billy Idol. Or is it Sting?"

"That is the look I'm going for."

"What color is it naturally?"

"Same color as my eyebrows." I waggle them in demonstration. "Red."

He drops his gaze, and then looks up boldly. "Do you have any tattoos?"

I laugh. "I do not." I can't tell him that vampire flesh and tattoos don't mix, that the ink bleeds out quickly, leaving us unblemished. It's a waste of money.

"What do you do for a living?"

I knock back the whiskey. "I don't work."

"Oh." He stares at me, probably confirming the rich kid assumption.

"Do you want to get out of here?"

He hesitates again.

"That is why you came over and spoke to me, right?" I bite my lower lip lightly. He can't take his eyes off my mouth. "Look, I think you're gorgeous. I also think you're lonely and looking for a little excitement."

"Am I that obvious?" He drops his eyes.

I take him by the chin again, bringing his face up. "Yes. But who cares?" I shrug. "You deserve some fun."

"I do?" He looks up at me, rapt. Then shakes himself suddenly. "I do." He places his hand into mine without faltering.

I am the instant before dying.

# CHAPTER 22

# INTO THE PALE

H ER NAME IS SARAH and it's the first time that she has used her fake ID. She bought it so that she could order wine with dinner when she went out with her ski bum boyfriend, but then he dumped her and went out with Kim-that-bitch.

That's how I receive these thoughts: *Kim-that-bitch*.

She looks at me, wide eyed and startled, as I slide onto the stool next to her. "I'm Zorah," I say.

"Sarah," she responds and I smile, light fingers in her mind. She is determined to get drunk, to get back at the ski bum, *I'll-show-him*.

"I love your hair."

"Yeah?" I smile at her. "Thanks."

"What kind of hair color do you use?"

I smile wider. "Oh, it's not colored."

"No, way!"

"Way." The bartender appears before me, and I tip my glass at him. He pours, and I catch him wondering about me. And Zeke. The way we had entered the bar together, ordered the same alcohol, and then spilt. He's wondering if we're swingers. I soothe his thoughts, taking away his curiosity, and see him smile softly to himself, comforted. *I don't want us to be remembered. We're pretty memorable.*

"You know, drinking alone in a bar is a bad sign," I tell Sarah and she laughs, a low and sharp sound.

"I'm not alone. Look at all these people."

She smells like a teenager, minty gum, cheap vanilla body spray, chemical hair care products. And underneath, sweet blood, sugary from the alcohol. The drink before her is blue with chunks of pineapple.

"Is that your boyfriend?" She nods toward the other end of the bar. I see Zeke tip back his glass for the last drops of whiskey, the line of his jaw sharp, mouth hardening.

"Boyfriend." I laugh at the word. "No. Zeke is not a 'boyfriend.'"

"He's gorgeous." Sarah sighs and takes a large swallow of the blue drink.

"Yes, he is." I watch as a man slides in next to him. His aura shines a beautiful dark plum, but Zeke's red aura devours it almost immediately, reaching out, reeling him in. I reach for Sarah in the same way.

She turns toward me, and her eyes have filled with stars. "You look like him."

"Yes, I have realized that."

She sighs heavily. "I am so tired of men."

"Is that why you're here alone?"

She rolls her eyes and takes another gulp of her drink. "There was this guy," she admits. "I really liked him. But..." She shakes her head gloomily. "He likes my friend Kim." She laughs, low and harsh. "Or I thought Kim was my friend."

I signal for another round of drinks. "Would you like something to drink that isn't blue?" I ask.

Sarah glances quickly at me, a flush rising on her cheeks. "It's just..." her words trail off, but I pick up the rest of the thought. *The only thing I knew.* She'd seen it on a television show.

"I'll have another whiskey," I tell the bartender. "And my friend will have a vanilla vodka and soda." Still a sweet drink but infinitely less adolescent.

"I just wanted to get out, you know?" she is saying. "Just go out and get drunk, and maybe flirt with a cute boy. Act my age for once."

I lift my eyebrows at this last, and she laughs.

"You know, do something stupid."

I laugh back at her, watching her light aura. It has contracted in very close to her body like a shimmering veil, withdrawing from mine which extends out from me, enclosing her. The red of it pulses, and I realize that it's in rhythm with her heartbeat, predatory and hungry. I feel desire coil through me, raising goose bumps on my arms. I want to drink her dry. Zeke had told me that the hunger is controllable just like any other urge. But this is a huge thing, like lust, like greed, the seven deadly sins coursing in my veins. The shield I use to shelter my mind drops, and color floods the world. I am over the edge, into the pale, the doors in my mind opening. I had been powerful before, bending reality to my will with little effort, but I sense the vampire beginning to transform me in unimaginable ways. I had not been able to raise the dead before, but I feel the storm gathering.

The bartender sets our drinks before us and I upend the whiskey into my mouth, swallowing twice. The sugar infuses me, but it is no longer enough. I look back at Zeke. His white head is bent toward the man next to him, tongue playing at the corner of his lip.

"Is he your brother?" Sarah asks, still trying to figure us out. That Zeke had come in with me but is now clearly seducing a man confuses her.

I turn back to her. "No, Zeke is not my brother." I smile. "Though we are the same."

"Brother from another mother?" Sarah snorts and takes a larger swallow.

She begins to bore me. "Do you want to get out of here?" I ask.

"I just got my drink."

I sense that her words are not a real protest. I do not frighten her, and judging by the green tinge to her aura, she is feeling the effects of the alcohol. She just wants to finish the drink I've ordered.

I flash my smile at her. "Drink fast," I suggest. "I have plenty more in the car."

"Should you be driving?"

I laugh. "I haven't had that much."

An adult would have questioned this claim – I've downed enough to lay most people flat – but she just shrugs and drinks faster. I glance back toward Zeke, but it is Alex who laughs at me from the end of the bar. I take in a breath sharply. He looks so real, solid, his dark eyes sparkling. I see the scatter of freckles on his cheeks, the whiteness of his teeth.

"What am I doing?"

I don't realize that I've said it aloud until Sarah says "huh?"

I close my eyes and breathe in slowly. I know what I'm doing. I chose this. I haven't lost him.

I open my eyes, and he's gone. Sarah watches me with concern. I smile at her. "Nothing," I say. "It's nothing."

I lay cash on the bar and stand up, looking toward Zeke. He stands as well, that smile I love so much flashing over his sharp teeth. His aura is very bright, scarlet and hungry.

Outside, the night is bitter cold, and Sarah hugs into her coat as the wind whips down the street, howling between the buildings. Above, the stars hang low and bright. It is quiet. The door opens behind us, and I turn to see Zeke, his face tipping down toward me, his lower lip between his teeth. I laugh, and he laughs back.

"Um ..."

I glance sideways at Sarah, and realize the small noise comes from her. Her eyes are on Zeke, her lips parting, eyes wide.

He pulls the man at his side forward, out of the shadow of the building and into the light. Zeke spins him and he twirls, drunken, laughing. I am not certain he sees me.

Zeke is on him fast, like a snake striking. He doesn't see it coming. Fangs are at his throat, and then he sags back. I see that he is smiling, eyes slipping closed.

This time I remember to watch.

The red aura surrounding Zeke parts as the blood flows into him, filling him with the man's colors. The white light from the crown of Zeke's head, the light I had seen before, shoots upward. To my vision it makes his face glow like the sun. The plum-colored aura flickers, pulsing in time, dimming as Zeke's brightens.

He blows out like a candle. One instant he is there and the next gone, clothes folding gently down upon themselves. The light shines bright from Zeke, and I watch his aura funnel though, exiting the top of Zeke's head, shooting upward. I crane my head back to follow as it zooms upward, and then disappears in a bright flash.

Zeke tilts his head back to follow my gaze and looks back, puzzled, when he sees nothing.

"What ...?"

I realize that Sarah stands beside me, still staring at Zeke, her mouth hanging open so far as to be comical. I spin her into me, pulling her back into my body, and sink my teeth in, not bothering to shield her mind. She screams, and I bring one hand up over her mouth, using the leverage to hold her close. Her blood floods down my throat, rich, and sweet. She tastes of bubblegum and virginity.

Zeke bends down and picks up the pile of clothes on the sidewalk. He watches me feed, a small smile playing on his lush mouth.

Sarah collapses in on herself, and I look quickly upwards. Sure enough, the energy shoots upward and bursts like a firework only I can see.

"What are you seeing?"

I look back at him. He stands looking up, rocked back on his heels.

"I see their energy. It flows through us when we feed, but then it exits up toward the sky."

His gaze comes back to me. "What? How do you mean?"

I search for the words to explain. "Okay, so you know how the crown chakra is on top of the head?"

A small crease appears between his eyebrows, but he nods.

"When you feed the last of their energy sort of ... flickers and channels through you. Your aura turns the color of theirs briefly but then it leaves you through the top of your head and flies up into the sky."

His red brows elevate a few centimeters. "No shit?"

I laugh. "No shit."

"What happens to it?"

"It bursts. Like a firework."

His eyebrows lift another notch. "What do you think that means?"

"I think it means that nothing ever dies."

His brows drop, and he narrows his eyes at me. "What do you mean."

I shake my head slowly. "I'm not sure. Something leaves them and reenters the universe."

"Do you think it's conscious?"

"I don't know. But I mean to find out."

"How do you plan to do that?"

I shrug. "I'm not sure. But now I have eons."

He clicks the auto locks on the car and places the bundle of clothing inside. I stoop to gather up Sarah's remains, smelling of bubble gum and cheap perfume. Strands of her hair blow away down the sidewalk.

"Zorah, why did you not just die? Isn't that the fastest way to discover the secrets of death?"

I look up at him, silhouetted against the sky, his features sparkling and cold and not human. I feel the madness tremble at the edges of my consciousness, threatening to overwhelm me again. Zeke must see something in my face because he takes a step toward me, but I shake my head slightly and he halts.

"I was getting there." It hurts me to admit this. The next confession hurts even more. "But I love life." I see affirmation on his face. Zeke loves life as well; he has admitted it. Loves being a vampire, loves the mortal coil, loves that he has been given a loophole.

"Even with all that's happened to me," I continue, straightening up, the bundle of warm clothes against my chest. "Even though, as you have pointed out, my tragedy is not that great, I'm afraid that death means the end." I struggle for the words to express myself. "Not that I'm afraid of ending. If my light enters the cosmos, or the universal consciousness, or whatever the hell happens, that's okay. Beautiful even. But I just wasn't ready." I take a step toward Zeke and his chin drops, lips parting. "I wanted to be ready. But I wasn't." As the words leave my lips Alex walks away from me down the street, turning the corner, disappearing.

"And so, you called me." Zeke's mouth curves sweetly up.

"And the instant I saw you, I knew you."

"Come on, pretty Zorah." He holds out his hand. "Let's go solve the mysteries of the universe."

I place my hand in his without hesitation.

# CHAPTER 23

# INTO THE BLACK

OVER THE EDGE, INTO the black, this is a dream that isn't. He is too real for memory, dark curls and flashing smile. I feel his hand in mine. He throws his head back and laughs, and I laugh as well, even as my skin begins to flake and crack, my fingers dissolving into cinders and dripping through his hands like lava. I blow away on the breeze. He wipes his hands together and runs away into the sunlight, and I can only watch him go.

All this power, all this vampire blood, and I cannot stop him. He is still lost, into the void, over the edge. The light blinds me, hiding him from sight, and darkness falls across my vision. Out of the darkness, shimmering like stars on water, Zeke comes.

His hair is the color of sunlight, but sunlight is not his domain. I pause on the edge of night, longing for Alex, but it is not he who answers my call. Instead, this new creature, this impossible thing, all sharp edges and cutting teeth, marble and ice and frozen blood. I had called to death and he has answered; I step into his embrace and it feels like recognition, like adultery, like deceit.

I awake in darkness. For a moment I am completely disoriented, and I automatically look with my inner eye, but only a faint gray glow appears. No auras, no light.

I remember that I have another way of seeing, and I look for heat signatures. Nothing, only a dim blue. I hold my hand before my eyes but can barely make out my fingers. I am the same temperature as the room.

I lie in bed alone. I slide to the edge and find the floor with my toes. Carefully I reach to my right to locate the corner of the bedside table and then the lamp. The light sends shatters across my vision, and I shut my eyes until I can see again.

"Zeke?" I know as soon as I call out that I am alone in the cabin. I get up and pull on jeans, tank, socks, boots before descending the stairs into the main room. I see light around the edges of the curtains, and I step to the window, pulling the fabric back.

The sun has just gone down behind the mountain, and the sky glows with sunset color. It's still so bright that my eyes burn. I allow the curtain to fall shut and go to the refrigerator.

I realize the mistake, a remnant of my human life, as I open the door, but then I pause. The interior is full of bottles. I take one and break the seal, and immediately my mouth waters. I upend it and blood, thick and cold, pours down my throat. I lick the residue off my lips and place the bottle in the sink. Human blood in the fridge no longer strikes me as strange. I take another bottle.

*Zeke?* This time I call out with my mind but still receive no answer. Perplexed, I go to the couch and sit, facing the curtained window. Deep silence surrounds me, and I place my hand on my chest. The heart there still beats but faintly, the rhythm slower than usual.

I have had dreams of Alex since his death. I have dreams of warning him in time, I have dreams of killing myself to step into his waiting arms. I have dreams of talking to him beyond the grave, I have dreams that he had never been born and had never died and never left me. This new dream feels different.

Alex had died on the highway, and I had not known. Nothing about the universe seemed altered or different until the phone rang, the voice telling me of his death. And through the grief that knocked me to the floor, had come the thought *How could I not have known?* How, with all my power, could I not have prevented this?

Alex had been beside me every step of the way as I learned and grew in my power. Until he wasn't. I searched and searched, reaching out with all my abilities to no avail. No glimmer of him remained, no lingering aura, no trace of thought, no whisper of his being. His body smashed on the highway, and he disappeared without a trace as though he had never been. I saw his ghost but that wasn't him. That was just my mind.

Or so I had thought. Then I had sensed those mighty doors on the edge of everything. I have seen how energy shoots upwards when the body dies. Our energy goes somewhere.

I crack the cap on the bottle in my hand and drink, feeling the heat suffuse my body. I watch my skin temperature rise past that of the room.

I allow myself to wonder if I have made a mistake.

Maybe I should have followed Alex into death, linking my destiny completely with his. In retrospect, hindsight being twenty-twenty and all that shit, I would. I would slit my wrists and fill the tub with all this blood Zeke finds so precious.

Death is the thief in the night, stealing dreams, futures. It has robbed me of everything. No growing old in a Victorian house filled with cats. No gray hair. No slipping into eternal sleep in one another's arms, the juices from rotting bodies mingling and drying to dust. We hadn't had time to get sick of each other, think *I wish I'd never met you.* We had been denied the chance to find the deepest reaches of one another's being. And it wasn't *fair*.

I fling the bottle in my hand at the wall as hard as I can. It disintegrates and falls as sparkling sand across the rough hardwood floor. The blood splatters spectacularly and runs down the wall in lurid drips.

I feel rage build in me and close my eyes, placing my shaking hands carefully on my knees, trying to control the surge of fury. I smell the blood on the wall and it does nothing to calm my surging emotions.

When Alex died the grief had paralyzed me, freezing me into a state near catatonia. I hardly remember the days between his death and the funeral, only Nicholas asking soft questions, *What would he want? Are these flowers okay? I'll have the wake at my house?* and nodding, yes to everything, just don't ask any more questions. I remember sitting in the center of our bed, staring at the polish flaking off my fingernails. People came, asked questions, put their arms around me, offered food, but I could only sit, motionless, knowing that if I moved it would be real.

I had moved for the funeral, of course. Moved when Nicholas came in, moved to put on the dress he handed me. Alex would have loved the dress, and I dimly thanked Nicholas. It was long sleeved and black (of course) in a heavy, velvety fabric that clung to me, enclosing me like a lover. I had stepped into heels, very high, and placed a hat over the hair that hung, unwashed and unbrushed, down my back. I remember ripping the curtain from the window—it had been a thin lace slip—and pulling the whole thing down over my head, over the hat, covering myself to the shoulders. Vanity had moved me enough to glance in the mirror on my way out, and I had been pleased with the result, very Jackie O. Alex would have wanted me beautiful.

I don't remember the service other than the closed casket. I remember sitting on a bed in one of Nicholas's unused rooms listening to the mourners below at the wake. The night passed and the booze flowed and they had grown louder, both in their laughter and their tears. I remember Nicholas's ridiculous wife pressing a small white pill into my palm and I had swallowed it with a bit of wine. Then I remember nothing.

Nothing until I had left Nicholas' house, some days later, just getting up and letting myself out at 2 a.m. The sidewalk had been very cold and I realized that I had lost the shoes somewhere. I had walked all the way home that night, a distance of some ten miles. I had come home in the sunlight, sweat drenching the black dress, blood on my feet. I had walked in my front door, peeled the dress from my body, collected a bottle of bourbon, and then my memory goes blank again.

The thing that wigs me out the most about grief is how it makes me feel as though I am dying. Slowly, in increments. Nothing I did made it relent, no matter how many times I told myself that death was a natural part of life, a beautiful one even, the final mystery. I tried to be intellectual, rational, but nothing makes it go away, this scratching, clawing, hungry thing that has taken residence in the core of my being, devouring me slowly. I fell into limbo, unable to die but unable to live or see how I ever could again. Eventually I had just given myself over to it, sucking in the alcohol like a drowning person reconciles themselves to breathing water.

And I hate it. I hate how grief obscures everything, how selfish it all feels. I cannot truly remember Alex, who he had been, how he had laughed, the weight of his warmth against me. The grief had devoured everything like .... well, like a vampire.

This is the hate boiling inside me now. Grief has driven me mad, over the edge, into the black, to place where all my rational thought sinks into the void. I could not decide to live or die, I cannot even think. Grief has reduced me to a primal, craving thing, and I HATE it.

I leap to my feet, dimly aware of a low snarling sound issuing from deep in my throat. At a glance, the curtains rip themselves apart and I stand in the blood light of the dying day, feeling it burn on my skin.

Fury coils deep in my belly in a tight, blazing knot and, unable to control it, I throw back my head and scream. I HOWL. The windows shudder and then it pours out of me, and I all I can do is stand and shake and let it come. I discharge all that rage, watching it stream from me in a dark purple burst that shatters the window, blows across the field, trembles in the trees on the other side of the clearing as a violent wind. I hear branches bend and break.

I want to kill, to destroy, to ANNIHILATE. I want to rip fragile flesh and hear bones crack. I want to tear screams from delicate mortal throats.

I throw back my head and scream, "I HATE YOU!" unsure if I am speaking to Alex, the grief, or myself.

The little cabin on the edge of the trees trembles.

I stalk to the door and throw it open so hard that the doorknob embeds in the wall. This feels GOOD, this feels like being GOD.

I unleash a stream of power, and the trees on the far side of the clearing burst into flame. Tiny living things flee before me, but I trap them easily and pull them in with just the power of my mind, pulling them to my ravenous mouth, eating them to ashes, one, two, three. Blood pours down my throat.

I run down the steps and into the field. Across from me the trees crackle, flickering firelight replacing the last light of day. I spin in a circle, lifting my arms above my head, and pull in more energy from the universe. The power surges into me and I scream again, dimly aware that the sound actually blows shingles from the roof of the cabin.

I turn toward the west and marshal all of the power that burns in my being. The west, the land of the dead, that cold home of the wind. "YOU WILL ANSWER ME!"

No circle this time, no protective barrier, no tools of magic. Just me. Just the universe. And it WILL bend to me.

"I will speak with the dead!" My voice roars up out of me. "I WILL!" It felt so easy now, what I had struggled to do before. I part the veils of reality with barely a thought; they rip back like the curtains and I pull. I PULL.

I hear something shriek, tear, but I only tug harder. "You gods are only dead metaphors," I whisper. "I am real." I scream it louder, "I AM REAL. And I will have my WAY."

The power rushes through me and it feels so GOOD. Orgasm frenzy, cannibal storm. Far away on the boundaries of my consciousness I feel something mighty flex. I grasp with every shard of my consciousness and YANK. Dimly I feel something in my head break and a gush of blood from my nose, but I pay no attention.

From the West I see a looming blackness, but I do not know if I see with my inner eye, normal vision, or the new predator vision I have acquired. I focus my will and rip. The black parts and the dead teem forth.

They come as shadows, dark against the black. They come as auras, wraiths sparking deadlight in my sight. Their thoughts fill my head, a barrage of images and sounds so sudden that I clap my hands to my ears without thinking.

So many. The long history of my species ... oh, wait ... the species I *used* to be, stretches before me. And they keep coming, bringing with them a riptide of images so fast and hard that I can not distinguish one from the next, just cry out helplessly as their emotions—rage-joy-lust-hate-misery-longing-confusion-wonderment-fear-grief-loneliness—wash over me. Dimly I feel my flesh part under their onslaught, the blood running down my body, soaking into my shirt.

"Stop." But it comes out as a whisper, my overloaded mind straining to process the assault of the sensory. Something in my left eye bursts, heals, and bursts again. I struggle to reverse the flow, push them back. But the flood in my mind makes it impossible to focus. Blood pounds in my head, and I realize that it streams from my nose and ears, a deluge of my stolen life dripping into the ground at my feet.

I open my mouth to speak again, to command as I had moments before. Nothing but blood escapes my lips. I sink to the ground, feeling them all around, struggling to find that still, quiet place at the center of my being, the place the power lives, but they block my way. My vision dims.

I do not immediately feel Zeke's arms around me, only become aware of his voice in my mind, a focal point in the screaming madness. I cannot hear his words through the tumult, but I latch onto his essence. His voice balances me, and I push away the barrage on my senses with all of my remaining strength. The battering of images and voices relents just enough for me to be able to hear him, feel that his arms encircle me, his flesh warm against mine.

He repeats my name over and over like a mantra. I reach into his being and pull power from the deep reservoir of energy containing the core of him, his vast well. I feel him flow into me, and I shove back against the tide of dead things – deadlights– with all my strength.

Slowly I stand, feeling the deep wheals in my flesh begin to heal. With a soft pop the flow of blood from my ear ceases, and my left eye clears. Again.

I look up at the looming thing, the great black gate. I do not call aloud this time, do not scream the words, only focus my power, Zeke's breath in my ear, and reach out my mind, envisioning an encircling net gathering the dead in. I began marshaling them back into the great darkness.

Now I can see them individually, though the sheer number still overwhelms me. As I bring each into line my mind touches them, what is left of them. Some seem to be only a single thought, repeating over and over – *why did I do it? Why did I do it? Why did I do it?* Others consist of a pure emotion with no thought, no image. Others seem more complete, their auras (deadlights) shifting colors like a human's, their thoughts layered and complex.

I begin searching for Alex. No, *no, no, no, no, no* – on it went. Hundreds of thousands, millions of shades, and none are him.

I draw Zeke's power through me and push them, PUSH, forcing them back into the black. They resist, pulling at me, clawing at my mind, images flowing through me in waves, impossible to ignore.

"You are not the one I want," I whisper, pushing each one, releasing them back into the void.

I do not quite dare to look into that blackness, the gate I had opened. As they flow past me my mind brushes something *alien*, something vast, something so *different* that I quail before it.

I reach deep into the recesses of Zeke's being and suck hard, drawing him into me, pulling on his strength. His breath stirs the fine hairs along my neck. I feel his lips against my throat, his teeth against my skin. His arms curl around my waist, his body curving into mine.

I draw my net closed, shoving the deadlights back into the stygian black that looks at me with unfathomable eyes.

I feel its alien gaze upon me, feel the recognition. It sees me, beholds my power, and I sense it stir, awaken. A chill works its way down my spine.

"What?" Zeke's voice whispers in my ear. "What is it?"

I cannot tell him, cannot make him see. I shift my body, futilely trying to impose myself between him and the Cthulhu eyes. Dimly I feel the strength draining through me, an unimaginable surge of power as I shove with all my might against the gates of the dead.

They go, giving way before me but slowly, so slowly. And as they leave, the gaze grows stronger, turns its force upon me. I feel my skin burn as though in sunlight.

Reaching deep into myself I find the rage I had felt so strongly before, blazing inside. "You may NOT!" I say, and slam the gates closed.

For a moment, the entire world seems to hold its breath, and then the breeze hits my face. Across the field the trees crackle and burn. I smell smoke and realize that a ravenous hunger roils inside my gut. I take a deep breath, and Zeke's arms relax and fall away. He crashes to the ground behind me.

# CHAPTER 24

# DESOLATION

I SEE HIM FALL, his eyes wide open, staring up at the sky. Blood gushes from his nose and, more horrifying, from his eyes.

"Zeke?" I fall to my knees and swipe ineffectually at his face.

*blood on the highway*

He stares up at me, his silver eyes filling with blood, his pupils very small in the light of the full moon rising.

"Zeke!" I pat his cheeks, the scent of his blood filling my nostrils, impossibly sweet. I can see his veins, dark under his white flesh. His pupils abruptly expand, eating the iris of his eyes, and his head falls sideways, his mouth slack. His muscles contract under me as his body seizes.

"ZEKE!" I grab the lapels of his shirt and shake him sharply. His head hits the ground with a thump. His hands come up, fingers hooked into claws, scrabbling at the air. His breath whistles.

I shake him again, but he only gazes up at the sky, his brow furrowing as though working through some difficult problem. The blood emptying from him mats his hair, black in the moonlight.

*blood in dark curls*

I do the only thing I can think of. Lifting my wrist to my mouth, just like I had seen in vampire films all my life, I bite deep into the artery there. My blood wells, and I hold the flow to Zeke's mouth.

His lips remain slack against my flesh, even as my body begins to heal. "Drink!" I shake him again, not caring when his head hits the ground. His aura, lurid and dark and red, dims toward black.

He has been alive for nine hundred years. How can he possibly die?

Then I feel his lips fasten against my wrist, and he swallows once and again. His eyes slip closed.

I realize that every inch of me aches. My very skin hurts, stinging from those great eyes. My blood seeps sluggishly from a thousand tiny lacerations, slowly healing. As Zeke pulls my blood into his body, I watch the veins appear beneath my skin and realize that he could drink me dry. I pull my wrist away and lick the pierced flesh to make it heal.

Zeke opens his eyes and sits up. Drying blood cakes his skin, and his pupils are dilated, eating the iris of his eyes. He seems even more pale, his skin translucent over the collapsed veins beneath his flesh. He looks dead.

"What happened?" His gaze slides over me to the place in the sky where the black gate had yawned only moments before.

I laugh shakily, relieved, hearing a note of hysteria in my voice. "I don't know."

His eyes shoot back to me, brows lifting. "You don't know?" He stands up all in one fluid motion, tension in every line of his body.

"I mean ..." I pause, trying to read him. His aura is darker than I have ever seen it. "I mean that I did it."

"Did what? What the hell was that?"

"I tried the spell again. I tried to access the dead. And it worked." He looms above me, and I stand up. He steps away.

"You call that 'worked'?" He spins to face me. "That," he stabs his finger at the night sky. "That nearly killed you. And you..." This time the finger jabs me sharply in the chest. "You nearly killed *me*."

His lips curl up, and then he spins and walks toward the cabin, fading into silhouette against the flickering light.

"Zeke!" I run after him.

He sprints up the steps and past the curtains billowing through the shattered window. The door crashes, and I hear the refrigerator open. Inside he stands framed in the harsh light from the door, his head tilted back, the dark liquid from a bottle pouring into his mouth. I smell it, delicious and sweet. Without pausing he holds a bottle out toward me. I spin the top off and drink deep as he opens another bottle and tips it into his mouth as well.

I feel the blood rush into me, and my flesh draws together, sealing the last of my wounds. I laugh aloud. "I can't believe that worked!"

Zeke sets the bottle he holds down so hard that the crack of the glass against the tile of the counter sounds like a gunshot. I flinch.

"You." He points at me again, his finger hard and sharp. "You will be the death of me." He looks out the window, his jaw hard, lips tight. The flickering light plays across his high cheekbones.

"Are you mad?" My voice comes out small and human.

He blows air out through his nostrils. "My woods are burning down."

I follow his gaze and behold a conflagration, the trees lit like giant torches. "Oh, shit." I reach out with my mind, finding moisture, pulling the clouds together. Lightning cracks, and then rain pours down. Great gouts of steam rise from the trees, and fog roils across the field toward us, bringing the scent of funeral pyres.

"Much better." He goes to the cabinet next to the refrigerator and extracts a bottle of whiskey. I smell the alcohol, sharp and sweet, as he pours a glass for himself. He doesn't pour one for me.

Outside, the thunder booms, a large and fearsome sound that makes us both jump. I sense its growing power. The wind blows through the gaping window, bringing rain with it.

Zeke takes a long swallow, shakes his head, and goes back to the refrigerator. He takes the last bottle and dumps a stiff shot of the red fluid into the glass with the whiskey. "Quite the storm you conjured up."

I laugh. I have been laughing too much. "Did I tell you about the time that I sent the rain away so Alex and I could have a nice day at the beach? The next day, a hurricane killed four people."

"Great. Does that mean that we're in for a hurricane?" He takes his glass to the window, his boots crunching in the shards littering the floor. The wind blows the curtains back and molds his shirt to his body, ruffling through his hair. "What the hell am I going to do about this bloody window? Do you realize that eventually the sun will come up?"

"Sorry." I hesitate. "Couldn't we, you know, call someone?"

Outside the lightning flashes, painting the walls with pallid light, and the thunder booms again. The rain picks up, coming down in a torrent.

"I don't think anyone could get through this even if it wasn't the middle of the night." The rain mists in and runs down his face in sparkling droplets. He seems not to notice. "So. Tell me. What did you do?"

I falter, uncertain how to explain it. "I ... I just decided to try again. I wasn't even sure it was possible."

He looks at me, eyes narrowed.

"I mean that I didn't even know if anything was left after death. I just knew that Alex..." I stop as his jaw ripples. "What?"

He takes a drink, the blood glistening on his lips. "Not a thing." He gestures. "Continue."

"Well, so I just decided to do it. But the gates opened and then they all just flooded out." I feel tears prick my eyes. "So many of them."

"And they're like ... what? Ghosts?"

"I guess. Most of them weren't really anything. Just like an emotion or a thought."

"You mean not sentient."

"Yeah."

"And?"

"And what?"

"Did you find what you were looking for?"

I hesitate. "You mean Alex."

He takes another swig.

"No. There were so many."

He sets the glass on the end table next to the sofa and looks up at me, his mouth hard. "Do you even know what you're doing at all?"

"What do you mean?"

"I mean ... do you have any idea what you're getting into? Any idea about the effects? Any idea at all..." His voice rises and he brings himself back under control, closing his eyes briefly, mouth drawing down.

"You are upset. I'm sorry, Zeke. I didn't know."

He reaches down and picks the glass up. Before I guess his intention, he flings it at me. I barely duck in time, and then it shatters over the sink, spraying me with glass.

"Hey!"

He comes across the room fast, anger pulling his mouth into a snarl, his eyes dark. Without slowing he shoves me back against the refrigerator door. The handle bites into my back. Outside, thunder roars.

"Enough, Zorah." I feel his breath against my lips. "I have had enough." He shakes me by the shoulders, none too gently. "Ever since I met you, my life has been in danger. Sunlight, ghosts, gates of death, but most of all," He shakes me again. "You. You are a hazard." He releases me so suddenly that I stumble.

He snatches the whiskey bottle from the counter and takes a long swallow. "This is not all about you, you know."

"I...I know that."

"Do you?" He spins toward me again, and I flinch. "Do you know that, little Zorah?" His mouth draws up over his teeth. "Because I don't think you do. I think that it's all about you and always has been. I think that pretty little Zorah has always gotten her way. I think that you have bent people to your will your entire life. Probably without realizing it." Thunder crashes so loud that my ears ring.

"That's not true, Zeke." I feel my defenses rise. "I always take other people into consideration."

He snorts. "Yeah? I have yet to see that side of you."

I stammer with bewilderment. "That's not true," I repeat finally, feeling like a child.

"Do you even like me?" He cocks his head to one side, lips tight and hard.

I laugh in astonishment. "Are you kidding?"

He shakes his head slightly. "Nope."

I lay my hands on the counter carefully and look him straight in the eye. "Zeke, I invited you into my home. Into my body. I *died* for you."

His eyes narrow. "That is one way to interpret your actions."

"There's another?"

He contemplates me for a long moment, his lower lip caught in his teeth. "Well, one could say that when I met you, you were drowning. You might have made it another year." He tips more whiskey into his mouth. "Maybe. A year, probably less, and it would have been suicide, alcohol, a dangerous man. Now you're technically immortal, but you're still looking for death. I didn't kill you, whoever made you a vampire didn't kill you, and yet you're still looking. So no, I don't think you're doing any of this for me. Or even that you're thinking of me at all." He set the glass down. "So, I'll ask you again, do you like me?"

I stare at him, dumbfounded. As much as I hate to admit it, I feel a small niggle of unease at how well he sees me. Even Alex … I drop my head, a chill working its way through me as I realize that even Alex had not seen me so well. I had manipulated people, even people who loved me, my entire life, just as Zeke said.  I feel my defenses rally and rise.

"Of course I like you."

He walks around the counter toward me. I fight the urge to take a step back. He places a hand on the counter on either side of me, trapping me in the circle of his arms. He leans in, his mouth descending toward mine. My lips part in response.

"You like me?"

"Yes," I whisper.

"Tell me."

I look up into his eyes, so silver and deep. "I like you." The words are hardly more than breath.

"You love me?"

The shock of his words shoots through my senses, and I draw in a sharp breath.

His mouth is so close to mine that I feel the warmth of his lips. "Tell me you love me."

I have never been frugal with endearments, but the words catch in my throat. The last person I had spoken those words to had blown away, ashes on the wind. And I am angry, the shocks of the evening wearing on me. Some mean part of me refuses to give him the satisfaction.

I shove against him, but he catches me quickly, and though I struggle I have forgotten his strength. "Let go of me!"

He laughs, a low growl in his throat. "Make me." The lightning is constant, a strobe through the window. The lights flash once and then go out.

I reach for the deep well of my power and find it, for the first time, empty. Though the anger courses through me I am tapped, dry. "Let go!" I say again, and then his mouth finds mine and, dear god, I cannot resist him, even for a minute, not even as his fingers bite into my shoulders, his teeth drawing the blood from my lips. His hand works its way into the top of my jeans and then rips, pulling my hips into him as the fabric parts.

The cabin creaks. There is a sharp *crack!* I am aware of rain lashing against my skin. The garish white flash of the lightning illuminates his face, and I find myself lifted, his fingers pulling away the shreds of my jeans, parting, penetrating. Water runs down his face and behind him, impossibly, I see the roof lift and spin into the night. Glass and splinters rain down. The curtains flap once and take flight into the sky. Rain streams over us, slicking our skin as Zeke bends me backwards over the counter. I feel the wood shudder, but his mouth consumes me and I lose myself.

I sit up.  Only shreds of my tank top remain; otherwise, I am naked, soaked. I pull the fabric off and discard it. The rain has stopped, though the air hangs heavy with moisture. No stars shine in the dark sky and the breeze, cold and smelling faintly of fire, lifts my wet hair off my neck.

Hardly anything of the cabin remains. The roof has entirely disappeared, and the front wall is fallen outward. The remaining furniture drips water. I stand up shakily.

From my left, what had been the front of the cabin, I hear wood scrape and then a crash as something overturns. Picking my way through the debris I go to the porch. One side is higher than the other, and it cants drunkenly.

Zeke picks up a piece of siding, from the front wall I think, and tips it off of the car. The vehicle appears relatively unharmed. He wears only his jeans and boots, his skin glowing deep blue in the darkness.

"Zeke?"

He turns toward me, and a dim flash of lightning glimmers in his eyes, dark and molten beneath red brows. He stands for a moment looking up at me, and then goes to the door of the car. Digging in his pocket he produces the keys.

"Daylight soon." He gestures toward the east, the still dark sky.

I step carefully down the steps. One has a spear of metal jutting from it that I skirt in my bare feet.

Zeke shakes his head, sending water flying from his hair. "I asked you to wait."

I stop, confused. "Wait?"

He stands in the open door, looking down. His skin is streaked with mud and blood. "I asked you to wait a month." When he looks up his eyes glisten. "Not long, even in human terms." I see a new trail of moisture against his ivory skin.

"Zeke?"

He gestures, taking in me and the destroyed cabin with one movement. "Quite the mess you've made." He steps into the dark interior of the car, the dome light glinting from the tips of his spiky hair.

"Zeke!" I run toward him. The motor roars.

"Have fun cleaning it up." He slams the door, and the tires spin as he reverses.

"Zeke!"

For a moment his eyes meet mine. A liquid drop falls from his chin. He shakes his head once sharply, and then spins the wheel, making the car shoot down the drive. The brake lights flash once and then he is gone, the roar of the motor fading.

# CHAPTER 25

# GRAVE THINGS

WHEN I SIT UP the soft, loamy dirt of the high mountainside crumbles and falls into my lap. The western sky glows with the last light of the dying day, the clouds lit from beneath with a gaudy, reddish glow. It is beautiful.

I stand, brushing the moist earth from my skin, leaving long streaks of mud. My hair hangs matted and filthy down my back. I had not been able to salvage clothes before the sun's death rays filled the sky, and I'd had to burrow naked into the earth. I feel a bit like a potato.

I look toward the cabin. Or where the cabin had been. It looks like a bomb had detonated. The roof has disappeared without a trace and the walls tilt outward, littering the surrounding field with debris. The loft had fallen into the living room, sending the bed crashing down on top of the couch. The refrigerator lays against the counter. It had cracked the sink into two clean halves, and water spouts sluggishly from the severed pipes.

"Holy shit," I say. No wonder Zeke's pissed. I shove away the memory of the look on his face and pick my way up the remaining steps. My immediate concern is clothes. I do not fancy spending another day beneath the dirt of the hillside and figure that hitchhiking into town naked is a recipe for disaster. In one form or another.

A huge scorch mark mars the floor. It burned through the wooden planks and left them sticking up in charred splinters. A lightning strike? One of my boots lies at the edge of the burn, but when I pick it up water pours out onto my feet. I sigh and toss it away. I don't see the other anywhere anyway.

Though the walls had caved out, and the loft had fallen into the first floor when the roof had taken wing, the main floor is basically intact. Except for massive amounts of debris. I toss paneling and smashed end tables and broken crockery out into the yard and manage to find one of the bags of clothing Zeke and I had liberated. No shoes but jeans and shirts, preserved in plastic and warmed by a day's worth of sun.

Dressed but barefoot I stand in the rubble. It feels odd to just leave, irresponsible almost. I keep wondering if Zeke will return, but I know, deep in my heart of hearts, that he isn't coming back. This place is finished for him. I take one last look around and start down the drive, walking fast.

In the woods, I unshield my mind and let the auras in to light my way. The moon hadn't risen and though the stars burn in the sky with cold fire, theirs is a dim and distant light. Except for the occasional warm flash of life in the brush, the temperature of tree and stone and frost is constant. But the auras are everywhere.

The forest seems uprooted, and I realize that the storm's damage is not isolated to the cabin. I count six trees struck by lightning, still smoking lazily, the heat in the wood glowing. Bushes had uprooted, bringing up sandy earth and stones. Water cut deep grooves in the roadbed and I hop over them, my feet sinking into mud.

As I walk, I think about what Zeke said. I had seen his rage in the red of his aura, the glint of his steely eyes. I wonder if he was right, if he had the right to be so angry. I'm surprised he left me. Does that mean he trusts me to figure it out? Or is he running far away?

I reach the highway and spin in a circle, remembering which way to take toward town. I realize that I can see faint heat rising from the highway, twin tracks of a lighter blue. The friction of tires against pavement. A vehicle had passed recently. I step out into the road and head west, walking between the fading tracks of light.

It makes me to ache to think about that last look on Zeke's face. I wonder where he is and reach out for him automatically. For a minute, I catch a glimpse of a highway unspooling in headlights, a flash of the last rays of sunset on a stark horizon. He is headed west, back the way we had come.

I withdraw the light touch of my mind and pick up my pace. I think he's going home, back to San Fran. I sense his anger, his sadness.

But knowing where he is allows me to focus on the immediate. I have turned fully, my mind is mostly restored, and I am in no immediate danger. I stop walking and look up into the sky. It feels good actually, to be here alone on this highway at night. I used to love being alone, the gentle crash of the world stilled. I would walk, and read, and nap, and cook. I could spend days alone.

Alex's death had left me alone in a new way. Bereft. For the first time since he died, I feel like I have time and space to breathe.

So I do: I suck in the air, noticing the scents of dirt, trees, and water as the cold burns through my sinuses. Alex remained dead and lost, but now I know there is an afterlife. And I have eternity to search for him.

"I need to get my shit together," I say. The night concurs with silence. I break into a run, delighting at how my muscles stretch, untiring.

It takes me less than an hour to get to Aspen. I run the whole way and not at a jog but at a full sprint. Arriving on the edge of town I slow and find my heartbeat steady and slower than it had ever been in my human life. I take a deep breath and hold it, feeling only a slight tightening in my lungs and then nothing. I count slowly to a thousand as I walk into town and never feel more than a passing urge to take a breath. It seems I no longer need to breathe.

"Cool," I laugh, and a family coming up the street toward me glances at me uneasily. I smile at them toothily, and they smile hesitantly back, picking up their pace.

The last time I had been here it had been past midnight. Now the sun has barely set and people throng the streets, window shopping, stepping in and out of shops that spill light and warmth onto the sidewalk, waiting in lines for tables at the restaurants.

Everyone turns to look as I walk by. Barefoot, clad only in jeans and a thin shirt, my hair tangled and muddy, I look like a disaster victim. And I have no money, no identification, nothing but the clothes on my back. I realize that attracting attention might be a problem. And I feel the first stirring of hunger.

Ignoring the stares, I make my way down the street, thinking furiously. And then I spot the Caduceus of a hospital. Perfect.

The nurse behind the counter starts to his feet, eyes widening, as I enter. I put on my most charming smile, light, soothing fingertips in his mind.

"Are you okay?" he asks.

"I am actually," I say. "I lost my way hiking, got separated from my friends. Can I just warm up a minute?"

"Of course." He comes around the reception desk and looks at my bare feet. "Why don't you come this way and we'll get you cleaned up."

I follow him into an examination room and sit obediently on the exam table at his direction, the paper cover crinkling pleasantly.

"How are your feet?" Pulling on examination gloves he takes one in his hand and gently swipes at the mud with a wipe.

"I think they're fine. Why?"

"You've been walking barefoot in freezing temperatures. It's a miracle you don't have frostbite."

"A miracle," I agree, watching the vein in his neck pulse.

"How did you lose your shoes?"

I think fast. "I took them off to cross a stream, but I slipped and they washed away."

He looks at me thoughtfully, and I wonder how plausible he will find this story. But he has no reason to suspect that I am anything other than a lost hiker. "You should be careful. Streams up here flood suddenly, especially after a storm like we had last night."

I nod.

"Where were you and your friends staying?"

"Just up in the National Forest. Camping."

He finishes with one foot and starts on the other. "Well, you're lucky. Tough feet." He grins. "You don't seem to have a scratch on you."

"Lucky," I repeat.

"Can I call someone for you?" He releases my foot and pulls off his gloves.

"Um," I think quickly. "We left a car down here. At ..." I rack my brain, trying to remember our trip down before. "That little hotel at the far end of town? Toward the bar? I just wanted to warm up."

"No problem." He snaps his fingers. "I can probably do you one better. Let me look in lost and found and see if there are any shoes. People leave stuff all the time."

I gaze at him gratefully. "That would be fantastic."

"What size do you wear?"

"Um, about a nine."

"Sit tight and keep your fingers crossed." He disappears, leaving me to contemplate a poster of the stages of lung cancer. Graphics depicted the advancement of the disease, crawling across the fleshy pink jello of lung tissue like tar.

He isn't gone long before coming back in with a pair of tennis shoes. "Eight and a half. Best I could do."

"That should work to get me to the other end of town." I pull them on and lace them loosely. "What do I owe you?"

He laughs. "Not a thing. My pleasure, really. I'm just happy you still have all your toes."

"Me, too." I slide off the bed and stand up, wiggling my toes in the confines of the shoes.

"You won't be cold?"

"I'll be fine." I give him a reassuring smile and let myself out into the night. My hair is still dirty, but I wrap it tightly back onto itself and under, forming an impromptu bun that hides most of the filth. Other than having only shirtsleeves in the rapidly chilling evening, I look more or less normal.

I speed quickly down main street, hugging myself as though cold. It takes only a few minutes to arrive at the little hotel I remember. I walk down to the end of the row of rooms, scanning for surveillance. I don't see any and cannot pick up the electronic buzz. At least not over the hum of the streetlights, the roar of traffic, or the thousands of voices that begin to whisper in my head the minute I lower the shield from my mind.

I lean against the corner of the building at the very end of the row of rooms, in the shadow cast by the upper story. And wait.

Patience has never been my strong suit. I simply make whatever I want happen, hurry things along. On the few occasions when I have had to legitimately wait for something I fidget like a toddler.

I remember waiting for Alex's ashes to be released to me. That had taken forever.

The memory brings more flooding in. I take a deep breath and allow myself to really think about what Zeke had said to me. For the first time I consider things from his perspective.

People have always fallen in thrall to me, and I convinced myself that it had nothing to do with my abilities. But even Alex had been fascinated with me to the point of obsession. It had blinded him to my faults, my selfishness, obstinacy, and pride.

Zeke is a creature as powerful as I, in some ways even more powerful. And I fascinate him, no doubt about that, but he has not fallen prey to my charms. He sees me, deep into me, I recognize that now. He has risked his life for me, facing me down in the height of madness. I cannot remember everything that had happened, but I do have a clear memory of his face, burned and charred, and the rage and pain in his eyes. And yet he had carried me to safety, his body bearing the brunt of my insanity.

All my life people have sought to be worthy of me, like the hero on a quest to prove their value just so I would deign to notice them. But I have to learn to be worthy of Zeke. And I'm not sure I know how.

I cannot just walk away and forget that Alex ever existed. His memory will fade with time, I know that, but the thought of his existence diminishing from my consciousness hurts me deep inside. I am not ready to let him go. And now I know that an afterlife exists in some form. If I could just know that he was okay, that there was a possibility of seeing him again.

Death is the thief in the night that robs one blind. I have eternal life and cannot live.

"Hey, pretty lady."

I start and look up to see a man, a suitcase in one hand and a bottle in a brown paper bag in the other. Behind him a battered blue pickup ticks softly as its engine cools in the chill. A hotel key dangles from one finger.

His aura shines a dull blue, a brackish green streak radiating from low in his stomach. Not old, not young. Average. He smiles at me slowly.

I smile back, taking him in. He wears a heavy flannel shirt against the cold, a baseball cap pulled low on his forehead. Patience, they say, is a virtue.

"Why you out here in the cold?"

I shrug. "Came out for a smoke. Didn't have any."

He sets the suitcase down and reaches in his breast pocket. "I can help you out with that."

I take the Camel he offers and bend my head over the flame, drawing deep. The smoke is acrid, and I can taste everything. It is rank and delicious.

He smells of smoke and sweat and something else, sweet. "Thank you." I eye the bottle. "Whatcha got?"

"Bit of rum. Why?" He lifts one brow. "Interested?"

I smile wider and watch his eyes on my mouth. "I am."

"Well." He seems to have difficulty tearing his gaze from my exposed teeth. "Come in then. We'll have a drop."

I push away from the wall and stand up. "That would be lovely."

He opens the door and picks up his suitcase again. "Ladies first." He stands back to let me enter.

"You're assuming I'm a lady." I go past him into a room paneled in dark wood, a green bedspread on the queen size. I step to the left to let him enter, and he sets the suitcase on the floor, turning to close the door.

I don't even give him time to turn around. His body slams into the door, the latch clicking shut, and my teeth sink into the tender skin at his throat, his blood pulsing into my mouth.

"Hey!" he says, and his fingers on the latch fall to dust, his clothes collapsing. I catch the bottle. Setting it carefully on the bedside table I pat through the jeans pockets and come up with a wallet. Keys fall from the front pocket into my hand. Opening the money compartment I find two hundred dollars, all in crisp twenties like he had just hit the ATM. "Jackpot." I remove the cash and put the wallet back without even looking at the rest. His blood coats my throat, telling me all I need to know. Wife, estranged. Two kids, girls. White picket fence. I sweep up the rest of the clothes and fold them onto the bed before picking up the suitcase.

I find another hundred in assorted rumpled bills in his pockets and nothing else. I fold everything and put it back into the suitcase. Kicking off the too small shoes, I pull my shirt, streaked with mud, over my head and step from my filthy jeans. Naked, I go to the small bathroom and turn the hot water on as high as it will go. The heat washing the dirt from my hair makes me sigh aloud with pleasure.

# CHAPTER 26

# FREEDOM

CLEAN, DRESSED AGAIN IN my jeans and a flannel shirt I had lifted from the dead man's suitcase, his baseball cap pulled low over my head, I pack everything into the cab of the truck. Leaving the room key on the nightstand, I brush my toe across the scrim of dust, the only thing that remains of his human life. It melts into the carpet like ashes.

"Thank you," I whisper, and shut the door.

The truck's engine rolls over a number of times before grumbling to life. I curl my bare toes around the clutch and back slowly out of the parking slot, taking care not to bash into the minivan to my right, parked too close. Pulling into traffic, I head west out of town.

Once again, a sense of freedom fills me and I laugh aloud, cranking the heater to full blast and rolling down the window so that the fresh air pours into the cab, replacing the must and faint scent of grease with the smell of juniper, loamy earth, and snow. I inhale deeply and realize that I am happy.

Before Alex's death I had been happy almost all the time. I had a job I loved, a partner who challenged and fulfilled me, a home. And the magic, of course, giving me anything I wanted.

The startling power filled me like fire, warm and comforting. I'd thought us invincible.

The traffic thins as I drive deeper into the mountains and I push the truck faster. By two in the morning, I have reached the on ramp for I-70. The glare of all-night fluorescents lights up the dark as I pull into a truck stop, glancing out the widow to locate the gas cap. Standing in my bare feet I top off the tank, breathing deep of the frigid air. I feel light, almost euphoric.

I worry that the clerk might notice and comment on my bare feet, but he barely glances up from a dog-eared copy of Penthouse. I know most gas stations are outfitted with cameras, theft prevention, and I wonder how I will pass unnoticed in a world filled with surveillance equipment. The man's truck is on the tapes and his absence will not go unnoticed forever. I pull a glamour over my face, hoping the cameras will only pick up a blur.

Back in the cab, I drive across the highway and into the massive parking lot of a Wal-Mart Supercenter. I can't remember the last time I have been in a Wal-Mart. I laugh aloud. Wal-Mart: shopping mecca for the poor and the vampire.

I angle the truck into a parking slot in the almost-empty lot and step out again into the night. It is late enough that no one greets me in the glare of the halogen lights suspended from the ceiling struts twenty feet above me. Under the onslaught of the lights, I change my direction and go to the accessories section. I have never been a fan of artificial light, but my vampire vision positively burns, everything jumping and buzzing under the fractured beams. I can hardly see.

A dark set of polarized lenses helps considerably. I make my way to shoes and chose a pair of white canvas sneakers and then pick up a full set of clothing: undies, socks, jeans, a white tee, and a fleece to go over everything.

Unlike the gas station attendant, the girl checking me out eyes my bare feet with bright interest. I gaze back at her with a slight smile from behind the safety of my dark glasses. The pulse in her neck beats steadily, and I realize that I will be hungry again soon. And I can't just leave a trail of missing humans in my wake. I need to take small sips. Make them forget. I'd rather that than eating pets and wildlife. Next time, I'll practice.

In the restroom, I strip to the skin and pull the tags off my purchases. I still have about fifty dollars left after gas and clothes – enough for gas down the road but not a lot else. This would have freaked me out back when I had been human. Now it just seems like a minor problem to solve. The sense of freedom intoxicates me.

Dressed, I shove my dirty clothes deep in the trashcan, retaining only the baseball cap. It covers my distinctive hair and keeps it out of my eyes. I appear almost normal. Except for the dark glasses at night.

On I-70 most of the traffic comes in the form of long-haul trucks, and I weave my way through these, descending toward the plains of the desert. Though the truck does not have a ton of power, the descent allows me to keep it at seventy-five and I make good time. I will be back in San Francisco in two nights. The only thing between me and home is daylight.

About four a.m., I pull of the road into a sleepy little town near the Utah border. Ahead stretches 106 miles with no services and daylight approaches. I drive slowly down the deserted street, passing a bright Super 8 and an oversized church, out of place in the tiny hamlet. And then, luck! Beside the road is a tiny motel, its shutters askew and FO SAL E hanging crookedly on its billboard. I turn around in the parking lot and drive to the church. Behind the building two busses are parked noses out. I reverse into the slot between them and get out. The truck is hidden from the road and from most of the lot.

I jog across the road and approach the deserted motel from one end. I still have not seen a single car. I pause on the edge of the street and look. The three types of vision start to come together, and I realize that I can make sense of the layers of sight. The auras and heat signatures blend and I can see through the walls, the slight variances in temperature radiating in a sort of radar pattern.

"Cool," I say to myself. "I've always wanted x-ray vision."

I choose the room on the far end, closest to the desert. Grasping the knob, prepared to exert force, it turns easily in my hand. "Not even locked." I let myself into a dusty room, corners gloomy even to my enhanced sight. I pull the curtains closed and flip the mattress off onto the floor. Leaning the box spring across the window and door I shake the blanket out and crawl beneath it, too tired to worry about the dust.

The truck runs out of gas on I80 just west of San Francisco. I let it roll down the incline I had been descending and then pull off onto the shoulder of the road and sit in the silence for a moment listening to the cooling motor tick. Finally, I turn the headlights off and pull the baseball cap low over my hair. I leave the keys in the ignition and climb out. I begin to jog west.

Traffic at two a.m. near San Fran can still be heavy, and tonight is no exception. I hold my thumb out as I jog, careful to regulate my pace, careful to look human. After a few minutes, I pull the baseball cap off my head, letting my silver white hair tumble down my back. Less than a minute later a late model Lexus sedan pulls over.

I hesitate. A Lexus means money, and a wealthy person who would pick up a hitchhiker at this time of the morning is either a nice guy or, more likely, a sleezeball. And anyone who drives a Lexus will be reported missing sooner.

I hop from foot to foot in a moment of indecision, and then decide to go for it. I can always magic them into behaving. I open the passenger door and look in at the driver. To my surprise, a young woman, no older than me, looks back and smiles. "Need a lift?"

I glance quickly in the backseat and find it empty. "I do, actually." I slide into the warm interior of the car, and the leather seat enfolds me. "Thanks for stopping."

"Not a problem." She pulls quickly back into traffic. "I can't let a woman hitch at this hour. Do you know the kind of creeps who are out?"

"I do," I reply with a grin. I can smell her, the fresh scent of soap and light perfume all over the metallic-sweet smell of her blood. My mouth waters, and I swallow convulsively. "You don't have anything to drink, do you?"

"See what's behind the seat."

I find a liter of water and swallow half of it. The ache in my belly subsides but does nothing for the urge building inside of me. I need proteins, sugars, calories.

"Where are you going?"

"Downtown, actually."

"Not a problem."

"Is it out of your way?"

She glances at me with a smile. "Not considerably. It's no problem, really."

She drives fast and well, guiding the car smoothly through the traffic.

"Do you want to know what I'm doing out here at this time of night?"

She doesn't glance at me this time, only quickly checks her blind spot and pulls around a diesel truck. "Only if you feel the need to tell me."

I study her profile, the strong line of her jaw, the pulse in her throat. "I don't."

Her lips turn up. "Then don't. I'm just happy to help."

I lean back in the seat, listening to the quiet music that comes from the car's sound system and wonder if I have managed to find the only genuinely good person out at this time of night.

She drops me on Esplanade across from the wharf. "Have a good night."

"Thank you. You do the same."

She tips me a wave and is gone.

I stand for a moment, bemused, and then turned toward home, scanning for a homeless person. The hunger has become a roar in my senses and I can feel daylight coming. Time to practice the small sip.

Turns out, it's easy. A light touch in their mind and they never even remember.

An hour later, full and satisfied, I stand on the walk to my little house, admiring the way the shadows fall through the ivy, making serpentine patterns in the grass. Home.

I fish the spare key out from behind one of the exposed rafters on the deck and let myself in. It smells musty, and I go from room to room opening every window, turning on every light until the place blazes.

My room smells of stale sex and old blood, the sheets rumpled and dusty, clothes tossed in a pile in the corner. I wrap my hair up on top of my head, secure it with a pencil, and go to work. I pull all the bedding off and cram the whole bundle in the washer. The clothing goes in the hamper for later.

I stand for an indecisive moment listening to the washer and then go to the big storage closet under the stairs and retrieve the largest cardboard box I can find. Grabbing a roll of paper towels, I start in the bedroom and begin collecting everything of Alex's. I start with the framed photos, the watch he had left on the bedside table, his journal still sitting with a pen marking the place he had stopped writing. I wrap everything in towels and pack them into the box, a series of shrouded packets.

Then I start on the rest of his belongings. Clothing and shoes first, then books and his various things scattered around the house. I fold everything into a series of garbage bags, lining them up next to the front door.

I pause for a moment to draw the curtains as the sun comes up and remind myself to get better window coverings. I leave the windows open, and the curtains stir in the breeze, forcing me to step around bars of light as I work.

Finished with Alex's things, I start on mine. All the dishes and cooking implements in the kitchen go first. I keep only the glasses and a big serving tray Alex and I bought in Italy. Everything else goes. I dump all the food in the fridge, now rotting and unrecognizable, into the garbage and scrub out the interior. I discard piles of clothing and shoes, keeping only items that I absolutely love.

By late afternoon the pile before the door has turned into a mountain. I carry the box of Alex's personal things to my closet and, taping it securely closed, place it on the floor in the back. Turning off the light, I leave it in darkness. Then I go to make phone calls.

I check my bank balance and discover that Alex's life insurance has finally been deposited. I call my bank first and pay off the mortgage and the late fees. Then I take care of the utilities, also late and incurring fees. I set up automatic payments for all the bills and pay off the seventeen hundred dollars on my credit card, wondering what I had purchased. Then I sit down at the dining room table to make a more difficult call.

Nicholas answers on the third ring and red tulips flash in my vision. "It's Zorah," I say and listen to him breathe.

"Thank god," he says finally. "Where are you?"

I see myself, deranged and screaming in his memory, and I wince. "I'm home."

"Are you okay?"

In his thoughts my mouth opens impossibly wide, a horror movie caricature. "I am."

"Thank god," he says again."

"Are you okay?" I ask. I seem to remember him hurt.

"I'm fine," he says. "Just got a cut on the head."

"Nicholas, can you come? Tonight?"

"Of course," he says immediately, and I remember why I love him. After all he had seen he will still come with no hesitation.

"Around eight?"
"Yes. Should I bring anything?"
"Just yourself," I reply and see him smile in my mind's eye.

# Chapter 27

# Unleashed

B Y THE TIME HE arrives, night has come on kitten feet, full of fog and warm breezes. I have moved the mound next to the door to the curb, neatly arranged for the charity truck that will come for it all in the morning. The house is spotless, the windows open to the damp air, and I have showered and dressed in long linen pants and a black tunic that leaves my shoulders bare.

Nicholas takes me in his arms, just looking. I hold my breath, wondering what he sees. After all he had seen, what will he see in me?

"You look amazing," he says finally and hugs me hard. "Are you really okay?"

"Yes." I pull away gently. "Please come in."

I lead the way into the kitchen to the breakfast table in the corner with the windows overlooking the shadowed back garden. I light a tall taper, and the dancing flame casts leaping brands of light on the walls, sparkling off bottles and glasses.

"How long have you been back?"

"A few days," I say. "What can I get you to drink?" I realize I can smell him, the rich scent of his blood, coppery and dark.

"I'll have a whiskey, if you have it."

I pour him a finger and a half over two ice cubes. I think about asking him about the last time he saw me, what that had been like. But I'm not sure I want to know. Before I can decide, he speaks.

"Zorah, what happened?"

I contemplate him over the rim of my own glass. The whiskey explodes warmth into my stomach. "I guess Alex's death finally caught up with me," I say at last.

He looks at me doubtfully. "Zorah, I know what I saw." He smiles without humor. "I'm not a stupid man."

I shake my head slightly. "I don't really remember it." A true statement. I don't remember it. Just flashes. Just my screaming mouth in Nicholas's mind.

Nicholas sets his glass carefully on the table as though afraid of making the ice clink. "You walked through the wall of the hospital."

I search my memory. Maybe remember falling. "I would be dead."

"Yes." His eyes narrow. "One would think."

I take another sip and watch him look at me, his eyes narrowed. Rule number one: never let them know you exist.

"There are legends, of course," he says finally. "And this is more Alex's field than mine, but there are folktales about poltergeist activity surrounding pubescence and trauma."

"Those stories exist in virtually every culture," I agree. Alex and I had read one another folk tales before bed.

Nicholas picks up his glass and takes a deep swallow. "Alex told me something once."

I keep my face carefully blank. "Did he?"

"Yes. He said that you could make things happen with your mind."

I smile in spite of myself. "Alex was a braggart." It is true – I had never met a more transparent person. Alex's enthusiasm energized everyone but getting him to keep a secret proved nearly impossible. It would slip out before he could catch it, running through his lips like breath.

"Is it true?"

Faced with the directness of the question I pause. Would I lie to my dear friend? If Nicholas knew at least a little of what I can do it will hide the deeper secret, the one that let me hear the pulse of his heart and the blood moving through his arteries.

"Yes," I say.

His lips curl up slightly, interest leaping on his face. "Prove it."

I reach out with my mental fingers and slam the window behind where Nicholas sits.

He jumps, making the cubes in his glass rattle. "You did that?"

"What else you would like to see?"

His lips part in wonder. "Make the chair move."

I imagine the ways chairs arrange themselves in horror movies, how they stack themselves into impossible designs, and then send the mental command. The three chairs we aren't using leap to the middle of the floor and pile themselves quickly one on top of the other.

Nicholas gasps and drops his glass. Luckily, he had been holding it a mere inch above the table, and so it lands with a clatter, sloshing the half-inch of liquid remaining inside of it.

Every time I use the power it gets easier. Before my transformation, it had taken minutes of concentration to visualize what I wanted. Now the process has become almost instantaneous. And effortless. Moving chairs is like exhaling. Opening the gates of death, now that had been difficult.

Nicholas gazes at me with something like rapture. I let the chairs topple.

"Zorah..." My name is like a prayer. "Do you have any idea what this means?"

"Means?" I shrug. "I guess not."

He slurps the last drops of whiskey from his glass, and I pour him another finger which he also drinks down.

"People have been trying to document things like this forever. There are whole television shows dedicated to the paranormal and all any of them have are shadows and mists and strange sounds that could be the wind."

I regard him doubtfully. "Are you saying that you want to put me on television?"

He laughs sharply. "No. It's just that ..." Words seem to fail him. "It's just..."

"That I can do magic?" I offer.

"Is that what you call it?"

I shrug. "It's as good a name as any."

He takes the bottle himself this time and pours a slug. He doesn't drink it though, just swirls the amber liquid in the glass.

"Nicholas," I place my fingers over his. "This isn't why I called you here."

He looks up at me, his eyes still dazed. "No?"

I remove the envelope from the pocket of my tunic and set it on the table between us. He looks at it suspiciously and rubs his finger over the thick, ivory paper.

"What is this?" he asks.

I take a deep breath. After all that I had been through, this still seemed like dying. "It's the deed to the shop."

He stares at me, his mouth dropping open in surprise.

"I want you to sell it for me."

"Zorah...you built that business with Alex. Why would you want to sell?"

"My life has moved on. I need to go with it."

"Are you sure?"

I nod. "This isn't an easy decision. I have spent my entire life working to be where I am now." I look down, the curtain of my hair slipping across my face. "But ... I have to do this."

"Do what?" Nicholas exclaims. "Zorah, something terrible happened to you. To lose someone the way you lost Alex, that's an awful thing. But you're still alive. You still have a life and a career. And people who care for you. You can't give that up."

I look up at him. "I'm not giving up." I shake my hair out of my face. "I'm moving on."

He finally takes a sip of his drink. The ice has melted, and he makes a slight grimace as the straight whiskey slides down his throat. "Does this have anything to do with Zeke?"

I hate that I hesitate. "No," I say, giving myself a sharp mental kick.

"Because that boy is a rebound waiting to happen."

I laugh before I can help myself.

He lifts his eyebrows at my mirth. "Well? Is he not?"

"Are you suggesting that I don't deserve a rebound?" This is deflection but it works, and Nicholas chuckles.

"I just don't want you to do this for the wrong reason."

"You mean for someone else." I lean back and take another healthy swig of whiskey. "You should know me better than that."

"I do know you, Zorah, or like to think I do. But I also know people. And I know what you've been through, and I know that this young man you've found is a deadly combination of beauty and strength. Just like Alex."

I hadn't thought of that. They are nothing alike. Alex had been dark and compact and brimming with humor and fun. Zeke is cold and remote. But Nicholas is right. They are both beautiful, strong, smart, oozing confidence and charm. And they feed off of it in the same way, basking in the attention. Alex because he was a shameful ham, always playing to an audience. Zeke because it sustains him almost as much as blood. Seen through Nicholas's sight they look disconcertingly alike.

"I'm not trying to replace him, Nicholas."

He smiles sadly at me. "Are you sure?"

I nod my head. "Yes, they are both beautiful and strong. But any man in my life would be. You know that, Nicholas. They are nothing alike."

He gazes at me shrewdly. "Your head knows that. But does your heart?"

I ignore his question. "This psychoanalysis is not going to change my mind."

Nicholas fingers the envelope again and then sighs and picks it up. "Oh, Zorah. I'm so sorry it's come to this."

I feel my eyes prickle with tears. "Me, too. But it has to be."

He refolds the letter and places it in the inner pocket of his jacket. "I'm keeping this until the end of the week. Give you a few days to think it over."

"Please don't." I take a deep breath and sigh. "Don't do that. I just want it to be over."

Later, when he has gone, I step barefoot into the garden, feeling the fog on my skin and the dew beneath my feet. The hunger has become a steady roar, but I ignore it the way I had sometimes pushed it aside back when I had been human. The first sliver of a waxing horned moon hangs in the sky, Isis in her lunar crown. After a moment I close my eyes against the night and reach out for Zeke.

He sits in his one room palace, his feet propped over a pillow on the end of his bed. He is nude, the sheets drawn over his legs and hips, and he is drunk. Very. I didn't know that it's possible for a vampire but apparently so. The alcohol roars in his mind, blurring the television screen. Something violent is on, all noise and explosions and brightly splattered blood. He sips from a glass, and I taste the scotch and blood in the back of my own throat. It is warm. His sightline shifts, and I see the girl at the foot of the bed.

She lies facedown, her dark hair falling over her face. She is alive, she has to be or she would be dust, but her flesh is marred with bite marks, seeping sluggishly. As I watch, an intruder in his mind, Zeke nudges her with the toe of his foot and she moans. He kicks her hard enough to send her toppling to the floor, eliciting a short scream that quickly becomes sobs as she comes to consciousness. She gets slowly to her knees and begins to crawl.

Zeke sits up so that he can see her more clearly. I sense the predator in him, from within him, and am chilled by its merciless hunger. He is playing with her like a cat with a mouse. He reminds me of Malachi.

She succeeds in making it into the bathroom where she tries to wedge herself into the space between the sink and the wall. Zeke grows bored and turns his attention back to the television. But then she whimpers, louder than before.

He leaps off the bed, his reflexes seemingly unslowed by the booze. Grabbing his belt from the chair where it sits atop the pile of his clothing, he storms into the bathroom and grabs the girl by the hair, hauling her out of the meager hiding place. So suddenly that I cry out from my place in the garden, he places his hands on either side of her face and spins her head sharply, breaking her neck. She crumples to the floor. Moving with ruthless efficiency, he winds the belt around her ankles and flings open the shower door. A hook I had never had the opportunity to notice is drilled into the concrete ceiling and he strings her up, leaving her to dangle headfirst over the tub. Taking a plastic five-gallon bucket from under the sink, he pulls a knife from the medicine cabinet, snaps it open, and cuts her throat.

The blood spurts out, and he catches it neatly with the bucket. The stream slows, no longer beat through her heart, and he sets the bucket in the tub under the flow, letting gravity do its work.

I open my eyes, severing the connection. What I had seen rattles me, but I do not fully understand why. I know what he is and I had seen him kill before. But the brutality of this ...

I stand, indecisive. My stomach growls at the thought of all that blood.

# CHAPTER 28

# RESURRECTION

I STAND BEFORE HIS door and hesitate. I sense him within, the glowing heat of him. His proximity raises the fine hairs on my arms and makes my stomach churn. I lift my hand to knock, pause long enough to control the tremble in my hand, and rap twice on the door.

Silence from within. In my mind, I see Zeke lift his head, his eyes narrowing. Then he sets down the glass in his hand and pads noiselessly to the door.

I feel him on the other side, a tense coil. I place my hand on the steel. He is fewer than three inches away, glowing within his cocoon dark aura.

He opens the door. He has dyed his hair blue, and it stands up in wild whorls and snarls, an electric halo that makes him look like a mad scientist. The color bleaches his skin, highlighting the fine network of veins at his temples. He does not look remotely human.

He wears only a pair of black jeans, and my eyes skate quickly down his body, unable to meet his flashing eyes or see the way his lush mouth tightens at the sight of me. My gaze lands on his bare feet against the concrete floor. I open my mouth with no idea of what I am going to say.

"You have beautiful feet."

I dart a quick glance at his face. He does not smile but his mouth relaxes. That tiny movement is the only thing that changes, otherwise he stands motionless as only a vampire can. No flutter of the eyelashes, no rise and fall of his chest with breath, no tiny shift.

"I'm sorry," I say.

His brows lift slightly.

"Can I come in?"

He stands so long that I'm not sure if he's going to let me and then shifts slightly to the right. Past his shoulder I see the unmade bed, a twist of clothing on the floor. I step forward and run into an invisible barrier.

It feels like running into a wall of clear jello. It gives slightly and feels a bit sticky against my skin, burning on my exposed flesh like a low electric charge. I have never felt anything quite so odd.

Zeke turns and walks away from me. I try again but still that firm, unyielding resistance. He scoops up the pile on the floor and shakes out a shirt. A skirt and a pair of lacy underwear fall to the rug. He kicks them nonchalantly aside. His back still to me he pulls on the shirt with quick, violent movements.

"Zeke..." I pause, questions jammed in my throat.

He faces me and sits on the edge of the bed, his eyebrows raised.

I select the most pressing question. "Why can't I get in?"

The corners of his mouth lift. "Because you're a vampire now, love. You need an invitation."

I digest this. "But ... I've been here before." I remember lying on that bed. Opening this door, running from him.

He shakes his head slightly. "So?"

"You don't need an invitation every time you come to my house."

"Nope. Just the one."

"So …" I blow out a breath in frustration. His smug look doesn't help. "So if I've been here before, why can't I get in?"

He leans forward and pulls his boots, the ones with the white flames, from beneath the bed. Tugging them on he says, "You weren't a vampire then."

I consider this. He watches me, that tiny smile still playing on his mouth. I know what he wants. And I don't want to give him the satisfaction.

But why had I come here? I had called death, and he had denied me. And so I had found another, but it had been Zeke who I turned to in the madness of my transformation. Not Alex. Certainly not Malachi. Zeke. So what do I want? Here is the choice in this pregnant moment and Zeke sits watching me from his bed, smelling of sex and blood and whiskey. I could turn and walk away, knowing that I had eternity. Or I can ask.

"Can I come in?"

He blinks rapidly twice but otherwise does not move. I hold my breath. Then he stands up all in one quick motion and comes toward me so quickly that I step back.

"Actually, let's go out." He strides through the door and pulls it shut with a slam.

He does not glance back at me but sweeps down the hall and takes the stairs two at a time. I shake my head, chagrined, and run to catch up.

His bike lurks on its kickstand at the curb, all black and gleaming. He swings a leg over and glances at me, his brows lifting. "Coming?"

"Absolutely." I climb on behind him, flipping out the passenger pegs and slipping my arms around his waist like so many girls have done to so many boys since the invention of the motorcycle.

I breathe deep as Zeke makes his way through city streets alive with nightlife. I can smell everything, the rain on the grass, smoke from outdoor grills, a hint of rot. All of the smells of life making my mouth water. Again, I feel content. Despite it all, Alex's death, Zeke's anger, my sudden and appalling transformation.

It feels as though a great pressure has lifted. I have time now. Eternity.

Zeke pulls to a stop at Golden Gate Park and leans the bike over on its kickstand. Through my triple vision the wide lawn blazes with color. Couples stroll through the damp evening air, their auras overlapping and intertwining. Children shout and run after Frisbees, their bodies radiating heat. Hawkers wind their way through the throng, selling tchotchkes, the veins in their throats pulsing. And I am a newborn vampire in love with the world laid open like a gift, made anew with predator vision.

I take Zeke's hand as we make our way up the gentle hill. He curls his fingers through mine and my heart sings.

The man waits on a bench overlooking the bridge, lit up and glowing in the night. I feel my eyes drawn to him, and a small niggle of recollection sparks in my memory. I remember him framed in sunlight, his hands against the bare flesh of my legs. His aura shines off of him in a bright golden glow, pulsing with health and life. And magic.

Then I see the women next to him. She puts her hand on his knee as her eyes meet mine, and I see the heat of her skin against the warmth of his jeans. The same radiant aura shines from her, joined with his in a pulsing yellow glow.

They have to be siblings, maybe twins. They have the same chestnut hair, the same brown eyes, the same heart-shaped faces. They are even dressed alike in khaki pants, hers Capri length, and black shirts.

Beside me, Zeke drops my hand and steps forward. "Thank you for meeting me."

*Me,* not *us.* I feel a wave of confusion, uncertainty. These two are clearly human. What does a vampire want with humans?

The woman turns to me, her face alight with curiosity. "You must be Zorah."

I'm not about to admit anything. "And you are?"

"Stefania." She turns to the man. "Sorin is my brother."

"Should I know Sorin?"

He smiles though his brown eyes remain wary. "The only time we've met you were screaming out of your skull."

My eyes narrow. "You bound me."

He shrugs in a don't-mention-it kind of way. "I did."

I step toward him, and his eyes flash, but he holds his ground. "How did you do it?"

I feel Zeke's hand on my arm and brush him off. But he just grabs me again, harder. "He helped me. He did what he did because I asked."

"I didn't ask *why*," I say in acid tones. "I want to know *how*."

Stefania turns to her brother. "She's powerful. And clearly one of us."

For the second time that evening, questions jam in my throat. I splutter and then continue with my original line of questioning, my eyes boring into the man Sorin's, willing him to answer me. "How?"

He glances quickly at his sister and then at Zeke and finally at me. "I made it so that magic wouldn't work on the chains."

His response surprises me so much that I bark laughter. "You didn't do anything to me. You did something to the metal."

He hunches his shoulders, smiling slightly. This time the warmth touches his eyes.

I laugh again, less harshly. "That's actually kind of brilliant."

"Thank you."

"Now, onto the second of my hundred questions."

Stefania nods encouragingly.

"You said I am one of you. What does that mean?"

She darts a quick glance at Zeke. "He hasn't told you anything?"

"The last several days have been rather ..." I search for the word. "Distracting."

This time it's Zeke who laughs.

"Maybe we should find somewhere to sit," she says.

"Lead the way."

She hesitates the barest fraction of a second, and I catch her thought, clear as if she had spoken. *Never turn your back on a vampire.* Then she does just that and heads deeper into the park. I notice that Sorin falls in behind us.

Stefania finds two benches facing one another in a quiet glade away from the lights and the people. When I sit, Zeke slides down beside me and drapes his arm across the back of the bench. I feel his warmth.

"So?" I prompt when we are settled. "I'm one of you."

They glance at one another, and then Sorin leans forward, his elbows on his knees. "Let me tell you what I told Zeke in our brief time together. Do you remember anything?"

*Falling. A woman with eyes of fire.* I shake my head.

"Well, this will sound quite mad."

I grin. "I'm a *vampire.* The whole world is mad."

He smiles. "Fair enough. In that case, here goes." He leans back. "Stefania and I are Romanian by birth. We come from an ancient family that has lived in the northern mountains for millennia."

"Like Dracula," I say.

"Indeed. Unlike most families, ours has kept very good records. We can trace our family back before the written word."

"How is that possible?"

"Before words there was art. Glyphs. Carvings and paintings on cavern walls."

"And what do these pictures tell you?"

"They speak of a war. Armageddon. The Book of Revelation."

"Wait." I interrupt him. "You're telling me the Christians are *right?*"

Stefania's laughter joins his. Zeke removes his arm and leans forward, intent.

"No. The Book of Revelation doesn't reference the future. It's about the past. It's about a war that already happened. Eons before that deranged prophet on Patmos. And it's only partially correct. Even we don't have the full story but ours is much more complete."

"So?" I find myself rapt in spite of myself.

"There was a war in what the Christians call heaven. We know that it was actually in a different dimension. Between beings of fire and beings of blood."

*Flesh magic and blood songs.* I shiver.

"A great rift opened in the world, a tear between realities. We were pulled, *pushed*, through. We..."

"Fell." I finish his sentence for him.

"Yes. The ones who fell...well...they were us. Magicians. Witches."

"Are you telling me that I'm from another *world*?"

He smiles. "In essence? Yes. When our people came here, we found beings much like us. But tied to this world. Theirs is a magic of innovation, evolution in the face of overwhelming odds. We seemed as angels to them. And we bred with the daughters of men. Our blood is compatible, but our children manifest remarkable powers. We can read minds, walk through walls. Each has our gift."

Zeke speaks for the first time. "Your blood provided a mutation."

"Yes. Of course, over the ages our blood has spread out. So our lineage is all throughout the world. We become sages, magicians, pranksters. In places our history is known. At least partially. But only in Romania has it survived almost intact. We became the keepers of history. Our job is to make contact with our kind no matter where they are in the world."

I lean back. It makes sense. Sort of. "Next question."

Sorin nods.

"Why are you here? I mean, how is it that you just happened to be *here*? Now?"

Stefania smiles. "I felt you. Several months ago I became aware of a gathering power. I sent Sorin to make contact. But, before he could, Zeke found you."

"You must understand," Sorin interjects. "Nothing like this has ever happened before. None of us have ever become one of them." He nods toward Zeke.

I select the most immediately pertinent question. "You said you 'felt' me."

"Yes." Stefania bobs her head. "That is my gift. I can feel our family all over the world. I feel when we are born, when we awake to our gift, when we work some great piece of magic. When such a thing happens, we like to send an envoy, someone to make contact. That's Sorin's job. And we've been waiting for you a long time."

I digest this. "So you can sense magical people. What else can you do?"

She blinks at me. "The gift blesses us in different ways. That is my power."

"You mean, that's all you can do?" I don't mean to sound incredulous.

"*All* I can do?"

I shrug. "Don't get me wrong, that's great. And it sounds as though you have a lot of range if you can sense people all over the world. That's cool." I turn to Sorin. "What can *you* do?"

He eyes me, a tiny smile playing at the corners of his mouth. "My abilities are quite precise. I can hear Stefania in my mind. And I can deflect magic."

"Making you an excellent person to make contact with magical people," I guess.

"You are correct."

Stefania is gazing at me. "So tell me, Zorah. What can *you* do?"

I hesitate. I do not know if I should show my full hand. But what can it matter? "I can do anything I want," I say.

Silence greets this proclamation. Beside me, Zeke sits as if carved from marble. Sorin and Stefania just look at me, expressionless.

Sorin sneaks a glance at his sister. "Anything? Really?"

Zeke places a hand on my knee. "As far as I can tell, Zorah is limited only by her desire."

"Okay" Stefania says. "Let's start simple. Can you read minds?"

I shake my head slightly. "Yes. But that's hard. Usually, thoughts are so layered and complex that they're …" I search for the word. "Muddy." I look at Stefania. "You thought *never turn your back on a vampire.*"

She chuckles. "I did at that. So what else? Can you fly?"

"Fly." I think about it. "I've never tried. But I can levitate." I stand up, take a quick glance around to make sure no one watches, and float up several inches off the ground. I test it and rise another foot. "It feels limitless. As though I could just float up into the clouds." I return to earth. "So, yes: I can fly."

Sorin turns excitedly to his sister. "See? I told you!"

"Can you control the weather?" Stefania asks.

I glance at Zeke who smirks. "Yes, but it's dangerous. It makes the weather in other places do weird things."

"A butterfly flaps its wings in Tokyo," Stefania murmurs.

"The main power that I have is that I see auras. Like light radiating out from people. That's the first power I know of having."

Stefania nods. "Our mother can do that a bit. She can diagnose illnesses and tell if people are happy or sad."

I feel a shiver of excitement at the possibility of meeting someone else who would understand what it's like to see the world through layers of light.

"Mama says it's like walking through a world of rainbows," Sorin says.

"Zorah opened a portal into the land of the dead," Zeke offers suddenly.

Stefania gasps aloud, and Sorin falls back against the bench as though struck. "*What?*" he breathes.

I see Zeke smile slightly under the force of their disbelieving eyes. "She did."

Stefania turns to me and I no longer see wonder on her face. I see fear. "You can't..." she stutters. "That's forbidden."

"According to who?" I ask.

"That's...you can't...do you know how *dangerous* that is?"

Sorin puts a hand on her arm. "When did you do this feat?"

"Three nights ago."

"*That's* what I felt!" Stefania exclaims. "I felt some huge disturbance. Fear." She shivers. "Madness."

"What happened?" Sorin asks. "Why don't you start from the beginning."

I hesitate. I don't want to tell these strangers what I had done, much less why.

"She opened a gate," Zeke says. "A massive portal. And all these beings flooded out. Like shades."

"Ghosts." Sorin shudders.

Beside him, Stefania breathes, "I had no idea such a thing was even possible."

"Why not?" Sorin asks. "Zabrina opens portals. Why not one into death?"

"Who's Zabrina?" I ask.

"Our other sister."

"Okay," I hold up a hand. "Wait just a minute. Portals into what?"

Sorin glances at Zeke and then back at me. "Our older sister can open doors into other worlds. She has traveled to twelve dimensions, each of them similar to this one. There are humans in each world, and some variety of animal species, though there are differences, due to evolution, I'm sure. Some species don't exist on some of the worlds and some have even more than this one."

"So..." I collect my thoughts. "Which dimension did we come from?" I note how quickly I have fallen into using "we."

Sorin shrugs. "We don't know. There are two worlds where everyone can do magic. Just like us."

"Harry Potter eat your heart out," I say.

Zeke shifts on the bench. "And there's one world where there is no sun."

I think of it, a world with no lethal light. In such a world we would be gods. "Are there vampires on all the worlds?"

"Yes. Even on the one with three suns."

Three suns. That would be difficult.

Stefania chimes in. "The vampires in the world of darkness are not like you and Zeke. They are monsters, pale and ravenous."

I cock my head at her. "Are you saying I'm not a monster?" That little girl. She had worn a pink dress with white polka dots.

She shifts uncomfortably. "I mean ... they're physically different. Zabrina was attacked there. The only way she escaped was to open a portal, and she pulled it through with her. Into sunlight."

Sorin looks grim. "She has burns down one entire side of her body from where it went up in flames. And the scars on her throat, well, those will never fade."

Zeke's leg bounces on the bench, and I turn to follow his gaze. He watches a young mother tend to her baby, lifting the child into the air, laughing into one another. But I see no tenderness on his face. When he looks at me his eyes are silver.

I feel hunger. Suddenly, all of this bores me. Who cares if some ancestor came from a different world? I have no stake in an ancient war. I am here now, alive and free.

I turn back to Sorin and Stefania. "You come tonight with tales of other dimensions. Of witchcraft. Vampires and monsters. You tell me that I am descended from an otherworldly alien race. You say that none like me has become a vampire. You tell me the things I do are forbidden." I leap to my feet. I reach for Zeke's hand and he stands up beside me. "Nothing is forbidden to me. I can do anything I wish."

"Zorah..." Sorin stands up. Beside him Stefania's eyes have gone round and alarmed.

"I am my own creature. I do not care for your family or your rules." I look up at Zeke. His head tilts down toward mine, his lush lips parting. "Come," I whisper. "The night awaits."

# CHAPTER 29

# REBORN

I DREAM OF SUNLIGHT on golden skin. But I awake in darkness and smile. Beside me Zeke sleeps curled on his side, his head cradled on one arm. I slip from bed and pass to the window and look out into the darkened yard. The fog twists in ghost shape tendrils between the trees, stealing over the garden walls and through the flowers on silent furry feet.

I pad down the hall to the kitchen and squint against the glare from the refrigerator as I reach inside for one of the tall red bottles Zeke had brought over the night before. I can taste fear in the blood, the sweet spiciness of it.

When I step outside the dew wets my bare feet, and I throw back my head, luxuriating in the night. Vampire fiction always speaks of the loss of the sun in a lament of grief and desire. But I don't care at all. The night speaks to me in shadowed whispers. It always has.

Maybe I will feel differently in a thousand years.

Zeke steps out beside me, and I watch his head go back, eyes slipping closed, a smile playing at the corners of his mouth. He loves it as much as I do.

"Do you ever wonder if the only reason you're attracted to me is because I make you?" I ask.

He grins behind closed eyes. "No."

"Why not?"

"Because I can feel when you try to do magic on me."

"You can?"

He opens his eyes and looks at me. "Yes. Like fingers in my mind."

"Good," I say. "I want you to trust this."

He takes a deep breath, smelling the night. "I do."

"Do you miss the sunlight?" I ask.

"No," he replies.

"Do you even remember the sun?"

His chin drops. "I remember everything," he says.

The blue hair looks black in the night, lightening his skin even more. The moisture in the air settles on him, the blue glow of water organisms under the red of his aura.

"Who are you?" I whisper.

"I was born as a human in the year 1113 in Greece. My father was a sailor in the employ of Rome. He married my mother, a Greek merchant's daughter, and she bore me."

"Did you have any brothers and sisters?"

He laughs. "Of course. We were Catholic. My mother produced a child every eleven to fourteen months. Nine of us. She died when she was forty." He smiles again, but sadly. "I had already turned by then, of course. I visited her grave and mourned her like a proper son. I brought night jasmine."

"What was your name?"

"Ezekiel. After the prophet. My parents were quite devout." He looks off into the night, his smile fading. "My name is the only human part of myself that I have not completely shed."

"How old were you when you turned?"

"Twenty-four."

I swallow. He had been five years younger than me.

"What?" he asks.

I laugh. "I was just thinking that I like younger men."

He grins. "Happy to please."

"So you were twenty-four. And married."

His smile fades. "To Yrsa. Yes. We couldn't have children, but we didn't care. We loved being just the two of us. I had taken a job in my mother's family business. I guess today they would be called importers. We lived in Athens. Near the docks. We ran a shop selling all sorts of things from all over the world. Pottery and copper and stone jewelry. Gold. Olives packed in jugs of oil. The finest fabrics money could buy."

"It sounds wonderful."

He looks back at me. "It was."

"So what happened?"

He shrugs and runs a hand through his hair. "I met a vampire. Of course, I didn't know that's what he was."

"Where did you meet him?"

"He came in the shop one evening. I was alone. He was foreign, Egyptian. He wanted to buy wine. I knew that there was something different about him, something off. His skin shone and his teeth gleamed so sharp." He smiles. "But I was fascinated. He was ... beautiful." He paces out into the garden, his back to me. "We drank then he took me in the storeroom and I screamed when he bit me. He drained me so fast and I lost consciousness. The next thing I knew he was pouring something down my throat, something so rich and sweet it tasted of heaven."

"His blood."

Zeke nods. "Like you, like everyone, I almost didn't survive. He just drained me the once and fed me what seemed like a liter of his blood. And then he left me. I drifted in a fever for a week and then fell into a coma. My family thought I had died."

I understand. "They buried you." I step sideways a bit, bringing his profile into view.

Zeke's eyes slip closed, his brow furrowing. "Yes. They buried me. I woke up in the dark smelling my own sweat and blood. I had never been so hungry. I was half out of my mind."

I shiver. "That's terrifying."

Zeke snorts laughter. "I was too hungry to be afraid."

"Good thing they didn't burn you."

He laughs. "Cremation isn't Christian, you know. The only thing that God ever gave me – eternal life."

"What did you do?"

"I dug myself out. I had to smash the casket, but it seemed easy. And the earth was loose. So I just pulled myself out." He pauses, and I realize that I have leaned forward, hanging on his words.

"Then what?"

"A vampire waited for me. He said something but I didn't pay any attention. I just ate him. To dust. Right there in that cemetery. He couldn't have been very old, or I wouldn't have been able to overcome him even all ravenous and newborn."

"So you never knew your maker."

He smiles dreamily.

I shift to another track of questions. "Nothing about you looks Greek."

He laughs. "You mean you haven't heard of the red-headed Greek line?"

I shake my head.

"My father was from the north. Ireland. He fled during the Viking attacks and traveled across Britain to Spain where he took a job on a merchant ship. All of my siblings had red hair. But I'm the only one with his blue eyes."

I feel the weight of his eternal life, unimaginable ages, history in flesh. "Your father fled from Vikings."

He shrugs. "Yep. They raided up and down the Irish coast for almost a hundred years before they were conquered, died out, or assimilated. We pretty much all have their blood at some point in the family tree."

"You're descended from Vikings."

He laughs. "I don't know if 'descended' is exactly the right word. I *am* Viking."

I blink slowly as that sinks in. "I'm going to have to entirely rethink the way I experience time."

He laughs. "It will come."

I look up at the night sky. "The night is young. Let's go out."

He bows slightly at the waist, one of his ancient, old-world gestures. "Your wish. My command."

The wharf crawls with summer tourists, beggars, hawkers, and San Francisco teenagers looking bored. The Golden Gate glows orange against the night sky, the lights on Alcatraz shining across the water beneath. Under the scents of candy, popcorn, sweat, and garbage lurks the heady aroma of pulsing blood.

"In here." Zeke guides me through a doorway into a shop of formal wear, vintage lace, moth eaten velvets, dull rhinestones. I laugh when he pulls a cloche hat over my eyes. "I loved this era," he says. "When men dressed up as much as women."

I pull a slinky pinstriped suit from the rack. The tiny stripes exactly match the electric blue of his hair.

"Hey, look!" He removes another suit of the same fabric.

"Dressing alike?" I cock an eye at him.

"Isn't that what all couples do?"

I laugh and duck into a dressing room.

Moments later we stand side by side before the three-way mirror to admire ourselves. In the matching clothes, we look eerily alike. I had added a blue streak to my blonde hair and with the white vampire skin and our blue eyes, I wonder if we share a common ancestor. My people were Nordic as were his on his father's side.

"We could be siblings." He rests his chin on my shoulder. "I like matching you."

I smile. "What an unbelievably romantic thing to say."

"I've had a lot of experience romancing people."

I shove him playfully. "Don't get cocky."

He shoots me a leer. "Isn't that what boys are supposed to do?"

I groan and smack him on the shoulder. "How'd you get so tall, anyway? Aren't people of your generation supposed to be short?"

He beats his fists against his chest. "Blood of Vikings, baby. Raised on rich food and sea air."

I laugh. "Okay, Viking. Shall we make some purchases and go feed on the masses?"

His eyes turn from grey to silver. "Excellent idea."

# CHAPTER 30

# COAT MY TONGUE LIKE ASHES

Z EKE STOPS SO SUDDENLY that I run into him. He grabs my arm to steady me.

"What's up?" I ask.

He closes his eyes and inhales, tilting his head back. "Smell it?"

Then I do. Jasmine.

"Vampire," Zeke says.

*Malachi*, I think.

Zeke heads for the dark doorway of a bar, his hand still on my arm, hauling me along.

"Wait." I resist him, twisting away.

"What?" He glances back at me, his brows coming down.

I scramble to gather my thoughts. "Why do we care?"

His eyes narrow. "What do you mean 'why do we care?'"

I shrug, feigning nonchalance. "What does it matter?"

He glares at me for a long minute. Then grabs me by the arm again, steering me into a narrow alley between the bar and the building next door.

"We need to know who this is."

I pull my arm away. "So, what? You're like dogs? Pissing on lampposts to mark your territory?"

He barks laughter. "Just call it my need to know."

I blow air out through my lips in irritation. "It doesn't matter."

Zeke pushes me back against the bricks but gently. "It does to me. Plus, I need to know what other vampires are around."

"Why?"

"Because vampires are dangerous."

"Dangerous to humans," I clarify.

He shakes his head. "We can also be dangerous to one another."

I remember. "You ate the one who made you."

"Yes. It's sport. Plus..." he hesitates.

"What?"

He lets out in an frustrated sigh. "Vampire blood is delicious."

I laugh incredulously.

"Think about it. You've tasted my blood. You've tasted human blood. Which is better?"

I don't have to think about it. "Yours, I guess. But I assumed that it's because it's *yours*, not because it's vampire blood."

He releases me. "Well, there are many of us who hunt and eat young vampires for the fun of it."

"But again, why do we care?" I touch his arm to make him look at me. "You keep telling me that I'm not like other vampires. I have all sorts of defenses."

"True." He spins away from me. "But I'm still going to find out who it is." He shoots me a silver look over his shoulder. "And why you smelled like him."

"This should be interesting," I say under my breath and follow Zeke into the depths of the bar.

The scent of blood and sweat washes over me, and I inhale the aroma of humanity, delicious, pulsating food. The scent of jasmine wafts under it all, sweet and beguiling. Kids in cheap vinyl, torn tee shirts, and metal studs shove against me, but I find it easy to keep my balance. They bounce off my hardness, shooting me curious looks. In my heels I tower over most of them.

"You are beautiful!" A boy in skinny jeans and a tattered Ramones tee shirt says, clasping his hands together prayerfully.

"Then bow down and worship," I retort and hear Zeke laugh as the kid sinks, rapturous, to his knees.

I catch up with Zeke standing before the stage, his arms crossed, conspicuously ignoring a circle of admirers shooting him coy and winsome glances. They pretend nonchalance, but their eyes devour us and I can hear their whispers.

*They're so beautiful.*

*Who are they?*

*Do you think they're twins?*

*They must be famous.*

"They worship us. We could start a cult. Start a religion."

The corners of Zeke's mouth twist up. "Vampires have tried that before. It's fun at first, but it ends badly."

"Yeah? How do you mean?"

He glances around, making brief eye contact with a girl who turns white and then very red under her pale makeup. "Humans are the real predators. They'll consume you, eat you up with their adoration. Their lives are too short to know what love is. All they have is obsession."

I think of Alex, how the very thought of him made me hungry, how I longed to touch him always, felt starved for him when we parted. Love? Or obsession?

Zeke leans close, his mouth at my ear. "When they realize that you won't turn them, they'll rip you to shreds."

"Lesson number one."

He nods. "Exactly."

The lights go out. The kids begin to scream. I inhale their scent, sweat and blood and cheap perfumes.

In the darkness a bass line begins to thrum like a heartbeat. A cymbal enters on the offbeat. A single beam of white light illuminates a small circle of the stage, and there he is.

Malachi.

His hair coats his shoulders and bare chest like oil, shadowing his face. He wears only black jeans and boots. His skin shines blue-white in the harsh light, rings glittering in his nipples and clavicles.

He lifts a microphone to his face, his hair sliding over his hands.

*I whisper you like water*

*And come to you like rain*

The children around me mouth the words with him, their breath coating my skin in the darkness.

A keyboard joins in, a high and wavering note.

*You coat my tongue like ashes*

*And I make you come...*

The music stops and he throws his head back, face turned up into the light. He has blacked out his eye sockets and smeared black lipstick across his mouth. The paint makes his skin even whiter. Rings shine from lip and nose and eyebrow. Around me the kids hold their collective breath.

"AGAIN!" He roars the word and the rest of the band crashes in. Around me bodies begin to move, and I let myself move with them.

Beside me, Zeke laughs. "He's beautiful," he says.

He is. In his element, skin shining, his green eyes shooting sparks in the stage lights, Malachi basks in the adoration pouring over him, hair flying like serpents from his head.

"A vampire pretending to be a human pretending to be a vampire," I say.

"How Anne Rice." Zeke casually pushes a girl's body away when she slams against him. She disappears into the sea of bodies.

I know the exact second Malachi sees me. The stage lights dim and the house lights come up and our eyes meet. I smell him, jasmine and sex.

He freezes for a split second, and I see the guitarist glance at him, her brow furrowing.

I smile. His eyes shift and land on Zeke. If at all possible. he grows paler. I see his pupils dilate, his nostrils flare. Zeke tips a salute, his lips drawing back from sharp teeth and then the lights go off again. Malachi brings the microphone to his mouth.

*You run through me in rivers*
*Your voice in my head it whispers*
*Everything about you shimmers*
*At your touch I blister*

I lean over to Zeke. "I think this song is about me," I say.

He smiles. "Everything is about you," he replies.

"I think you scared him."

Zeke laughs. "Well, now I know."

"What do you know?"

He reaches out and draws me into him. "I know who turned you. I know how you did it."

"Happy now?"

He shrugs.

"Can we go?"

He grins. "Let's stay for another song."

Around us the bodies shift, and the music picks up tempo into a driving beat led by bass and drums. Malachi drops his head, pulsating with the rhythm, the beat in his body. The guitar player, a girl with long blonde dreads, crouches next to him, moving in sync.

Zeke draws me in, his hands running up under my jacket across the flesh of my bare back. I feel him against me, his body hard and cold. And aroused. His lips trace down my throat, pausing over the pulse in my jugular, but he doesn't bite. Only traces the heartbeat with his tongue, sending shivers down my spine.

"Pretty Zorah," he croons. "For nine hundred years I have walked this world alone and now you. You make me feel so..." He nibbles along my collarbone, his fingers pulling my collar back.

"So what?" I ask, breathless.

He grins, his teeth sharp and gleaming in the pulsing light. The shadows swarm in the hollows of his eyes and beneath his wicked mouth. Around us the music crashes and booms. Bodies slam into us and then career away into the gloom.

"So what?" I ask again.

His lips descend to mine. "Human," he whispers and then he is on me, in me, one with me, and I rise to meet him, my hunger matching his.

Standing in the darkness in the alley behind the club I look up at the stars and laugh. Zeke, standing behind me, his arms around my waist, looks up too.

"I don't think I'm seeing what you see," he says.

I press my wrist to his mouth and gasp as he bites, pulling deep. Then he licks across the wound and I heal. He looks up.

"Oh..." he says and I laugh again.

The sky shines with auras and the heat rising from the lights and the humanity of the city. A cacophony of color, a beautiful assault.

"I am reborn," I say.

Behind us the door opens, and Malachi steps out. He freezes when he sees us and seems to consider going back the way he had come. But a crowd of people, beautiful in their artful tatters and smeared makeup, swarm out behind him and the door closes and locks.

"We love you, Malachi!" one of them cries, embracing him. "We follow you on TikTok!"

Beside me Zeke chuckles under his breath. "Of course he's on TikTok."

The group flashes selfies and Malachi grins, hamming for the camera, all sharp teeth and gleaming edges. Then the fans run away down the ally, the glow of phones lighting their way, and we are alone with him.

I hear him swallow and then he says, "I see it worked."

I hold my arms out, smiling. My shin shines pale and glistening in the low light. "It did."

His eyes shift to Zeke's face and then back to me. His lips curl up. "Does that make you my daughter then?"

"Only according to American vampire films," Zeke says. "And they have vampires that *sparkle*."

I laugh at the disdain in his voice.

Malachi shifts his weight nervously from foot to foot. Zeke steps around me and their auras overlap, red on red. The white light spiraling up from Zeke's crown shines much brighter, but Malachi has it too, a brilliant glow radiating. In appearance. they look completely different, but their skin gleams with the same pallor, silver in the shifting city light, their eyes shining from the shadows that cling to both of them.

"How old are you?" Malachi asks.

Zeke smiles. "Older than you."

"By several hundred years, I'd guess."

"Indeed. You're what? Less than a hundred?"

Malachi hesitates. "Eighty."

I watch Zeke's tongue dart along his teeth as though tasting the air. "You're a baby. An infant. Who made you?"

"Raven and Crow."

"Really." Zeke shoots a glance at me. "Twins. Almost as old as me." His gaze goes back to Malachi. "They do like pretty things." He reaches out and strokes a strand of Malachi's black hair. Malachi does not so much flinch as quail. "Where are they now?"

"Overseas. I'll join them there eventually."

Zeke's eyes narrow. "This is the first time that you've been out by yourself, isn't it?"

Malachi draws himself up. "I've been on my own for ten years."

Zeke throws his head back and laughs. "Ten years! Ooh, you *are* all grown up."

Malachi stiffens. "I made her, didn't I? When you couldn't?"

Zeke cocks his head sideways like a leopard playing with prey. "Are you questioning my vampire machismo?"

Malachi's eyes dart quickly to me.

"You did quite a number on her." Zeke wraps the long strand of black hair around his finger and tugs, forcing Malachi forward, into Zeke's space.

"She asked for it."

Zeke yanks on the hank of hair and Malachi's head dips, though he makes no sound. "Said so many rapists about so many victims."

"It's true." Malachi looks toward me, and Zeke follows his gaze.

I shift under their eyes.

Zeke reaches out and draws his fingertip along Malachi's chin, close enough to kiss, their cool breath mingling. Malachi looks up into Zeke's eyes, trapped. I see his pupils dilate, hear his breath catch. The energy builds between them, the violence, and it makes the new predator in me burn.

"Well," Zeke says. "Zorah can take care of herself." His breath stirs the fine hairs at Malachi's temple.

"She told me to draw it out. Said it was more likely to work."

"Did she tell you to torture her?"

Malachi lifts his hand to where Zeke's is twined in his hair. "She didn't tell me not to."

Zeke cups Malachi's face in his hands. "I'm sure we both know that Zorah has many talents. Now, my money's on her." His eyes shoot sideways to me. "I don't know if I should kill you or kiss you for making that." Zeke sharply pushes Malachi away.

I bristle. "Hey! I am not a 'that.' I am not a thing."

Zeke regards me coolly. "Shut up, Zorah. If he is an infant, you are zygote."

I remember him telling me that he has centuries to forgive me. I see the anger in him and feel weary at the thought of trying to win him back. I want to erase his anger, but I can't: he knows when I try to work magic on him. "You just said that your money's on me!"

They have the same expression on their faces, brows lifted, lips parted, as though they can't believe my impunity.

I stamp my foot. "Well? Didn't you?"

Zeke tilts his head so that his temple rests against Malachi's, two fallen angels, beautiful and dangerous and deadly. "The newborn are so ..."

"Human?" Malachi suggests, and they both laugh.

I glare at Zeke. "Didn't you come here to drive Malachi out of your territory?"

Zeke glances at Malachi through his lashes. "Is that what I said I'd do?"

I feel a tense ball of conflicting emotions, wound too tight.

Zeke stalks toward me down the alley. "You know what I think?" His voice purrs, mocking. "I think that you want me to kill him while you watch. I think that behind the vampire in you, underneath the witch, there's a human girl who wants the two beautiful boys to fight over her. You want to be the epicenter of the lovers' triangle."

Behind him, Malachi leans back against the wall and lights a cigarette, squinting his seawater eyes against the smoke.

"I thought you said that vampires are dangerous to newborns."

He narrows his eyes. "And you said that you're not like other newborns. A fact I agreed with."

I deflate. "You're right." Was he? Did some part of me want them to fight over me? Like some middle schooler?

Zeke turns back toward Malachi. "Women," he says despairingly.

Malachi shrugs. "I don't understand any of it."

Zeke laughs.

I know they are baiting me, but I don't understand how they're on the same side suddenly. Of anything I imagined about the two of them meeting, this is not it. "Fine," I say. "You can have each other." I turn and walk away, hating myself for wanting him to call after me, hating that he didn't.

# CHAPTER 31

# THE DOOR IN THE WEST

MY CONFUSION GROWS AS I walk. Is Zeke right? Despite all of my self-awareness and insight, am I still just a little girl socialized to think that the only outcome of a meeting of men who know me is violence?

I kick off the high heeled shoes and run, loosing all of my vampire strength, running from my questions and confusion. The wet streets streak past, and I turn down darker side streets. The trees drip as I dash by. When I finally stop, I am soaked. The suit clings to me, and my hair sticks to my cheeks.

I look around. I am across the street from a church, one of the old stained-glass affairs that I love for its elaborate architecture. A tiny cathedral in stone and glass. A late mass must have just let out; people stream down the steps, many of them pausing to speak to a cassocked priest who stands in the doorway.

I remember what Zeke said about faith, about its ability to repel vampires. He'd said that he would love to see me in a church. I let the auras flood in and gasp at what I see: the church glows with vivid purple light radiating upward from the spire. It is almost too bright too look at. I have never seen this before. I wonder if it is part of my enhancing vampire sight. I push my wet hair off my face and walk across the street toward the light.

The last congregants look at me curiously as they make their way down the wet steps but without fear or concern. I just look like a girl who has been caught out in the rain.

I push open the heavy wooden door and step into the narthex, leaving wet prints on the stone floor. Three large arches open into the nave, and I walk through the middle one, pausing next to the fount of holy water. Hesitating only a moment, I dip my fingers into the liquid

A sharp shock runs up my arm, and I pull back. But the tingle fades, and my flesh appears unmarred. Power there, but not a lot. I put my wet fingers into my mouth and laugh around them as my tongue goes temporarily numb.

The priest and another man turn at the sound. "Can I help you, dear?" the priest asks.

I eye him warily. If Zeke is right, this man could have some sort of power.

He walks down the aisle toward me. The other man picks up a stack of papers and disappears through a door to the right of the lectern. "Are you okay?" the priest asks.

I can't resist. I hold my arms out, palms up toward the high, timbered ceiling. "Forgive me father, for I have sinned."

He stops, sensing something off. "The church welcomes all people."

I sigh and drop my arms. "Well, that will be a problem." I remember my mother, accusing me of demonic influences. I push the thought of her away and take a step toward him. "You see, I am not exactly human."

He holds his ground, but I see the blood rush to his face in a sudden adrenaline flush. "All things are equal in the eyes of God."

"Now, that is part of my issue." He is almost close enough to touch. I see stubble of a dark beard on his chin, and I realize how cute he is. How young. Dark hair and eyes, pale skin, full lips, wide forehead. Just my type. "Is it equal in the eyes of God when a woman is raped? Is that equal to a child being born? Or to falling in love? Is that equal to genocide?" I take another step forward.

He folds his hands in front of him but does not retreat. "It's complicated."

I laugh. My voice echoes weirdly in the cavernous space. "So is that 'all things are equal in the eyes of God' just shite you tell the natives? Is it a lie?"

He draws himself up. "What you're asking is called The Problem of Evil. Theologians have been asking your questions forever."

"Not forever!" I bark at him. "Only since some twit came up with a definition for God that made Him all-powerful, all-knowing. *That* is what created the little dilemma you call The Problem of Evil. But you know what I think? I think the solution to the problem is really quite simple."

He stares at me. "What do you think, dear?"

I roll my eyes. "Don't call me 'dear.' Do know how condescending that sounds?"

He almost smiles. "Sorry. Habit." He gestures expansively. "Please continue."

"Thank you." I smooth my hair back, spattering droplets of water on the floor. "As I was saying, it's really quite simple." I lean forward, and he tilts his head down toward me. "Your God doesn't exist," I whisper.

"Ah." He nods. "So you don't believe in God."

I shake my finger reprovingly. "Of course not. But do not dismiss my thoughts on the matter just because I'm an unbeliever." *Unbeliever.* That was the word my family called me. They thought it an insult.

"Enlighten me."

I start to like him. He has pluck. "What's your name?" I ask.

"I am called Father Andrew."

"How biblical. I have a cousin named Andrew. But I didn't ask what you are called. I asked your name."

"We give up our birth names."

I blow a sigh out in frustration. "Fine. What *were* you called?"

I watch him consider whether or not to tell me. "Aiden," he says finally.

"Now, see? That's a perfectly lovely name. Why on earth would you give it up?"

"We give up our identity in service to Him."

"I know that," I say, irritated. "I understand the logistics. I just don't understand why anyone in their right mind would believe in the fairy tale that is Christianity."

He looks at me sadly. "You think it's a fairy tale?"

"It comes complete with magic tricks and people coming back from the dead." I think about it. "Although I suppose that can happen, actually." I laugh. "Maybe it's all just fairy tales."

"All of what?"

"Belief. Faith." I gesture at the room. "Reality. All of it. Maybe we give it power."

"Faith is not a fairy tale."

"Then life is!" I yell.

He regards me, his eyes sad. "Can I call someone for you?"

His concern irritates me. I reach out with mental fingers and pull the tall double doors of the church closed with a bang. "There is no one for me."

He looks uncertainly past me toward the doors. "No one? Who are you?"

I step around him in a circle. He follows me with his eyes. "I told you." I lean into his ear, my breath stirring the dark curls at his neck. "Not human."

He laughs with only a hint of nervousness. "What do you mean?"

I reach out, letting my mind skate across all of that harnessed power, all that purple light. I feel it like a vast well, my regard causing ripples on the surface, like water. I close my eyes and breathe deep of it.

I walk toward the altar, looking up at the massive panes depicting white Jesus suffering on his cross. I feel the power well up inside me, firing my blood. It comes so easily now, pouring through me. I am invincible. I reach out and smash the huge windows down.

They fall with a mighty crash, exposing a stone wall and backlighting. All just façade. Behind me Aiden yells in alarm. The other man bursts through the rectory door and stops dead, his shoes sending glass shards tinkling down the step that sets the podium up off the floor. I reach out with my mind and drag him to me. His toes skate across the wood, and he cries out in alarm. I laugh and reel him in, wrapping my hands around him and turning back to the priest, the other man in front of me like a shield.

"Do you believe in evil, Father?" I bite deep into the man's jugular, holding him by the hair with one hand, the other pinning him to me. The blood splashes up, spurting across my face, running hot down my shoulder.

But only a little of it. The rest pumps into me in a wash of image and sensation: sun on skin, beach sand underfoot, the velvety texture of an old leather Bible. His strong heart beating in rhythm with mine.

The father's eyes bore into me, his mouth falling open. He reaches out, but I send him sliding backwards along the hardwood floor. He fumbles at his waist and comes up with a cross that he holds out toward me like so many priests had done to so many vampires throughout time. I see his lips move.

I feel the man's heart stop. I draw him into me, more his essence than any substance. Beneath my fingers his skin dries and cracks. He falls to dust.

I clap my hands briskly together, sending up a puff of white ash that clings to my damp skin and the streaks of blood running down my arm. I walk toward the priest.

He sinks to his knees, the cross still held before him. "Though I walk through the valley of the shadow of death, I will fear no evil," he says.

"For thou art with me," I finish. "Tell me, father. Aiden. Tell me how, if your God is so all-powerful, so all-seeing." I lean down to bring my face level with his. "How does He suffer something like me?" I reach for the cross he holds before him, feeling heat radiate from it. It is a heavy, ornate thing. I wrap my fingers around the top of it.

I feel the burn immediately, my flesh beginning to blister. But I just grip tighter.

I stare into the priest's eyes, so close that I see myself reflected in his pupils. "Your God is a myth," I whisper. "And I will prove it." I rip the cross from his hands and send it spinning across the floor and into the shadows.

I hold him still with a thought, pinned to the floor, and turn toward the West. Around me the power ripples and sparks. I draw it into me and picture the massive gates in my mind. I consider what lies beyond but the power of this place pours through me like a river, intoxicating.

"I will have what I want," I say. Before me the gates shudder and begin to open.

"Zorah!" Zeke's voice cracks through the air like a whip, making me jump. My focus wavers. He stands on a pew near the doors. He is covered in blood. It streaks his white skin, clots around his mouth, drips from his cuffs. He had been caught in the rain as well, and his hair stands up in wild wet tangles, dark with gore.

"How the bloody hell did you get in?" I demand.

He grins. "There's a side door."

I reach out for it with my mind, see it sanding open. I slam it shut. Aiden gasps at the sound.

"Well ... where the fuck is Malachi?"

Zeke wags a finger at me. "Shame on you. Cursing in church."

I stamp my foot. "Well?"

He licks blood from his lips. "Well, what?"

I stomp again. "Where is Malachi?"

"Why do you care?"

"Zeke!" I glare at him.

He laughs. "I have no idea where Malachi is, love."

"Whose blood is that?"

He gazes at the red streaks on his hands. "I have no idea about that either. I can't read their thoughts like you can, remember?"

I look back at Aiden. He has closed his eyes, his lips moving in prayer.

Zeke jumps to the floor and stalks up the aisle.

Before me the gates yawn. I feel the gathering dark. Lifting my gaze I see them, the doors, superimposed over the west wall of the church.

Zeke follows my gaze, and his skin turns even paler. He sees them, too. "What the bloody fuck do you think you're doing?" He leaps toward me.

"Now who's cursing in church?" I stop him with a thought, and he halts as though hitting a wall. "What I was born to do."

I see real fear in his face. "Zorah, you are going to kill us both. Or get us sucked into hell." The fear on his face turns to anger. "Would you stop. Please." The last word comes through gritted teeth.

A flicker of movement in the narthex and Stefania appears, Sorin behind her. My attention slips, and the stygian doors open another crack. I feel them now, the looming dead.

Furious, I shout, "How the hell do you people keep getting in here? For fuck's sake." I reach out and bring the lintel stones down with a mighty crash. The twins in the doorway sprint up the aisle as cement dust chokes the archway. I bring the stones down. All of them, over the arches framing the nave, behind the alter to block the door off the chancel. Sorin and Stefania kneel between two pews, their arms around another in the crashing chaos. Zeke leaps forward onto another pew as a stone rolls past him.

My attention on bringing the stones down, the western gates shudder open another fraction. I shove back against the mighty doors and, my focus diverted from him, Aiden stands up. I push him back down with a snarl. He falls with a whimper, his feet sliding through glass.

"Zorah!" Stefania calls my name in the sudden quiet. "You can't do this."

I whip around to face her. "I am sick of people telling me what I can and cannot do." I stalk toward her. She stands her ground, and I slap her across the face.

She cries out and falls back against her brother, a red welt standing out along her jaw.

I turn back toward the gates. "If you people don't stop distracting me, this is going to get really interesting."

Zeke hops off the pew. "You don't have to do this, Zorah."

"Please do shut up." I concentrate, visualizing a circle around me, encompassing me and Aiden, shutting out Zeke, Sorin, and Stefania. Zeke stops again, grimacing, as he encounters the barrier. I close my eyes. In my memory, Alex dances.

He had been such a good dancer. His body against mine, the scent of his hair in the back of my throat, the taste of his sweat on my tongue. I can feel him against me, his hands lifting me, the texture of his skin against mine. In my memory, he smiles.

I open my eyes. Zeke's mouth moves, but I pay no attention to his words. The gates loom before me. I draw deep of the well of power encircling me. Aiden whimpers but I ignore him.

*I am the danger in the darkness. I am the diamond spell. I am the voice from the shadows. I am the blood that wells.*

The gates open.

# CHAPTER 32

# DEADLIGHTS

S TEFANIA SCREAMS BUT THE sound seems far away and unimportant. I see Zeke step forward into the periphery of my view. His head tilts back, his lips parting, as he gazes upward into the black.

The dead surge forward, but I hold them at bay. This time it feels effortless, that purple light flowing into me.

*Alex.*

I call him. But he does not answer. Instead, another steps forward. I see her at the entrance of the stygian depths, a slight, dark thing. She wears a simple white shift of rough fabric, a band of copper holding back the black sheet of her hair.

She holds out her hands, her brown eyes on me. *Zorah,* she says.

"Who are you?" I ask.

"Yrsa," says Zeke.

My concentration falters. The gates gape, and I feel the surge of dead things from beyond. So hungry. So lost.

Zeke lifts his hands, and she steps down as though descending a stairway.

"Zeke!" I hiss, but he does not even glance. He sees only her.

*Ezekiel.* Her hands slide into his, and I falter. I have ceased to exist for him like I blew away on the wind.

He does not speak, does not ask any of the questions that I would have, that I have dreamed of asking Alex. My lost one. *Are you okay? Did you miss me? Can I help? can I...? do you...? will you...?*

He only takes her hands, and I see her take shape, gain corporeal form, her fingers curling over his. He looks down into her upturned face as though drowning.

I die again.

I had died when they came to tell me. He had left like a whisper as I lay dreaming, and yet I had known the instant I opened the door to the face of a young police officer. I had seen it in his face, in the way he called me "ma'am."

This is not how it's supposed to happen, this couldn't be how it ends. His face tilts down toward hers. "Yrsa." He says it again. Deep inside the rage wells up like the last time I had tried this. The last time when Zeke had ended up on the ground with his blood leaking out of him into the freezing mountain air.

This is not what is supposed to happen.

ZEKE. I put all of my power into that command, and he looks. He finally looks at me.

She does as well. *Zorah,* she says. Her feet step toward me over the glass and dust, but it does not stir. He follows, his fingers still linked through hers.

WHERE IS ALEX? My lips move but the real power of the words flows from my mind.

*He's not here.*

I DON'T BELIEVE YOU.

She smiles at me then, a look of compassion. Pity, even. *This is just a holding place, Zorah. Not all the dead stay.*

STOP SAYING MY NAME.

*I've been watching you.* She glances at Zeke. He stands beside her and seems unable to wrench his eyes from her. *I've been watching him forever. I watched him meet you.*

"I'm sorry, Yrs," he says, and the sound of his voice is strange in the midst of our silent conversation. "I'm so sorry."

Something inside me breaks at the anguish in his voice. I see tears spring to his eyes and feel the prick as moisture rises in my own.

Her fingers skate down the plane of his cheek, barely brushing his skin. She is hardly here. "There is nothing to be sorry for, my love." She speaks aloud to him in return, her voice faint and insubstantial. "It was my choice."

"But we didn't know the price." The tears fall now, slipping in crystalline droplets down his cheeks.

"No one ever knows the price of their actions," she says. "If we had succeeded, how many people would I have killed?"

His lips part to answer but instead a sob emerges, and I watch his features crumble. His head drops over their linked hands. Her face turns up toward his, and he rests his forehead against hers.

Such an intimate, private gesture. Rage leaps inside me, a living, hungry thing. This is not how it is supposed to happen. I send Zeke sliding back. He cries out as his hand is ripped from hers.

"Be gone, evil thing."

The voice comes from behind me, and I spin to see that Aiden has retrieved the cross I had sent spinning from his hand. How did he move? My focus has faltered.

He holds the heavy thing toward Yrsa. "The power of Christ compels you," he whispers.

Unexpected laughter bubbles up in me. He sounds like a B horror movie. "Don't you realize?" I bend at the waist to bring my face down even with his. "Your God has no power here. Here, I am the only god." I focus on the cross, and it bursts into flame, the fire licking around the priest's hand. He yells and drops it.

*Zorah.*

I spin to find Yrsa right in front of me, close enough to touch. I see the freckles on her nose, the way that her lashes tangle at the corners. I try to shove her back.

*You have no power over me.*

That voice in my head. I snarl at her, but she doesn't recoil. *I feel your pain. The way that grief tears and devours. But he isn't here, Zorah. He came, and then he went.*

WHAT? HE WAS THERE?

*This is only purgatory, Zorah. A place of holding. Waiting. The dead come and go, some quickly. Others stay forever.*

I struggle to make sense of what she's telling me.

*He came, and for a while he waited. I only noticed him when Zeke noticed you. We watched together.*

"What do you mean?" I stare at her, mesmerized. She has a tiny fleck of gold in her left eye. Zeke steps up behind her, and she reaches back for him without looking. His hand slides into hers. He draws close behind her, his head down. I cannot see his face. He just stands behind her, seeming to breathe in the scent of her hair, motionless as stone.

*We saw everything. You were something new. First to me and then to him.* She glances over her shoulder at Zeke, and her next words are not for me. *I had never seen you like that. I could see your fascination. Your attraction.* She turns away dismissing me. *Now it is only him.*

*I watched you fall in love with her.*

He looks up at her now, tears on his cheeks, leaking from his eyes. Emotion flushes his face, and his mouth parts, glistening. I have never seen him like this, so vulnerable. 'You make me feel so human' he had said, but I have not done anything to him like she does with her mere presence. Her impossible appearance.

"I'm sorry," he says.

She smiles. "For what? For loving her? For moving on? Never be sorry for love." She caresses his cheek. "I'm happy for you."

I remember Alex asleep, curled on his side, his dark curls fanned across the pillow. I always bought sheets to compliment his coloring, and I see him now against cream colored fleece, his cheeks flushed in dreaming, his clever fingers intertwined with mine.

"Where are you?" I whisper.

At the sound of my voice Yrsa turns back to me. "He watched you become a vampire." She smiles suddenly, and almost laughs. "He loved that."

"What? He saw that?" I remember Malachi, his teeth in me, the violence of it. My cheeks flush.

"Death gives one a certain..." she pauses as though searching for the right word. "Perspective. The terrible things of this world are not as important." She glances at Zeke. "I have watched for over nine hundred years."

"I'm a monster," he says, tears in his voice.

She shakes her head sharply. "I would have been a monster, too. Remember that I chose. Had I turned, I would have killed and pillaged my way across the world beside you."

At her words, Zeke's vision seems to clear. He shakes his head slightly as though awakening from a dream and brings his sleeve across his face, wiping away the moisture there.

She looks back at me. *But you change everything.* Her voice in my head. *In all his time on earth, Ezekiel has always been alone. Even with lovers and paramours, queens and concubines, his journey has been solitary.* She steps toward me. *But you are a new thing.*

I cannot look away from her dark eyes. I had thought to possess Zeke, make him mine, the lover who could not die. But now I realize that I never will. This woman has parts of him that I will never know, never see. So I ask the only question left to me. "Where is Alex?"

She smiles at me but sadly. "He's gone. He's moved on. He said that you would have wanted it that way."

"Gone where?"

She shrugs. "Beyond. There are doors into the different worlds. They open and people enter and stay for awhile. As soon as they're ready, they depart."

I feel a great falling emptiness inside of me. I become aware again of how the power of this place channels through me, the immense amount of will that it takes to hold the circle, keep the doors open, and the dead at bay.

"So that's it then." I am so tired. "He's lost."

She shrugs again, the slight movement of her shoulders. "As to that, I cannot say. Some dead simply wither into nothing. Some leave, to be reborn I would guess. But there are so many worlds, so many paths to tread. He went on."

"Of course he did." I feel ridiculous. In the nights that followed his funeral I had told him again and again to go on, to continue his journey. I had felt nothing, no whisper of him, but he had been there, watching. He had merely done as I asked.

"You have eternity to find him, Zorah. You did before only you didn't see. You thought that maybe this life was it. Well, it's not. There is so much more. And no religion in the great infinite expanses of reality have any clue. We get to choose. He chose to leave. I chose to stay." She turns back to Zeke. His tears have dried, and now he looks straight into her face, his eyes silvering.

"I think that our time has finally drawn to a close, my love," she says.

His brow creases. "I never thought to see you again."

"I know." She glances at me. "It's quite the gift that this one has afforded us."

She smiles, this time in joy. "We get closure."

"What do you mean?"

"I believe that the time has come for me to move on. To see what's next."

He takes a sharp breath.

She looks at him with some complex combination of sadness and elation. "I have watched you for a millennium. I have seen all that you are. And now it is time for me to continue."

Tears spring to his eyes again. "I..." He stops, lost.

"This is the choice, my love." She glances up at the door, where it yawns, an impossible thing, a tear in reality. "You could come with me."

His eyes widen, and my breath stops, every part of me clinching in terror. She holds out a hand to stop him as he steps toward her. "In which case this body would die. You would cross over."

My knees buckle. Everything seems too bright, the light flickering. I think I might faint.

"Or," she continues. "You could stay here. Continue this wondrous life you have found."

*Stay*, I try to say, but my voice has departed completely.

"The choice is yours."

He finally looks at me. I make my expression impassive, hide the roiling turmoil in my stomach. But I have fallen to my knees, and he looks down at me. Then he looks up at the yawning door, indecision in every line of his body. He looks back at her.

She says nothing, her eyes soft, the small smile on her lips.

For a minute, I think about just letting the doors close. The effort of keeping them open has begun to strain me, a great fatigue taking over my mind. But that will trap her here. And he has to choose. If I make that choice for him, we will be ended. I will lose him, too.

"We have eternity," he says, and she nods.

"Nothing ends."

A small shake of her head. "Never."

He steps toward her and her arms come up. Her head fits beneath his chin as though it had been there forever and his eyes slip closed as her body rests against him.

I glance around. Two faces watch us from over the back of an overturned pew, and I start. I had forgotten Sorin and Stefania. Their faces wear identical expressions of shock, mouths hanging open, skin pale.Blackness creeps into the edges of my vision. I shake my head sharply. The doors slip and swing inward. I catch them, but barely. They are so heavy.

"Safe travels," he says but it seems that his words come from a great distance. He kisses her forehead. "Until the next life."

In a dream I watch her step way. She smiles, a look of joy and love I cannot comprehend over the scream that has overtaken my mind. The purple light wavers.

«Σε αγαπώ» she says.

"I love you, too," he replies.

Then she turns and ascends invisible steps. She pauses once to look back, her gaze sweeping the scene and lingering on him. Then she looks up into the blackness and does not look back again.

I release the doors and they slam shut, disappearing in the same breath as though they had never been. I lean over and vomit up a great splash of black blood. When I stand up, he is there.

"How...? Why...?" Nothing makes sense, and the room spins, but he catches me. His hands on my shoulders, and he pulls me in, wrapping me in his arms, his cold body, the desert scent of him.

The sobs come with a suddenness that overwhelms me. All the grief, the anger, uncertainty, and terror streams out. Zeke's arms tighten around me, his breath on my hair.

I look up at him, eyes streaming. "Why did you stay?"

He grins. "And miss all this?" He snickers. "I have to see how this ends."

I wipe my eyes. "You wanted to see what I would do in a church? Now you know."

He throws back his head and roars laughter up at the ceiling. After a moment, I join him.

He glances around, mirth still flickering in his eyes, taking in the pile of stones before the door, the glass on the floor. His gaze comes to rest on Aiden. "Who the hell is that?"

"He likes to be called Father Andrew," I say.

"Why is he here?"

"I was going to try to break his faith."

"I think it worked."

I look at Aiden. He sits on the floor, his knees drawn up against his chest, rocking slowly back and forth. His eyes are fixed on the place the door had been, but his gaze is wide and vacant.

I kneel beside him and place a hand a hand on his shoulder. At my touch he jumps and gasps, his eyes flying to my face. He tries to speak but only emits a moaning sound.

"It's over," I say.

He takes a deep breath. "For thine is the kingdom and the glory forever and ever."

"Amen." I say it with him.

He looks at me. "I don't know where God is."

"You don't know?"

"No." He rocks back on his heels and stands up suddenly. "It is not my place to question His plan."

I laugh. "How do you think I fit into his plan?"

"You're not one of His."

"Oh, no? So ... I'm what? One of Satan's?" I think of my mother again. I think of eating her.

"The Bible speaks of an adversary. The serpent. You are a demon in flesh."

I nod. "In which case, how does the demonic fit into the divine plan? If your God is so powerful, I must exist at his pleasure. I must be a part of that plan of which you speak."

His eyes dart away and land on Zeke, watching with interest. "I ... I don't know."

I look at Zeke. "He doesn't know," I say. Zeke shrugs, and I bite back a chuckle.

I reach up and take the priest's face between my hands. I feel the heat of his faith, but I do not burn or blister. "Your God isn't real," I say gently. "And neither is your devil. I can kill because there's no one to stop me. There's never been anyone to stop things like me."

"I don't believe you," he whispers, and I see tears in his eyes.

"It doesn't matter," I whisper back. "As you clean up your church and sweep up the dust that was your friend, you'll start to believe."

I release him. He falls to his knees again but not in prayer. In despair.

I turn to face the exit, chocked with rubble and dust. Drawing on the last of my energy I send the stones up into piles, opening a way through. Sorin and Stefania still crouch between pews, their hands linked. Like the priest, they seem broken, lost.

I take Zeke's hand and start up the aisle. I pause before them and Stefania shrinks back against Sorin, their dark eyes upon me.

"We're finished," I say. "If I want you, either of you, I'll come to you. Until then, you better be ghosts."

Sorin nods. "Yes," he says. Stefania just looks at me, her eyes devouring her white face.

Zeke pulls me into him. "Burn it down," he whispers against my mouth.

I let the power come, surging out in a line of fire that races across the floor, lighting pews like kindling. I feel a great weariness, but the fire still comes at my command. The twins leap to their feet and run, their hands intertwined like children in a fairy tale.

"Come on." Zeke takes my hand and we follow, out into the rain. Behind us, a window explodes outward with a crash.

Zeke pulls me along the streets, dark and sodden. The water sluices down, washing us clean. When he draws me inside his apartment building, the air feels very warm. He drags me down the stairs, then releases my hand to fumble the key into the lock. Throwing the door wide, he runs inside.

I stop at the barrier, feeling the buzz against my skin. He turns in the middle of the floor, his chin dropping, blood dripping onto the rug. He grins, lips pulling back from sharp teeth, eyes silver and burning in his face. Lightning flickers through the window at the end of the hall, and I feel it, the gathering storm.

He holds out his hands to me. "Come inside, then."

# Epilogue

T HE WATER LIES STILL and smooth as glass, reflecting the stars. The Milky Way glimmers above, reflected below, and I feel as though I am free floating through space, drifting in the void. Far away on the distant horizon a storm flickers, lightning forking through the distant clouds, but I know it is miles away. According to the GPS in the control room, anyway.

I walk along the railing, listening to the faint creak of rigging, the soft lap of the water against the hull. In the silence every sound is magnified, echoing across the calm water. I lean on the rail and gaze down into the starry depths. She has been down a long time.

"Zorah," I call softly, and listen to my voice carry across the stillness of the becalmed Atlantic. She does not answer, of course. I pad inside to the galley, all shining and gleaming clean. The only thing we use is glasses.

I take one, a heavy crystal thing, and pour a stiff shot of whiskey into it, topping it off with blood from the industrial size refrigerator. Glass milk bottles line the interior, each carefully sealed. Their interiors shine scarlet.

I take my drink outside and return to the rail. Reaching in the pocket of the linen shirt I wear, I extract a packet of Dunhill cigarettes and light one, drawing deep. "Fuck cancer," I whisper, and laugh softly to myself. The smoke burns chemical in my throat. I taste it as no mortal ever can.

When she surfaces Zorah rises straight out of the water, hands at her sides, as though lifted from beneath. Water runs down her bare skin, pooling in her navel, dripping with tiny splashes from the tips of her toes. She is like a nereid, a goddess born from the sea. She levitates even with the deck and then floats through the air until she can step on board. She wrings water from her hair, allowing it to splash over the side, sending ripples through the stars.

"I heard whales," she says.

"You were down a long time."

"The starlight reflecting down through the water distracted me," she replies and walks to me, her hips undulating. The silver light refracts off her wet skin. She is coated in light, crystalline droplets hanging from her nipples, glinting from her pubic hair. She takes the glass and swallows one dainty sip before handing it back.

"Where in the world do you want to go?" I ask, reaching for her.

She steps into my arms and lays her wet head against my chest. I feel my shirt dampen. "In the world?"

"Anywhere in the world you want to go."

"I want to see blood sacrifice on the Kalighat in Calcutta. I want to lie on the floor of the Sistine Chapel in the moonlight. I want to swim with dolphins in the dark waters off Maui. I want to crawl into the graves beneath Westminster Abbey. I want to drink wine in the catacombs of Paris."

"You want, you want, you want." I smile against her hair.

She looks up at me. "And then I want to go to Romania and speak with a woman named Zabrina about other worlds."

"I want that, too."

She gazes out across the water. I wonder what she sees there with her impossible sight that I can only glimpse in the fleeting taste of her blood.

"Are you ready to get underway?" I ask.

She looks up at the stars. I see the Milky Way reflected in the dark depths of her eyes. "I am."

"Come then, lover." I smile at her. "The world awaits."

ACKNOWLEDGMENTS

I used to have magnetic word poetry on the back of a door in my house. When we had people over, it would often move around. One morning I came downstairs and read "watch and whisper as those above fall." So my first debt of gratitude goes to whichever guest rearranged the magnets to spell out that compelling phrase. It rattled around in my head for several years and ultimately resolved itself into one of the major themes of this book. Not saying this book wouldn't exist without you, mystery guest, but it would be called something else!

I owe my love of reading to my parents, especially my mother. She read to me my entire childhood. My dad pushed me to read on my own, and also imbued me with a love of knowledge. I am who I am because of the two of them. I won the lottery when it comes to parents.

My partner Greg supports me, challenges me, makes me laugh, and is my constant companion through this adventure that is life. I couldn't do it without him.

I have an incredible circle of supportive friends, a coven who brings magic and wonder into my life, and great colleagues in the good work of education. Thank you all for being awesome.

Three years ago, when I decided to get serious about writing horror, I joined a writers' group and it was one of the best decisions I've made. I workshopped this book in group, and it is what it is largely because of Heather, Kat, Janette, Sandra, and Luis. They understood what I set out to do, and pushed me to think deeply, examine each word, and believe in the work. They are the reason I had the courage to pitch the book to Winding Road Stories.

My editor, Michael Dolan, also believes in this book. People kept telling me that the vampire market is "saturated" (they're not wrong), but Michael understands that there is an audience hungry for this type of book. He also understands that this story isn't really about witches and vampires. It's about grief. It's about power, and what people are tempted to do when they have it. It's an exploration of what someone with power might do to bring back someone they love. The price they're willing to pay. Vampires and witches are just the vehicles I use to explore the soul-eating nature of grief. Yes, there is an Alex. His name is J, and I love him still.

Finally, I ask forgiveness for playing with the geography of San Francisco to make it suit my needs. Writers rewrite the world as we see fit!

Catlyn Ladd loves alliteration, the sibilant slip of similar sounds. She blends metaphors and archetypes from the shadow self, illuminating the monsters that gestate there. Catlyn worked as a stripper before becoming a professor of philosophy, religion, and women's studies. Her fiction has been published in a number of anthologies including ones by Black Hare Press, Dark Lit Press, and Skywatcher Press. Her nonfiction book, *Strip: The Making of a Feminist*, is published by Changemakers. She lives with her partner and cats in Colorado. She can be found at www.catlynladd.com and on Twitter, Instagram, TikTok, and Facebook as Catlyn Ladd, the Eclectic Academic. Subscribe to her newsletter at catlynladd.substack.com.